WARNING!

Adult Fiction

Sexually Exquisite

*If you are not eighteen or older,
do not, seriously, do not read this book.*

SINGLE HUSBANDS

HoneyB

GRAND CENTRAL
PUBLISHING

NEW YORK   BOSTON

Copyright © 2009 by Mary B. Morrison

Excerpt from *Who's Loving You* by Mary B. Morrison published by arrangement with Dafina Books, a division of Kensington Publishing Corp. Copyright © 2008 by Mary B. Morrison.

Grand Central Publishing
Hachette Book Group
237 Park Avenue
New York, NY 10017

Visit our Web site at www.HachetteBookGroup.com.

Printed in the United States of America

First Edition: March 2009
10 9 8 7 6 5 4 3 2 1

Grand Central Publishing is a division of Hachette Book Group, Inc.
The Grand Central Publishing name and logo is a trademark of Hachette Book Group, Inc.

Library of Congress Cataloging-in-Publication Data
HoneyB.
　　Single husbands / HoneyB.—1st ed.
　　　　p. cm.
　　Summary: "Another steamy erotic tale from Mary B. Morrison, writing under the pseudonym HoneyB, about three men who marry for all the wrong reasons"—Provided by publisher.
　　ISBN: 978-0-446-58230-8
1. African Americans—Fiction. I. Title.
PS3563.O87477S58 2009
813'.54—dc22

2008030403

Book design by Charles Sutherland

Before you say, "I do,"
I'd like to say to you . . .

Date:

Given To:

Given By:

Personal Message:

Dedicated to the women who will not marry single husbands.

There may be a·shortage of men, but there is no shortage of SEX.

Instant Message From the HoneyB

I'm asking ALL adults to support me on sharing this very important message:

Educate, Don't Procreate

There is no reason ANY teenage girl should have a baby. None. We have too many teenagers getting pregnant—for all the wrong reasons. It's time for adults to stop undereducating young females and start empowering them. I'm most concerned with the females because most of the males are not accepting responsibility for their actions.

I understand that most African-American women suffer from postslavery sexual trauma. Whether it was our parents misinforming or undereducating us, our being molested and raped, battered and abused, and our being taught that sex out of wedlock is sinful, it's time for a monumental epiphany in the way women of all nationalities view sex and our bodies. As a woman who is comfortable with her own sexuality, I want to spark an empowering sexual movement for other women.

Young girls should be educated about their bodies and their hormones. They need to know safe sex practices. They need to know they are in control, not the guys.

I hope you join me in imparting this very important message to our young girls.

Sexual Knowledge Is Powerful

Introduction

Is there a loophole in marriage vows?

What wedding vows did you, or will you, exchange? Do, or will, these words sound *somewhat* familiar to you?

> In the presence of God, our family and friends, I offer you my solemn vow to be your faithful partner in sickness and in health, in good times and in bad, and in joy as well as in sorrow, forsaking all others, keeping only unto you for as long as we both shall live. I promise to love you unconditionally, to support you in your goals, to honor and respect you, to laugh with you and cry with you, and to cherish you for as long as we both shall live.

I encourage you to re-read the aforementioned paragraph verbatim—but don't stop there. Read the vows you exchanged or are about to exchange at the altar, then read all the marriage vows you can find and e-mail me any preexisting marriage vows where it states, "I promise to exclusively have sex with you," or any vows that explicitly include fidelity. I have yet to find vows that state married couples shall not or will not have sex outside of their marriage.

I can imagine that most, if not all, of you are clinging to the words "Forsaking all others, keeping only unto you." Forsaking means to renounce or turn away from entirely. All includes your family, friends, coworkers, pastors, exes, strangers, etc. It is humanly impossible to forsake *all* others and keep only unto one person for the rest of your life. The vagueness implies one is to keep unto one, but it doesn't clarify in what capacity? Sounds nice, but I implore you to think twice about the true implications. Wedding vows are so obscure, they are essentially left to one's interpretation.

Moving along . . . There was a woman on *Oprah* who sued her husband's mistress and was awarded a monetary judgment, I believe, in the amount of $500,000 against the mistress but settled for $50,000. I believe in that case the mistress constantly pursued the woman's husband, knowing he was married, and I believe the husband did not act or respond favorably to the mistress's countless written and verbal solicitations.

In any case, even if a married person faced with similar circumstances would have engaged in sexual intercourse, I pose these questions: "What do you feel should happen to a married individual who engages in sex outside of his or her marriage? Why?" Should a married person go to jail for emotional and/or sexual infidelity? How would one measure such a crime? By the number of wet dreams, orgasms, or partners? What if the sex was bad? What if the woman outside of the marriage gets pregnant?

Your marriage is your commitment. If you choose to quote words or phrases such as "vow to be faithful," I ask that you first seek the definition of the word "faithful," then pay close attention to how the word "faithful" is being used in conjunction with other words in the vows.

There are beliefs rooted in Christianity like "Thou shall not commit adultery" and "Thou shall not covet his neighbor's wife," but to my knowledge or lack thereof—correct me if I'm wrong—none of the Ten Commandments are quoted in marriage vows. And even if they were, everyone is not a Christian. Some individuals are atheists. So I must ask you, the reader, because you are intelligent, "Is there a loophole in wedding vows regarding fidelity?"

The three couples in *Single Husbands* made a commitment to one another, but somewhere along their journey after saying, "I do," Herschel Henderson, Brian Flaw, and Lexington Lewis took detours. Or did they? Now I want you to take a moment to think about whether people change after they are married, and how. These three men didn't honestly deviate from their premarital behavior. Most people don't. What had happened was that the women they married thought signing a marriage license would miraculously turn their unfaithful fiancés into faithful husbands.

Have you ever thought about the definitions for "marriage" and "license"? Marriage is the state of being united to a person of the opposite sex as husband or wife in a consensual and contractual relationship *recognized by law*—not by your girlfriend, your ex-man, your best man, your spouse, your mama, your daddy, or a stranger—by law.

There are no prerequisites to getting married. In reality, it doesn't matter if the parties exchanging vows respect, love, or hate one another. Who honestly cares? The law rules above all hearts. The law doesn't care if one is under duress, secretly miserable, constantly unhappy, or clearly unsure as he or she journeys down the aisle or stands before the altar. One's credit score, IQ, and bank account can collectively be below zero and in the red and he or she can still find someone to marry.

License means a permission granted by competent authority to engage in a business or occupation or in an activity otherwise unlawful—a document, plate, or tag evidencing a license granted. Does this mean being single is unlawful? If having sex outside of wedlock is unlawful, then 98 percent of adult Americans (which probably includes you and definitely includes me) and a substantial number of teenagers need to be placed under house arrest. I find the concept of marriage ludicrous, because most people, married or single, don't have the decency to respect the person they're in a relationship with. No stamp of approval can successfully debate what I'm saying.

A license is a document. Every license—except a marriage license—must be renewed, can be revoked, suspended, or terminated for failure to adhere to the laws under which the license was granted. A marriage license can either be annulled (reduced to nothing) or dissolved (to become decomposed or to cause to disappear), which ends in divorce.

A marriage license is a façade. It's a piece of paper granted not by the parties involved but by authority (the law) to the parties who have no enforceable control over their spouse. In many cases, people are marrying strangers. What's my point? People who decide to get married are disillusioned because they believe they have entitlements, when in actuality they have zero authority to hold the other person accountable to anything that the individual does not desire to commit to. You don't marry a piece of paper. What you commit to is marrying an imperfect being whom you somehow expect to become perfect when you hear, "I now pronounce you man and wife."

Did you catch that "man and wife" part? What male chauvinists slipped that in on women? Not "husband and wife." But "man and wife." What does that mean? Sounds to me like the individual conducting the marriage is saying, "Women are married to men who are not married to them." Actually, that's about right. What are women signing up for when they etch their signatures in permanent ink on a marriage license?

To me, a marriage license is synonymous with the enforcement rights of a birth certificate. It simply identifies a person's status as having a legal commitment, but the license does not, cannot, will not, shall not, make anyone whole, complete, secure, or happy. If you get caught running a red light, you've got to pay. If you don't pay, you get a warrant for your arrest. If you get caught fucking around on your spouse, you get to stay married and fuck up again. But you can literally break all the laws of marriage and never be penalized. Which brings me to, "What are the laws of marriage?"

Hit me up at HoneyB@MaryMorrison.com with your responses.

You can throw in the towel and cut your losses, but you

cannot bring forth charges against a cheating spouse unless you're perhaps married or living in the state of Florida. I ain't gon' mention no names, but I wonder if the famous multimillionaire couple—that once upon a time lived in Florida—if their double affairs suddenly became hush-hush when the man allegedly impregnated a woman out of wedlock. Hmm? I'd better shut the shack up. I meant, shut the fuck up. Anywho, what good is a marriage license? Now, if you marry the right person, a license may make you wealthy, but how much will it cost you emotionally? Will you lose your self-identity? That's assuming you took time to know yourself before getting married.

The law cannot make any married person accountable; it merely grants an immeasurable tool with no accountability. In fact, singles have more enforceable rights than married individuals. Hmm, how many married women by law can make the husbands take care of the kids physically and/or financially? Any divorced woman or single parent who is not receiving child support means she fucked the wrong broke-ass man.

Every license in America, except a marriage license, has built-in requirements for renewal, or else it does what? Expire. A marriage license is granted in perpetuity. So when a couple decides to get married, they need to think logically if the commitment is one they're willing to keep forever. Forever . . . ever? Hmm. Not many couples stay married forever, and the ones that do? A lot of them are unfaithful, unhappy, and they die unfulfilled. A woman who defers her dreams for many years to care for her husband and kids can suddenly find herself abandoned, alone, and divorced. I wonder if the fine print on a marriage license lists children as an asset or liability. What good was the marriage license when you receive a divorce decree?

I encourage every woman and man to really think about what I'm conveying. Define marriage for yourself. Write your own vows. Maybe what you want isn't marriage at all but a mutually dissolvable cohabitation agreement and a power of attorney granting your partner certain rights, should you become mentally, financially, and/or physically incapacitated. Couples may want—and I highly recommend—one joint bank account (calculated on a percentage of each person's income or a 50/50 split) to meet the household expenses and two individual accounts in case shit don't go your way. At least you won't have to worry about your spouse running to the bank to close out the joint account after you've had an argument.

More important, as my daddy told me, "Speedy, always have enough money to leave. There's nothing worse than being in a relationship that you desperately want out of but can't afford to go." Now I don't know if my dad told me that because he'd beaten my mother until she killed herself or what, but I listened to his words of wisdom.

When my ex-husband laid hands on me, immediately I had him arrested, removed from our residence, divorced him, and started dating men who cared about my son and me. I've met some really nice men along my journey through life. When my soul mate proposed to me, I gave back the ring. He felt because he was the man he had the right to physically discipline my son. Fuck that! Beat your own damn kids that don't fucking live with you. I refused to allow any man to beat my child or me. A big dick and a set of balls don't make a man the boss in HoneyB's world. For me, a man has got to come, and have cum, with integrity. People need to know who or what they honestly care about before getting married. Know your core value system and share your values with your mate.

The piece of paper the marriage license is written on came from a living tree that once upon a time, (before it was chopped down . . . killed) released life-sustaining oxygen to human beings who destroy most everything around them, including other human beings. Why do people carelessly and vindictively hurt one another? A pussy pocket is the *only* pussy a man can ever own. And, ladies, if you want to own a dick, take a trip to the pleasure store and buy one.

What did Oprah say on one of her shows? "Hurt people hurt people." I hope you take this message to heart, and the next time you feel like hurting someone, you have a change of heart. In our paranoia-driven, socio-economic, political, conscious-less culture, marital status, just like money, ranks above health and happiness.

Are you happy with yourself?

Are the women in this novel happy? What the women in this novel get is what they have had all along. Instead of dating a single man, these women voluntarily licensed . . . *Single Husbands*.

Single Husbands . . .

Three men who married for all the wrong reasons.

Herschel Henderson said, "I do," to have access to his wife's money, Lexington Lewis vowed for his better and her worse, and Brian Flaw meant until death do we part. Herschel has a mistress that he sexes more than his wife, Lexington is making love to as many women as he can at the sex clubs, and Brian is fucking women of every ethnicity because he's a man who loves pussy. The one thing these men share is despite being married, none of them will give up the sexual freedom they enjoyed as single men.

SINGLE HUSBANDS

CHAPTER 1

Brian

Emotionally unavailable . . . to all women, except his mother and his wife.

The countless number of women he'd fucked before saying "I do" easily doubled during his ten years of marriage. Pussy was his vice. Anal sex too. Damn, his dick hardened as his eyes beheld his wife easing her red thong out of the crack of her butt, then over her ass. Irrespective of his discreet infidelity, he'd kept his wedding vows; he'd kept all of them.

He didn't marry his wife's mother. He'd married her daughter. Yet, somehow, Michelle's mother deemed it her responsibility to hold him accountable to his vows. Perhaps because her husband hadn't kept his vows, or maybe she wanted a happier life for her daughter than the one she'd had. Framed by his wife's mother, hung by him on their coral reef–painted bathroom wall, centered above their double vanity, were his exact words:

> I, Brian Flaw, take thee, Michelle Thibodeaux, to be my lawfully wedded wife, to have and to hold, from this day forward, for better, for worse, for richer, for poorer, in sickness and in health, to love and to cherish, until death do us part, and thereto I pledge thee my faith.

Brian's passion for life and his marital commitment were straightforward. His desire for love juxtaposed with his insatiable appetite for sex created a dichotomy that perpetuated an internal struggle within him. There was absolutely nothing his wife could say to keep him from being attracted to, and having sex with, other women. Nothing.

His lustful struggle, all too common among married and single men, was one that most women found incomprehensible. A hard dick needed to rest its head in a pussy. Brian was a grown man with no intention or desire to live up to anyone's expectations, except his father's. Brian's life was his own. Not his wife's. His decision to share his dick with other women, and to share his life with his wife, was a conscious commitment to share, not to give.

Reared in the South, New Orleans to be exact, Brian was taught by his wealthy parents that sharing was a good thing. "Share with your sister. Share with your brother. Share with your friends. Share with those less fortunate." His wife knew he had a philanthropic heart when they'd met at a charitable fund-raiser hosted by Les Gens de Couleur Libres, The Free

People of Color of New Orleans. Brian's primary purpose for attending the event was to meet his future wife, a woman whom his dad would approve of.

Considering there was a shortage of men at the event and everywhere Brian had traveled, his sexing multiple women was quite gratuitous, fulfilling a greater humanitarian purpose. If only in their orgasmic moment, Brian sexed more women into happiness by selflessly making them come, preferably first.

Brian's upstanding ways were deeply rooted in his upbringing. Unlike many New Orleanians, he wasn't the descendant of slaves. His father, grandfather, and great-grandfather, dating back to the 1800s, were free French-speaking men— Republicans, lawyers, and journalists—part of the Comité des Citoyens speaking out about *Plessy* v. *Ferguson,* writing about *Brown* v. *Board of Education,* constantly fighting for separate but equal rights for blacks.

Brian came from a legacy of light-skinned, successful, thinking men who would rationalize their behavior and the aggressive discipline of the white people around them. His ancestors declared success teaching—more often preaching to him—that "Light-skinned Creoles unequivocally married light-skinned Creoles." His forefathers constantly reminded him, "The darker the skin, the harder the fight for constitutional rights." Unanimously, the first time in Flaw history, every voting member of three generations of Flaws voted for Obama.

Everything was both debatable and negotiable. Respect ranked second on his patriarchal list of values, right below family values and above self-preservation. With freedom came liberties. And the Flaw men came rather frequently. The one forbidden rule was no bastards were allowed in the family tree. Flaw men took impeccable care of their kids and their wives, no exceptions. Brian's eyes scrolled from his wife's smile down to her protruding shaft.

"Baby, my pussy is puckering," she purred, spreading her lips for him to witness her arousal.

He lusted for a lick of her coconut-tasting secretions, thinking, *That's mine. I own that shit right there. Her lips, her clit, the blood engorging her shaft, even her orgasms, exclusively belong to me.*

Pussies. Suckable. Fuckable. Spankable. Lovable. Big. Small. Fat. Tight. Strawberry. Creamy. Cherry. Vanilla. Raspberry. Juicy. White chocolate. Blissful. Neapolitan minus the chocolate. Wet. Dry. Hot. Loose. Sweet. Fishy. Every pussy other than his wife's was just a pussy, a warm place to dip his dick for a minute until he made his way back home to his wife and kids. Family was first, always.

Like his father, who'd stayed married to his mother for over forty years, marrying Michelle was Brian's greatest investment. No amount of money could yield a greater return than the love of, and from, his wife. She was his everything.

Eagerly Brian wanted to slip the head of his hard dick inside his wife's sweet, hot, juicy, fleshy volcano and make her pussy erupt with white, creamy cum hotter than the bubbling praline mix his grandmother constantly stirred atop her gas-burning stove whenever his family visited her and his grandfather in Amite, Louisiana.

His wife's moans. Her shivers. Her whispers. Her pleasure was his gratification. "Take care of home first" was his family's mantra. Its creed included sexual satisfaction. Brian's stiff tongue circled inside his watering mouth, then relaxed behind his teeth. Slowly his lips parted, curving upward at the ends as he stroked his chin then smiled, watching his former Louisiana pageant queen step into the shower. Brian danced in behind her, then closed the door.

Beholding her immeasurable beauty, he admired his wife as she tilted her head backward, allowing the warm flow of water to glide over her pale face then in and out of her mouth.

"Your flight to Houston departs at two o'clock from Miami International," she said, swiping the water away from her eyes. "Your driver will be here at noon to pick you up. Don't forget to review the most recent stats and articles I e-mailed you on Marcus Monty. You know he's going to sign with you. We've already claimed that. Those other sports agents can't handle him off the court like you can, baby. Be sure to take your vitamins. I've laid them out for you and packed a daily supply in your carry-on. And most important, kiss the kids good-bye as soon as you get out of the shower, because your mother is picking them up in a half hour. Oh, and my mother reminded me to upgrade our cell phones with the new GPS, so I did yours last night," Michelle rattled.

Staring at his wife's tantalizing lips, he hadn't heard most of what she'd said and definitely tuned out everything after he'd heard her say "mother." Standing beside his wife underneath his separate showerheads, Brian closed his eyes, then

5

exhaled a long "ahhhh." Then he said, "I love you, woman," thankful that he had a competent and considerate wife. No matter how exhausting or demanding her day was, Michelle always made time for the little things that she didn't have to do, like keeping his schedule.

His wife became quiet. At times, their silence spoke louder than words. The energy swarming around his heart was all for her. Energy. Brian separated his feelings for his wife into three categories: Love. Sexual. Spiritual. The three could at some point exist independently, intermingle, or consume him all at once. There was never a time when at least one of his feelings for Michelle was not present.

The water glazing over her kissable, thin lips made his dick stand tall, damn near touching his navel. Lathering his body with Very Irresistible shower gel for men, Brian realized Michelle was the irresistible one, not him. His parents were crazy about her the minute they saw her, knowing their grandchildren would be light-skinned with good hair too. Closing his eyes again, he felt her magnetic spiritual energy beaming toward him. Slowly opening his eyes, he peered at his wife, teasing her protruding bubble-gum-pink nipples.

Brian smiled, then whispered, "Damn, that's my shit."

"Yes, it is, baby," she reassured him. "And this is mine," she said, squeezing his dick.

Not exclusively, but yes. His dick was her dick. "I miss you already," Brian said, pressing his lips against hers.

Closing his eyes once more, he imagined sprawling his fingers over the crown of Michelle's head right before bearing down, guiding her to submissively kneel before him. He loved whenever his wife demanded that he take total control in the bedroom, insisting, "Take me, Brian. Fuck me any way you want."

Anything he wanted to do with or to his wife was okay with her, except inviting another woman into their bedroom. He agreed. With a woman as amazing as his wife, he didn't need another pussy spread across his face in her presence. A ménage à trois with two other women would be nice to experience one day.

There were times when Michelle would let him say, "Bitch, give me my pussy. Sit this sweet fucking watermelon pussy on my face and rotate it in my mouth." Watermelon "Eat some now, save some for later" was his favorite candy. Sometimes he'd say to her, "I want you to come hard or you gon' make me take this big-ass dick and fuck the shit out of you." Then he'd cup his palm and slap her firm ass until it blushed the way he liked it, and say, "Answer me."

Suddenly he heard his wife softly say, "Earth to Brian."

Opening his eyes, he exhaled, "Ahhh," again returning to the image in front of and not behind his corneas.

With the warm water flowing from his showerheads beating against his chest and her showerheads sputtering water against the back of her head, his wife firmly gripped his hard dick. "Yes," he grunted, placing his hand on the crown of her head. This time he wasn't imagining. He thrust his dick in and out of her mouth before tracing her succulent lips with his precum.

"Fuck me," Michelle moaned, standing. She pressed her lips against his, surrendering her tongue to his suctioning jaws.

"Not yet, baby. Not yet." Brian's sexual appetite was brewing. His spiritual energy marinated in his wife's love for him. He wanted to get his mind right so he could please Michelle first. "I want to watch you play with your pussy, baby," he said.

"Umm," she moaned, spreading her lips once more. Her middle finger traveled in tiny circular motions over her pink pearl.

If he touched his lovely wife right now . . . "Damn. Fuck this."

Brian slammed her creamy titties and blond pussy hairs against the teal tiles. "Assume the position," he commanded, putting her hands high above her head. He covered both of her hands with one of his, pressing her palms against the wall. His foot swept her feet wider apart. His body meshed flat against hers, forcing her stomach against the wall.

"Ah, yes," she moaned, submitting to him. Her left ear and cheek were flattened against the tiles. Warm water showered his back. "Fuck me real good, Brian."

They weren't going to see one another for three days. He'd always leave her more than satisfied. The last thing he wanted was for his wife to lust for another man to fuck or love her. After tucking the kids in last night, they made love off and on until they made their way into the shower a few moments ago. One more explosive orgasm for the road would hold him until he arrived in Houston tonight.

Bending his knees, he held his shaft, positioned his hard-ass dick at the opening of her pussy, and with one long, continuous thrust he entered his wife. His dickhead throbbed up the walls of her vagina until he reached the roof of her cul-de-sac. He tiptoed, penetrating her deeper. As he stood still, his dick marinated in his wife's pussy as he lowered his lips to her mouth. They kissed. He pushed a little deeper. Within five minutes, a thick stream of cum oozed inside her pulsating pussy while the warm water caressed his back.

"I love you," he said right before her pussy muscles ejected his dick.

Turning her to face him, he covered her mouth with his, dancing with her tongue. Michelle was the only woman who drove him mad with sexual desires. That's why he had to marry her. No other woman he'd met had measured up to Michelle's brains and beauty, and his parents' approval.

Inhaling deeply, Brian held his breath for five seconds, then released, saying, "I'm good. You good? I had to release that—"

Interrupting him, Michelle smiled and then whispered, "Hush. I know, baby. I know. Yes, I'm real good." Then she kissed his lips.

Brian scooped a healthy portion of mixed plain yogurt and turmeric from the crystal dish perched on the shower ledge and began layering Michelle from her neck to her toes. She stood away from the showerheads, allowing the homemade mixture to dry and tighten her skin. Lathering her hair, he massaged his fingertips into her scalp. He loved the silky feel of her long, thick hair between his fingers.

"Ou, wee," he exhaled, reminiscing how she brushed her sandy-colored hair all over his body last night.

Two hours after his, Michelle's business flight was departing from Fort Lauderdale International Airport. "Is there anything you want me to do before I leave?" he asked, scratching her scalp.

"Umm," Michelle exhaled. "That feels wonderful. No, baby. Everything is in order. My mother will check on the house while we're away."

Rinsing his hands, Brian kissed his wife's lips while she rinsed her hair and body with cold water. He kissed the nape of her cool neck, then slid his hand between her butt cheeks.

"Baby, I swear you've got the prettiest ass God has ever given any woman. Damn!" he said, kneading his fingers into her shoulders. "Let's get outta this bathroom so I can taste my sweet pussy."

"Kiss the kids first," she insisted.

Michelle's body dripped with wetness as she smoothed coconut oil onto her skin. Gently drying her off, Brian pressed his lips to the nape of his wife's neck once more, wrapping his arms around her waist. Sliding his pubic hairs side to side against her ass, he glanced at his sexy-ass wife in the mirror.

They were an amazing power couple that spent more time on the road working than at home with one another. The quality time they invested in one another made the sacrifice for their careers worth it. Being away from Michelle three to four days out of the week made him appreciate her more.

Their fabulous home on The Island in Biscayne Bay mirrored Brian's life. He was a public figure residing in a private neighborhood in South Beach, Miami Beach. The guardhouse at the entrance of The Island resembled Brian's conservative personality. He had the illusion of being private and exclusive with his wife, although he wasn't. Like the guard on duty twenty-four hours a day, Brian would do all within his control to protect Michelle's heart from shattering if she found out about his numerous affairs.

"Baby, you are so beautiful. I love you. You are good to and for me." She truly was his foundation. Brian would rather die than live without Michelle.

That was factual—not debatable or negotiable.

CHAPTER 2

Herschel

top choking me so tight, baby." Nikki wheezed, struggling
to pry Herschel's fingers away from her throat.

"Shut the hell up, woman. You know you like this big dick
knocking the bottom out of your tight-ass pussy," Herschel
countered, repositioning his huge masculine hands for a
firmer grip and deeper grind.

As Herschel's thumbs pressed hard above his wife's pitu-
itary gland, he hoped to suppress the gland's ability to secrete
the endorphins that would make Nikki scream with pleasure,
skip to the shower, then coldheartedly leave him once more.
He wanted his wife to stay at home with him. His thumbs
dug deeper into the base of his wife's brilliant brain; he was
determined to evoke excruciating pain. The veins in her neck
swelled with blood.

"Why do you tell me to manhandle you, then beg me to stop? Make up your mind. You want me to stop or not?" he asked, fucking Nikki harder. Too bad her head couldn't pop off her body. He was fed up with honoring and obeying her. That was his wife's role.

As he pumped his pelvis against her buttery smooth, slick ass, her titties banged his knuckles. Nikki had the softest skin, which layered over the firmest muscles. Her preferred doggie style was cool, but Herschel was more of an old-fashioned missionary-style kind of guy who enjoyed kissing and looking into a woman's eyes while sexing her. He needed a woman who wanted him as much as he craved her. Once upon a time, early in their marriage, that woman was his wife. Not anymore.

Herschel was dog tired of role-playing in and out of bed with Nikki, pretending that he was happy. Secretly he hated his wife. If no one—like her mother, sisters, or clients—would notice Nikki missing, he'd kill her. Right here. Right now. Then throw her body in the bay. "Hate" was such a strong word, but the sight of Nikki disgusted him more than it pleased him. Not because she was unattractive. Nothing was further from the truth.

Nikki was five feet ten inches, a curvaceous size-twelve, with wide child-bearing hips and a round ass, plump titties— firm and perky like fresh giant nectarines—flawless mocha skin, short jet-black wavy hair on her head and her pussy, and sparkling white teeth. Nikki used to be the perfect woman for him. But once Nikki got that ten-page spread in a national magazine showcasing her culinary skills, the bitch thought her shit didn't stink. Flying all over the damn country, some-times abroad, she joyfully left him home alone every possible moment she could disappear for business or pleasure. If it weren't her house, he'd put her ass out.

Nikki stretched her neck enough to clear her airway, then said, "Herschel, I want a divorce."

Forget that. He was the one who'd stood by her side at the altar. He was the man who encouraged her to continue her multimillion-dollar business and career after they'd married. He was the one on her arm at all those humdrum invitation-only galas sponsored by Nikki's clients for their well-to-do friends. He couldn't care less about folks who spent their money and their lives pretentiously hugging, kissing, and boasting to impress one another. One of Nikki's friends told him, "Did I show you the picture of the diamond collar and convertible Porsche my husband bought our darling Yorkshire terrier, King MaxB? Oh, come see. Let me get my camera."

No, they did not spend the equivalency of my annual salary on a damn dog! Herschel had politely walked away from her. He was preoccupied living his own life, trying to get promoted at his nine-to-five, eight-hours-a-day, five-days-a-week job. He did not want to see pictures of a spoiled dog that lived better than most people.

Angrily Nikki shook her head, trying to crawl away from him. Her knees dug imprints in the mattress.

Good. That's right. Get mad. Slide. Slide your legs flat along the mattress so you can fall on your face and choke yourself, Herschel thought, clutching his fingers around her neck. She had the audacity to have gotten upset with him for fucking another woman. What was he supposed to do with his depressed dick when his wife was always gone? She was lucky he hadn't moved in a concubine or two to satisfy his sexual appetite.

Damn! What the fuck did his wife expect of him? Didn't she realize he was a man? A man with a dick that got hard every damn day, sometimes six times a day. Whenever his dick got hard—he wasn't different from any other man—Herschel wanted to stick his dick in his wife, and since most of the time his wife wasn't available, then he'd stick his dick in whatever pussy was ready, willing, and immediately available.

Nikki should've called ahead and told him she was coming home a week early. The argument Nikki started six days ago was old but far from over this morning, or tomorrow morning, or the next day after that day. Herschel knew he was the man in, not *of*, his house, because shit between them was never resolved until Nikki said so. Why in the fuck did he have to sleep on the sofa six nights in a row to appease her ass when she adamantly objected to having his baby? Wasn't his wife supposed to bear his children?

The nursery room had been decorated for ten years. They didn't have guests occupying the other four bedrooms. Why did he have to call her ass from the home phone every damn night she was out of town just to prove he was at home? Wasn't like he stayed or slept at home after hanging up the phone with her. Last night was his last night sleeping on the couch.

"You know I love you, so why do you keep disrespecting me and threatening to leave me?" Herschel asked, squeezing a little tighter.

"I can't breathe." Nikki whimpered as she struggled to

wedge her fingers beneath his. "You're"—she gasped—"choking me"—she gasped again—"too tight, for real."

Herschel had zoned out. He wanted to let go of Nikki, but he couldn't. He did love his wife. His mind said, "Let go, man," but his fingers tightened more as he penetrated Nikki deeper. Maybe if she lost consciousness, became brain-dead, then died an accidental death of unknown causes, he'd be free to marry Ivory and move his mistress into Nikki's home. No, actually, Nikki's place on The Island was a mansion.

Their two-thousand-square-foot master bedroom overlooked the Biscayne Bay. The porch outside their bedroom had a tropical theme that complemented living in South Beach. The tangerine stucco walls with high-arched cutaways allowed the perfect amount of sunlight to shine onto the outdoor covered patio and into their bedroom. Tropical punch sofas and burnt orange wicker chairs sparsely scattered about the patio made Herschel want to fuck his wife outside in their flaming red hammock every morning. He imagined bending Nikki's naked body over the waist-high stucco wall and sticking his hard dick inside her wet pussy.

When the sun wasn't shining, the track lighting lined along the patio ceiling created a purple-blue nighttime atmosphere more seductive than the day. The mural of tall palm trees clustering the ceiling reminded him how his wife's confidence could outlast his greatest storm. Why should Herschel stay home alone in such a romantic space while Nikki whisked her ass in and out of Miami International Airport like the terminal had a revolving door exclusively for her?

Herschel braced his forearms against Nikki's shoulders,

pulling his wife toward him as he slid his dick deep inside her. He couldn't deny that stroking Nikki's pussy felt like dipping his dick in warm milk and honey. Loosening his grip, he slipped his finger into her mouth, imagining it was his dick, then grunted, "Suck it for me, baby."

Nikki clamped her teeth around his finger, refusing to let go.

"Ow!" he screamed, praying his knuckle was still attached. "Goddamn! What the hell's wrong with you, woman? You almost bit my finger off!" Herschel yelled, pushing Nikki flat against the bed. He wanted to call her a "bitch," but the last time he'd done that, shit got really bad for him when Nikki threatened to put him out and call his boss. That was too much testosterone power for a woman. In a few minutes, she could've made him both homeless and unemployed. His $250,000 white-collar annual salary was less than the yearly interest on their joint bank account.

Facing him, she rammed her knee into his balls.

"Ahhh! Woman, are you crazy! What the fuck . . . uhhh . . . is wrong with you?"

Patting her neck, Nikki gasped for air.

Falling into a Z shape, Herschel grabbed his nuts; then his bald head fell onto the mattress. Shifting his eyes to the corners, he stared at Nikki as she got out of the bed. Orange tiger-striped imprints of his hands remained embedded in his wife's flesh. He saw his fingerprints spiral her neck like a choker necklace tattoo. Damn, he didn't mean to do that. Herschel witnessed the bruises darkening to a deep red. *Fuck.* The taping for Nikki's prime-time television sex-talk show was tomorrow. It was the middle of spring, and if the bruises hadn't disappeared by then, she'd have to wear a scarf around her neck to cover up what she'd made him do.

All his wife had to do to keep peace with him was give him some time, undivided attention, and genuine affection every now and then. "Baby, baby," Herschel repeated, then said, "I'm so sorry. I don't know what got into me. It wasn't me. It was some demon inside of me that unleashed. Please forgive me. Nikki, don't you see how much I need you." Stumbling toward her, his lips pressed softly against hers. His mouth circled hers, trying to pry her thick, luscious lips apart with his tongue.

Honestly, if Nikki had contracted to do a normal talk show or a cook show even, he would've been okay with that. But why did his wife have to be the acclaimed Sexpert for Sexcipes? Why did Nikki have to interview good-looking, wealthy men about how her natural aphrodisiac, high-protein appetizers and entrees would ignite their sex drive without the aid of penile-enhancement drugs? Wasn't like she cooked at home anymore or catered to his dick. Herschel was a man, and he knew how other men viewed women. The thought of his wife laughing and giggling with men who also wanted to fuck her drove Herschel insane. How many times had his wife succumbed to being a tramp, then come home offering him her sloppy secondhand pussy?

"Umph, umph," Nikki groaned, placing her hand in the center of the chiseled chest she used to drizzle her edible heated wax on, then lick it off. "No, not this time, Herschel." *Smack!* Nikki's palm landed against his face. "You need to go be with that bitch you had up in my bed when I got home! All we have left between us is great sex once a month and you've managed to fuck that up too! You can't even fuck me right. Unleash this!" Reaching behind her, Nikki kept her eyes on him as he walked away from her.

Fuck. It was a good thing he had quick reflexes. Herschel ducked just in time to dodge the hand-sized crystal ball that came zooming toward his head like she was a professional shot-putter. *Crash!* The sparkling ball stuck into the Sheetrock, looking like an intentional creation.

"You are so fucking crazy, Nikki! Stop this shit. Baby," he said. Racing toward her and snatching her biceps, Herschel rattled Nikki's body, trying to shake common sense into her. Couldn't she look into his dejected eyes and see his aching heart crying out to her? Probably not.

Swiftly turning her shoulders side to side, Nikki couldn't break free unless he wanted her to. Herschel didn't believe in hitting women, but Nikki was pushing him to do the unthinkable . . . kill her.

"Herschel, please," she pleaded. "I just want you to take your things and get out of my house. Let me be. We're both miserable. Why can't you just let me be?"

Oh, now that she'd made it, she didn't need him anymore? Was that it? If she really wanted him out, Nikki would have to buy him out. "Baby," Herschel said, wrapping his chocolate muscular arms around Nikki's long, shapely torso, "listen to me." He glided his hand over her short hair, which was neatly tapered around her mocha face. "That bitch that was here don't mean shit to me. I was lonely. I miss you. I mean, like, fuck, you're pissed off at me and it's like you're the one who's never home. I miss my wife. Damn, Nikki, you're gone *all* the time. You're never here to fall asleep in my arms at night. You're never here to let me make love to you. Coming once a fuckin' month is all I get and you're the one pissed off. A nut a month is all I'm worth? Let's work on rekindling our marriage. I need you, Nikki. Baby, please, let me make love to you right now like we're on our second honeymoon."

Staring at him, Nikki frowned.

The woman who was in their bed six nights ago honestly didn't mean anything to Herschel. But *he* meant everything to Ivory Henderson. Truth was, Ivory wasn't legally his wife, but he'd given her the title "wife" and unofficially he'd given Ivory his last name. It was a mind-control game to keep Ivory faithful to him. He wasn't serious about leaving Nikki for Ivory. But if Ivory had had half the money and assets Nikki had, Herschel would've never married Nikki, because while he did love his wife, Nikki had become too mannish for him.

In spite of her callous ways, Nikki had gotten what she'd paid for: companionship, a fine-ass man to escort her to public events, and a damn good lover. Those were the things Herschel still wanted to offer his wife. He hadn't changed at all. Nikki had done a one-eighty, turning her back toward him.

Backing Nikki onto the bed, he knew his wife wasn't finished coming. This time, Herschel climbed on top of Nikki missionary-style. His muscular thighs parted her legs nice and wide, pressing her legs against the mattress. The head of his dick slithered over her pussy hairs and along her shaft. He held his hard dick against Nikki's clit until he felt her pussy pulsating.

Feverishly Nikki kissed him, panting with her mouth covering his. The heat in her breath was the passion that had drawn him to her on their first date. Maybe if he got himself together, he could make things right between them again.

Mindful not to place his hands anywhere close to Nikki's mouth or neck, he cupped her ass while roaming his lips all over hers. He eased his dick inside his wife, slowly penetrating her the way she liked.

"Deeper, damn it," Nikki moaned, grabbing his ass, pulling him into her. "Fuck me harder. Fuck me harder, I said."

The day Herschel proposed to Nikki, he promised Ivory he'd never leave her—no matter what. He wasn't serious about Ivory. In case things didn't work out with Nikki, he wanted to make sure he could hit his backup pussy anytime he wanted. Having two lovers assured Herschel he'd never be alone.

The day Herschel stood at the altar with Nikki, he'd recited the same vows later that night at the hospital for Ivory. Role-playing had gotten him into more trouble than he'd imagined possible. Sex with Ivory had gotten better than sexing his wife. Herschel laughed with Ivory, cried with Ivory. They dreamt aloud together. Unlike Nikki, Ivory believed in him. Every man needed a woman who believed in him. But there was one thing he'd regret the rest of his life, and that was missing the delivery of his son with Ivory while he stood at that altar with Nikki.

Why couldn't Herschel respond when the pastor said, "If anyone has cause why this man and this woman should not be joined in holy matrimony, speak now or forever hold your peace"?

Herschel slid his entire body up and down over Nikki's, trying to figure out how to emotionally reconnect with her. His lips began to glide from hers down to her chin. Was his once-a-month rationing sympathy sex? If so, he'd take whatever he could get. Gently he kissed her neck, noticing his fingerprints had slightly faded. He traced her collarbone with his tongue. Positioning his mouth over one of her breasts, then squeezing her other nipple, he suctioned her nipple between his teeth. Firmly he drew her areola into his mouth, while twisting her other nipple back and forth.

"That feels so good." Nikki moaned, loosely wrapping her arms around his shoulders.

Slowly his mouth trailed down to his wife's navel, to her pussy hairs, and onto her shaft. He cupped his mouth over her clit, pausing for a moment to inhale the sweet aroma of her juices mixed with his. The taste of pineapple-honey-coconut swarmed all around his mouth. Nikki knew all the right foods to eat to taste sweet. She knew which foods heightened a woman's libido.

Nikki's culinary skills started out being for the palate at the dinner table; now his wife was a sexpert: a cunnilingus culinary chef one day and a fellatio cuisine queen the next, and in unbelievably high demand by singles and couples—straight, lesbian, and gay people—all around the world. Nikki's clients didn't hesitate to meet her demands of fifty grand a day, plus travel expenses. She was booked for the next two years and had already banked $10 million in nonrefundable deposits.

Licking his wife's pussy, Herschel thought, *Maybe I should learn how to do the same thing. Bet if I made more money than her, she'd love and sex me crazy.* He'd have to find another way to get rich quick. Nikki's niche was secure—she refused to give anyone her sex recipes, including him.

Standing at the altar on their wedding day, Herschel should've looked Nikki in her eyes and said, "Baby, I don't love you enough to marry you." But that would've meant no all-expense-paid vacations for him with his boys, Brian and Lexington. No single-family three-bedroom home for Ivory and his son. And Ivory would've had to stop lounging around the house all day and get a nine-to-five job like him. As long as Herschel kept their agreement and lived off Nikki's interest, Nikki never missed the monthly mortgage payments from their joint bank account.

Swallowing every drop, Herschel savored the juices oozing from Nikki's clit. Easing his finger inside his wife's pussy made her hotter and wetter. His dick leaked precum onto the sheet. Frantically strumming her G-spot, Herschel felt Nikki's back arch. His mouth took in her entire shaft. He suctioned her shaft as if he were drinking one of those mouthwatering piña coladas at Deco Blue in South Beach. Nikki's legs started trembling uncontrollably. Swiftly he probed her G-spot . . . deeper . . . and deeper . . . until he tapped her squirt zone. Nikki's fluids showered his face, pissing clear fluids all over him.

Hell yeah! That shit turned Herschel the fuck on! No matter how hard he'd tried, he never could make Ivory squirt. Few men could make a woman squirt and most women didn't know much, if anything, about female ejaculation. Until Herschel had met Ivory, he'd thought every woman at least knew she could ejaculate.

Nikki collapsed against the bed. Herschel lay beside Nikki. With all the money they had, he didn't know how to keep Nikki happy anymore. Eventually the inevitable would happen. Divorce. Then he'd find out how much he truly loved Ivory.

Nikki whispered, "Herschel, don't ever fuck some bitch in my house, in my bed. If it happens again, don't say a word. I'll personally pack your shit and put your ass out."

Correction—now that they'd been married ten years, it was their house and their bed. A divorce was the least of his worries. Keeping his love affair with Anthony a secret was Herschel's biggest challenge.

Herschel wasn't stupid. If it weren't for what she'd have to pay, Nikki would have divorced him a long time ago. The longer she stayed in the marriage, the harder it had become for her to force him out. And the other woman in their bed wasn't some bitch. She was a one-night stand he'd met at the gym, and Herschel couldn't remember her name.

Just in case Nikki was serious, Herschel softened his voice. "Baby, I'm sorry, and I mean that," he lied again. "Please forgive me." Raising his right hand, he continued, "I swear on my mother's grave, you are the finest, the sexiest, the most beautiful black woman in the world, and I am so fucking proud of you."

Herschel *was* proud of Nikki, but he also despised that she didn't need him. He knew that shit. Nikki could have any man she wanted. Why she'd married him? Herschel knew the answer to that too. He'd spoken all the words Nikki and every other successful, single, sexy woman wanted to hear. There were a lot of lonely women in the world. So lonely that they'd marry down just to have a man in their bed, in their life, on their arms, and to have bragging rights over their single girlfriends. A woman like his wife would stay in a fucked-up relationship to avoid being alone. Nikki wouldn't admit it, but he knew he filled a void in her life. He was like her favorite shoes. She didn't wear them often, but she'd have a fit if anyone threw them out.

"Herschel, hush. Your mother is not dead," Nikki said, getting out of bed.

"Well, she will be one day," he said, rolling over and pulling the covers up to his chin.

CHAPTER 3

Lexington

Lexington Lewis lived for the weekends. Thursday. Friday. Saturday. Sunday. And occasionally Monday. Saturday night, singles night, was his favorite night out. Dancing in the shower, he flossed twice between all twenty-eight teeth, including the gap in his two front upper teeth, then brushed for four minutes, one minute per quadrant. Roaming the bristles between his upper lip and gums, then doing the same at the bottom, he swiped under his tongue, then back and forth across the roof of his mouth. Filling his mouth, he swished the warm water between his teeth, then spat the water into the circular drain centered between his fourteen-inch-long-feet. He thoroughly rinsed his toothbrush, placed it inside the holder, then tossed it on the shower rack, picking up the bottle of citrus mouthwash. He filled the cap, poured the tingling tangy contents into his mouth, swished it around, and began lathering up his face towel.

Lexington bobbed his head as he scrubbed the inside of his ears. He intensely washed behind his earlobes and around his neck. He cleansed his broad shoulders, his slightly hairy chest, and rotated the towel six times under each armpit, singing, "Meet me at the club, I'm going down . . ."

"Humph. You gon' mess around with some bitch and catch something you can't get rid of. And you want to know why I won't give you any pussy or suck your dick," his wife, Donna, said, entering the bathroom. She hiked up her thin cotton robe, sat on the toilet, then began pissing.

What happened to his wife? Donna used to be happy, self-assured, and ladylike. Now she acted more masculine than he did. She could have used any of the other five bathrooms in their home, or even her side of their double master bathroom, but she didn't. Invading his privacy was his wife's way of protesting his going out. Complaining out loud to herself, she'd either gotten accustomed to his leaving most nights or tired of discussing the topic with him, realizing nothing she'd say or do would change his mind. Donna flushed the toilet and his warm water instantly turned cold.

"Humph, look at cha. Big ole dick ain't worth shit," she said, staring at him.

Lexington frowned. Was she referring to him or his dick? His dick shriveled in protest, trying to hide behind his balls from his wife. Lexington stood still, waiting for his wife to get the fuck out of his space and close the damn door.

Spitting the mouthwash down the drain, Lexington

resumed showering when the water returned to warm. He scrubbed his dick and pubic hairs repeatedly before doing the same between the crack of his ass. He twirled the tip of his finger inside his soapy asshole, then rinsed again and again.

Stepping his six-foot-six frame outside the shower, layering baby oil with aloe vera and vitamin E over his wet body, Lexington dried off with a plush white towel, removed the oversized shower cap from his head, shook his locks behind his back, then made his way into the bedroom. Donna was propped up like a blow-up doll in their bed, pretending she was watching television.

Sarcastically his wife said, "Don't forget your condoms. You already have more mouths to feed than you tend to. When was the last time you picked up the girls from school?"

Lexington could have replied, "When was the last time you took your lazy ass to a gym?" or "I take them to school every morning that I'm not out of town on business," but that was what Donna wanted. Any reason to keep arguing. Instead, he said, "I love you too," putting on his black linen slacks.

She knew he had three kids and three baby mamas before she married him and gave him two more. Did Donna think a marriage and more kids were going to make him settle down? After ten years of marriage—seven of them unhappy—her staying home most nights was her problem, not his. Besides, she'd stopped sexing him three years ago. So what was the point of lying in bed next to a dry, sour pussy he couldn't fuck?

"Why don't you just stay gone this time," Donna said. "You're more of an emotional liability than an asset to us anyway. Leaving me here with the kids every night, like somebody else is their father."

What the hell was she complaining about? The girls were asleep, and they'd still be sleeping when he got back before sunrise. "Haaa," Lexington exhaled, buttoning his linen collared black shirt. He tugged his waist-length locks from under his shirt, dropping them behind his back, and proceeded to twist them in a bundle. He wrapped his locks in black linen, sprayed on his Sexual Fresh cologne, slipped on his leather sandals, then left his bitter wife where she belonged—home alone.

Donna knew he wasn't going anywhere. Neither was she. The one thing Lexington wasn't was a deadbeat dad. Growing up in New Orleans with both of his parents in the house, Lexington's father was always a gentleman. He took out the trash, washed the cars, mowed the lawn, gave Lexington's mother money for groceries, clothes, jewelry, outings with her girlfriends, and anything else she wanted. His dad never forgot Mother's Day, his mom's birthday, or their anniversary. Outside of doing those things, his father went off to work and came home to play with his wife and kids. Lexington started out treating Donna the same way his father had respected his mother, but Lexington was no babysitter. His mother took care of them, and it was Donna's job to take care of the girls.

Lexington reenacted his father's ways of always providing for his children. He didn't visit his three kids outside their home, but Lexington generously paid child support for each of them. He provided a separate allowance for each of his five kids, making certain they didn't want for anything. He missed his only and oldest son, Lexington the second, but not seeing his son was easier than seeing his son's mother. He didn't love his son's mother. He was still in love with a woman who'd never had his baby.

Donna should be happy to suck his dick every day. Lexington earned enough money to retire Donna from slaving over hot stoves in a crowded Louisiana kitchen. He paid his staff to set up Donna's online business, selling and shipping body products, from their South Beach home. Donna's money was all hers and she could do whatever she wanted, including divorce him and marry someone else. What was she waiting for? Surely not for him to fall in love with her again. That was a wrap.

Hopping into his SUV, Lexington started the engine, cruised out of his driveway, and bypassed the guard shack of his Biscayne Bay home for a thirty-minute trip to his favorite swingers club in Fort Lauderdale.

Why won't she leave and go make some other man miserable? If the poor, unfortunate, unsuspecting man had any sense, he'd run like hell from Evilena Donna. No man wants a woman, girlfriend, or wife who complains all the fuckin' time about every damn thing.

Their life was like a movie script. Donna would say, "Why don't you stay home with us?"

Then he'd ask, "And do what?"

She'd reply, "I need some help around here."

"Help doing what?" he'd ask.

What did she want him to do? Put a cushion underneath her ass? Listen to how her day at home went while the kids were at school and while he was out running his technology company? His girls had more interesting topics to talk about than his wife. That's why the girls stayed in their rooms after school. Donna emotionally drained them and him. Maybe if his wife used some of those sweet, sexy-smelling body products she sold to their neighbors—Nikki, Michelle, and a few of the other women on The Island—he'd fuck his wife instead of masturbating while thinking about fucking Nikki. Herschel was his boy, but Herschel didn't deserve Nikki.

Merging onto the Florida Turnpike northbound, Lexington mumbled, "Donna better make sure she doesn't fuck up or let me catch her fucking another man while wearing my wedding ring, or she'll be a single parent on her own, like my other baby mamas. Whether I fuck my wife or not, I pay for that pussy."

His exes learned the hard way that Lexington Lewis didn't share his private pussy stash with any man. In business and marriage, he didn't believe in leftovers or second chances. It was Lexington's prerogative to fuck as many women as he wanted, especially since he earned enough money to pay all the household bills—mortgages, cell phones, car notes, water, electric, credit cards—including all of the bills for his ex-wives. He didn't need a judge to tell him how to be a man. But once Lexington was done with a woman, he was done for life. There was no backsliding in his world. And Donna knew that because she saw how he'd dismissed all of his baby mamas.

Until Donna started making some real contributions to their household—like cooking, cleaning, sucking his dick, riding his shaft, or paying half the mortgage—her pussy could shrivel up like a raisin in the sun and fester. Lexington did not give a fuck. Not anymore.

Taking a right turn onto West Commercial Boulevard, Lexington stopped at the liquor store on the corner of Rock Island Road, in the strip mall near Natural Trend Setters, where he went to let Yanique wash, condition, and twist his locks once a month with aloe vera gel and natural shea butter straight off the block. Pointing at the large, clear truffle-shaped bottle of tequila with the lime-colored ribbon, Lexington placed a hundred-dollar bill on the counter. Dude behind the counter kept spitting his lyrical rap.

"Keep the change and give me one of your CDs," Lexington said, encouraging him. "You gon' get your big break one day, man." Lexington glanced past the barbershop, down to the salon. The lights were off, so he kept things moving.

Pulling up to his spot on West Commercial Boulevard, he handed the valet attendant his keys. One line of succulent women dressed in corsets, thongs, garters, thigh-high stockings—some in stilettos, others in high-heeled boots—was standing near the podium, waiting for their cars.

"Hey, Lexington," one of his blackberry hotties said. She must've coined the phrase "The blacker the berry . . ." because her pussy tasted like raw sugar.

Lexington nodded toward the door and she handed her car keys back to the valet saying, "My lover man just got here. I'm going back inside."

Entering the club, with her right behind him, the swingers club was a revolving door of sex-crazed couples and singles

willing to mingle with complete strangers for gratifying fun—
no strings attached.

Why couldn't Donna fuck him the same way? Who gave
a damn if she was pissed? His wife's duty was to keep him
sexually satisfied. If he ever married again, Lexington was
including in his vows: "I promise to suck my husband's dick
and fuck him whenever he wants." Then he'd make her sign a
contract—if she reneged, he could bring home another woman
to fuck him.

Lexington flashed a smile at the club monitor behind the
front desk, then said, "What's new?"

"A few," he replied, reaching for Lexington's bottle of top-
shelf tequila.

"I'm expecting a newbie tonight. She's a goddess, man.
Trust me, she stands out. Let her in when she gets here," Lexington said, handing him $10 to cover his guest's fee. "She'll
ask for me by name."

The guy in the corner who was completing his online
membership application leaned over the counter and asked,
"Do I have to enter the name and address exactly as it is on
my driver's license?"

Lexington smiled as the club monitor nodded.

The guy watched other members walking in, handing the
monitor their membership cards and bottles of alcohol, then
asked, "Was I supposed to bring my own alcohol?"

Lexington smiled as the club monitor nodded again.

"Maybe I should come back next week. I don't think I can
loosen up without a drink, man," he said.

"No worries. Let him drink on me tonight, man," Lexington said to the club monitor.

"He's got you covered on drinks. Your admission fee is seventy-five dollars."

"Seventy-what?" the man asked, watching a woman hand the club monitor ten dollars. "Why come she gets to pay ten dollars and I have to pay seventy-five?"

"Because she has a pussy and you don't. Look, either you want in or go someplace else. You're holding up my line."

Reluctantly the man gave the club monitor $75, the last $5 in singles, as though that was all the money he'd had in his pocket. The guy was obviously married and it was clearly his first time at the club, and probably not his last. Men would spend their last dollar in hopes of getting their dicks sucked by beautiful women.

Swaggering toward the swinging double doors, Lexington glanced at the posted sign he'd read each Saturday night: *If nudity or live sexual acts offend you, do not enter.* That sign must've been for women like his wife, because none of the men Lexington knew were offended by lude, nude, or rude sex acts, especially his boys, Brian and Herschel.

Five days a week, after he sat on his nuts for ten, sometimes twelve, hours a day, his dick warranted unadulterated orgasmic pleasure, especially on weekends. Lexington wasn't a sex addict; he was an alpha-male sex fanatic on the prowl for all the pussy he could suck and fuck before the club closed at four in the morning. That would give him less than five hours, and, hopefully, there would be at least a half-dozen sets of puckering lips swallowing and riding his dick. But there was one special woman he'd invited. He doubted she'd keep her promise to come check out his favorite spot.

Smiling at the hotties at the bar, squirming their naked, bodacious booties on high stools, Lexington looked at the bartender, circled his finger in the air, then pointed at the new guy. R. Kelly's "Bump 'N Grind" resounded in the background while XXX videos played on flat screens throughout the club.

"Man, I know you. I got you. Him too?" the bartender asked for confirmation as he lined up ten plastic cups.

Lexington nodded, watching the bartender splash shots of tequila without a measuring cup. "Ladies and gent, this round is on Lexington," the bartender announced, serving them to all the women seated at the bar, plus the guy Lexington had pointed to.

Generously sharing his alcohol with women gave Lexington premier pick of any honey at the bar, but he didn't hang around waiting to see which ones were most interested in him. The boldest ones would find him at some point before the night was over.

Lexington recalled his father telling him, "Son, you never want to find out what kind of pussy broke-ass men have to dip their dicks in. Make as much money as you can, as fast as you can, and as honest as you can."

Lexington handed the bartender a $50 tip and picked up his usual double tequila mixed with watermelon pucker. His boy Brian, the most prejudiced white-looking black man he knew, had turned him on to palatable watermelon flavors.

Swaggering away from the bar, Lexington sat at one of the

tables in front of the dance floor and watched two women seduce the strip pole while caressing one another's titties. There were two other women dancing like they were at a nightclub, instead of a sex club, never touching one another. They must've been first-timers. Then there was a man squatting pussy-level, with two women gyrating in his face, and another grinding her pussy hairs against the back of his head. Was she coming, rolling her pussy on his head? Yep, his hair was definitely wet, and not from sweat. Damn. Lexington smiled. He'd better enjoy the moment, because soon, around two, the pendulum would swing in favor of the women once the multitude of horny men filed in from the casino and nightclubs.

Unbuttoning his linen shirt, Lexington exposed the silkiness of his chest. He unzipped his pants and pulled out his dick, laying it atop his lap, thinking, *She's not coming. I might as well get my stroke on.* Loosening his head wrap, Lexington leaned his head back, then closed his eyes, fingering his long, luscious locks.

"Hey, Daddy," an unfamiliar voice resonated from behind.

Lexington glanced over his shoulder. Three gorgeous Latina women had surrounded him. His locks always drew women to him like metal to a magnet. "Mind if we join you?"

He smiled at them.

"I'll catch you next week. I'm going home," said the woman who'd followed him back into the club.

Lexington stood and gave her a hug. "No problem. Drive safe," he said.

Opening his arms, Lexington stepped between the Latina women, saying, "Excuse me, ladies," then walked up to his invited guest. He kissed, then hugged her tight. "So you did make it. Did you pay to get in?"

She shook her head, smiling at him. "Of course not. A real woman never pays for a man's pleasure or his pain."

Smiling, Lexington clinched his bottom lip between his teeth. *True that.* She didn't have to pay for anything when she was with him. He'd happily prepaid her fee. "I didn't think you were bold enough to come out on a sex play date with me at a club. Where's your husband?" he asked, not caring.

"Probably fucking your wife," she said, passionately kissing him. "Why you got my locks hanging out like that?" Picking up his head wrap from the back of the chair, she proceeded to tie the wrap over his hair.

The Latina women had dispersed elsewhere in the club. He noticed one of them shaking her head in protest at the guy he'd given a drink to. Dude would have better odds taking off those cheap clothes and going over to the all-nude side of the club.

"I see somebody is happy to see me," his invited guest said, massaging Lexington's dick.

"That's his job. He's part of the welcoming committee," Lexington said, watching his dick harden. "See how glad he is to see you. Damn, you look hot! That's a sexy-ass thong teddy." He lowered the cup, uncovering her nipple, then sucked her breast.

She licked her lips, then kissed his.

Covering her nipple, she kissed him again. "Give me a tour. I wanna see where all of those people with towels wrapped around their asses are disappearing to," she said, gliding her fingernails up and down his back. "Hold up," she said, staring.

A man sat at the table next to them. A voluptuous woman wearing a black leather corset with garter straps, stockings, a thong, long black gloves up to her biceps, a mask covering her eyes, and stilettos stood in front of the guy as she slapped a black cat-o'-nine-tails in her hand.

"This is going to be good," his date said, sitting down like she had a front-row seat at a sex show. "She's definitely a dom. I've always wanted to do this."

The voluptuous woman danced seductively to "Darling Nikki" by Prince. Setting her breasts atop the bustier, she jiggled them in front of the guy's face, gliding the leather strips over her cleavage. Licking the straps, she grabbed his ears, pulled his face into her pussy, stuffed her clit into his mouth, swayed back and forth, then commanded, "You've been awfully bad. Suck me." Turning around, she bent over, sticking her ass in his face. Slowly she slid the straps over her pussy. "You wanna eat me, don't you?" she asked.

Frantically he nodded.

"You don't eat my pussy until I tell you to eat my pussy," she said. "Stand up. Bend your ass over the seat," she demanded.

Lexington watched his invited guest stare in amazement at the couple. Her breathing pattern altered from normal to slow, deep, heaving breaths. He could tell the couple turned her on, but his eyes trailed her eyes to the woman's nipples. From the way she watched the woman, he couldn't tell if she was more turned on by the woman or the man.

"Pull down your pants," the woman said.

Whack!

The cat-o'-nine-tails whipped across the guy's ass.

"Down," she said, and the guy knelt before her, then stared at the floor, his hands clamped in front of him.

"You want a drink?" Lexington asked. He'd seen enough.

"Whew! *Need* one. But I shouldn't. I'm on antibiotics," his guest replied.

Lexington led her to the bar. Alcohol didn't prevent antibiotics from working. His guest was having a drink on him.

She stared at the woman seated at the bar on a high stool, with a man stooping in front of her, licking her pussy, then watched another woman straddle the rail across from the bar and begin masturbating with a pocket rocket clit massager.

"This place is too hot! You should've invited me sooner," his guest said.

"Too hot or fucking hot?" Lexington asked, twirling his finger in the air to the bartender. Next he held up two fingers, signaling for a double shot of tequila, straight up, then pointed at his date.

His date unzipped his pants at the bar, shoved him against a stool, got on her knees, grabbed his dick, and proceeded to lick his balls.

"Aw, shit! You haven't even had a drink yet," he said. He wanted her to enjoy herself. That was why he'd invited her. Watching a lot of people freely having sex did strange things to all of the women he'd invited.

His guest had on her teddy and he still had on all of his clothes, including his sandals. His unbuttoned shirt exposed his chest. Lexington rubbed his own nipples. At Trapeze, there was no such thing as over- or underdressed as long as the attire was presentable for men and sexy for women.

She spat on his dick, then stroked his shaft. Her tightened fingers slid all the way down to his nuts, then she locked a firm grip, trapping the blood inside his shaft, making his dick nice, long, and overstuffed like boudin sausage.

Her mouth opened wide. Her throat bobbed up and down over his head. She suctioned him in, massaged him with her tongue, then eased him out of her mouth. Again she tightened her jaws around him, bobbing up and down his dick like he was chocolate melting in her mouth.

"Baby, ease up before you make me fucking explode in your mouth," Lexington said, nudging her forehead.

He picked up the chilled double shot of tequila, poured half of it on his dick, and the other half down her throat. Opening her mouth wide, she sucked his dick faster. Immediately his dick got ten times cooler *and* hotter at the same time. His new discovery of tequila aiding in an awesome blow job was the shit!

"Fuck, baby. You ready for this third shot?" Lexington asked. He was so fucking ready to let go of the sperm dying to be released. They knew not their own fate. His body would reproduce more sperms that would bring him ultimate ecstasy, hopefully again tonight.

She shoved his dick deeper inside her mouth, stroking and sucking him, until his legs weakened, then trembled.

Shooting cum over her sexy mocha lips, Lexington whispered, "I love you."

Lexington doubted it was the tequila warming his heart. It

was his date. Lexington was down with, and for, Nikki ever since they were high-school teenagers growing up in New Orleans—him at De La Salle and her down the street at Sacred Heart. Unlike his wife, Donna, who'd graduated from Xavier Prep, Nikki, with all of her money and success, didn't give a damn about what people thought about her. After all the years they'd been together, Nikki was still willing to try something new just for him. Nikki was the sole reason Lexington relocated his business from New Orleans to South Beach and bought an estate near hers on The Island.

He didn't want to live without sharing his life with his first and only true love.

CHAPTER 4

Nikki

Money equaled power.

An established, successful woman was more powerful than her male counterparts, and she was entitled to the same privileges as any man. Last night wasn't about Nikki fulfilling Lexington's fantasy of her sucking his dick at a sex club. Last night, Nikki felt liberated, knowing she could have satisfied her sexual craving or fulfilled her fantasy with the man or men of her choice. She chose Lexington. He did not choose her.

Last night, she could've been that exotic woman dancing on the pole, or the dominatrix woman slapping that man, or the woman sitting at the bar getting her clit licked while sipping on a drink. Ironically, Lexington's urgent desire to leave came at the exact moment when a group of tall, sexy Puerto

Rican men invaded the club, overshadowing all of the other dicks.

Women weren't that different from men. New dick to a woman was just as thrilling as new pussy to a man. All of Nikki's lips puckered the second those succulent, edible, delicious Puerto Rican men ripped off their shirts, whipped out their dicks, with conviction, and made her pussy drool.

"Let's get out of here," Lexington had said last night.

Nikki had glanced over her shoulder just in time to see some of the most impeccable, glistening asses she'd ever witnessed.

Oh, well. Maybe next time she'd go back with her best friend, Venus.

Nikki somberly eased out of bed, dragging her feet to the kitchen in search of damiana tea, fresh peaches, and figs to reinvigorate her dwindling libido. As much as Nikki enjoyed the taste of soy milk and coffee, both soy and caffeine spiked serotonin. An elevated level of serotonin decreased a woman's sex drive. Stimulants like ginkgo and ginseng were great for her male clients' sex drive but had the opposite effect on a woman's libido.

"What time is it?" she wondered, pausing in the living room to stretch her hands high above her head. The house was quiet. Good. Maybe Herschel was gone.

Entering the kitchen, she saw him leaning against the counter in front of the appliances. Nikki exhaled a dry "Good morning."

"It's way past morning," he grumbled. "And I've been thinking. Nikki, seriously, I want us to have a baby," Herschel said, standing tall, as if his posture would make her agree with his request.

Silence. Everything was quiet. No usual buzzing from the huge double-door stainless-steel refrigerator. She couldn't hear the ticking of the grandfather clock in the living room. In the moment of not responding to her husband, life for Nikki was peaceful within her. Why couldn't she be serene within all the time?

Herschel stood in front of the fresh avocados, figs, and peaches, then folded his arms across his chest. He knew her diet. He knew those were three of the foods that definitely increased a woman's sex drive, along with garlic, oysters, and chocolate truffles.

Reaching around her husband, Nikki lightly squeezed a peach with her fingertips. She selected a ripe one and placed it on the cutting board on the island. She eased a knife from the holder and laid a pineapple sideways next to the peach. Slicing off the top and the bottom, she pushed them aside, then inserted her pineapple cutter, removed the center, diced it into cube-sized chunks, then tossed the pieces into a bowl. Standing in front of Herschel, she waited for him to move out of her way.

His lips flattened. His eyes stared into hers.

Nikki placed the bowl of fresh pineapple on the island, stared into Herschel's piercing brown eyes, then said, "Please. You can't possibly be serious about this baby issue. You're not in love with me. You need to quit bringing up that conversation. I'm never having your baby. What you really want is for me to slow down long enough for you to catch up. It's too late. That's not happening," Nikki said, walking away from him.

She opened the refrigerator, scanning for the orange juice that she wanted to blend with peaches, pineapples, and strawberries for a fruit smoothie. She exchanged the orange juice for yogurt. Glancing at the clock, she saw it was well after three in the afternoon. Her late night with Lexington had left her feeling mellow and happily exhausted.

"Herschel, move from in front of the blender," Nikki said, nudging him in his side. "You don't support the bastard you've got. I do."

Herschel's jaw dropped. He quickly stood straight, then closed his mouth.

Nikki continued speaking. "What? Kwan is ten years old, looks exactly like you, and the last time I went to church with you, Ivory and Kwan sat next to me in the pew and your stupid ass let them, 'cause what? You think you're slick? You think you're smarter than me. Never that, sweetheart. I know everything about you. Everything."

Herschel reached out for her. Nikki stepped back, then said, "Don't touch me. Am I supposed to appease your ego by throwing up for months with morning sickness? Am I supposed to give you the opportunity to decide whether or not you seriously want to be a husband and father while I wobble around pregnant for nine months while you tag along as a gofer with Brian and Lexington to the golf course to stroke eighteen pussy holes? Or kick it with your girlfriend Anthony?"

Herschel held his breath.

"Um-huh. That's right. I called you on your shit," Nikki continued. "There is no way I'd gain over twenty-five pounds, getting stretch marks on this body, waiting for you to come home late at night, trying to stick your dick in me—to prove what? That you love me? Yeah, right. I was foolish to believe you'd ever keep the wedding vows you made at the altar."

"Baby, I did keep my—"

"Herschel! No, you have not! You have a fucking boyfriend, a mistress, and a son. Do you know how embarrassing it would be for me if my clients and family found out your ass is bisexual? Get out! Just get out of my face! Out of my house and go live with them! I'm not about to change my lifestyle to give you a damn baby you won't take care of." Pausing for a moment, forcing back her tears, Nikki said, "Fuck you, Herschel. Stand in front of the blender all damn day if you want to. I'll be back tomorrow."

"How'd the show go? Who were your guests this week?" Herschel asked, stepping aside.

Forget the smoothie. The hunger bubbling in her stomach boiled with disgust. Rolling her eyes at her husband, Nikki replied, "The taping was two days ago."

She knew her husband knew the answers to both of his questions. Her tapings always went well. Why wouldn't they? If he was indirectly inquiring about her bruises, the artist applied makeup to Nikki's neck to camouflage the remaining discoloration. Nikki hadn't bothered explaining how she'd gotten the marks. Her private life was nobody's damn business, and Nikki—like Brian, Michelle, and Lexington—had done a great job of maintaining a positive media image. If protecting her reputation meant quietly staying married to her bisexual husband, then that was exactly what Nikki Henderson would do.

"I know. But I've barely seen you over the last two months," Herschel said, narrowing his eyes at her.

"I've got to go. I'll see you whenever," Nikki said, leaving the fruit and the yogurt on the counter. She went into her spacious walk-in closet and tossed a red bikini into her oversized purse. Scanning for something to wear, she reached for her lavender halter-top dress.

Standing directly behind her, Herschel's hands covered hers. "Whenever? You come in here after five this morning, sleep all day, and now you're leaving until whenever? I thought you had to cater a party tonight." Snatching the dress from the rack, he said, "You are not wearing this dress out of this house."

"Haaa!" Nikki exhaled, clenching her purse. She didn't feel like arguing with Herschel again. What was she thinking? That dress didn't match her swimsuit anyway. She quietly excused herself from the closet, exited the bedroom, left the house, hopped in her car, then sped out of the driveway. The loose-fitting mint-green cotton shorts and tank-top T-shirt she'd slept in last night were fine. She could stroll South Beach topless if she wanted and she'd be among the majority of the women getting perfect line-free titty tans.

Why—oh, why—didn't she stay single? Nikki didn't enjoy disrespecting her husband; it was her way of maintaining her power. During her marriage, Nikki had grown her own set of balls. No more pretending with Herschel, catering to Herschel, being inconvenienced for Herschel, or lying around her house with him when she didn't want to be there with him. Herschel was lucky Nikki hadn't told him about her affair with Lexington. The only reason she hadn't told him was that it would destroy her friendship with Donna.

She'd known Donna before they moved one mansion away from her and Herschel. Nikki had prepared appetizers for Donna's girls' birthday parties in the last few years. Lexington talked about wanting to spend time with his kids. Nikki agreed, but if that meant time away from her, she'd support—not encourage—his planning. Nikki had her own problems with financially providing for her husband's illegitimate son. Herschel did not want another child. Her husband wanted her to relinquish her dominant position. Would her husband be happier if she were confused like he was?

"I'm crazy in love with my job. I'm damn good at it. And I pay the bills in my house. Not Herschel," Nikki said, driving past Lexington's estate.

Shit. She needed a baby like a fish needed a blow job. As she cruised by the guard shack, that thought made her laugh. Nikki sat at the red light, watching cars speed along US 41. Maybe she should've just bought herself some fish instead of getting married. Driving along Fifth Street, Nikki took a right at Collins, left at Fourth, then another right. She cruised along Ocean Avenue in her convertible, checking out the sexy-ass PRCLs—Puerto Rican, Cuban, and Latino men—at the sidewalk cafés. She wondered if marrying one of them would've been better than walking down the aisle to let Herschel put an incarceration ring on her finger. It was a ring she only wore because she was trapped in the eyes of lurking paparazzi waiting to exploit her and the husband she once loved . . . She didn't love her husband anymore.

The attractive men she saw couldn't be worse than Herschel. At least not the PRCLs she'd fuck—not giving a fuck about more than coming, so she could go about her day. The one thing each of her PRCL lovers had in common was they were all passionate. They were crazy about her; they satisfied her sexually; they had a zest for life; they enjoyed what they did. That was more than she could say about her discontented husband. What would it take to make her husband happy again? Who? What? When had he changed his outlook on life? *Despite . . . in spite . . .* she'd remained his lawfully wedded wife. The question she needed to answer: why?

Herschel wasn't passionate about his job, he wasn't happy with Ivory or Anthony, and he hated Nikki. Which was exactly why Nikki was headed to Nikki Beach for a late lunch, not with the man she should've married, but to connect to the universe and lay with her feet in the sand.

Nikki parked at valet and handed the attendant her keys. She started to bypass the gift shop but decided to step inside. "I'll take these," she said, laying the cutest sheer purple pants on the counter. Dashing into the restroom, Nikki removed her clothes, covered her body with Hawaiian suntan oil, slipped into her sizzling red bikini, stepped into her pants, then exited the ladies' room.

"Oh, excuse me," she said, almost bumping into a kissing couple standing in front of the restroom door.

A kiss was never just a kiss. She wondered if the man who was kissing the woman was equally as passionate about her as she appeared to be about him. Had they just met? Did they travel to South Beach together on vacation? Or was the guy in town on business in search of some fun and she just so happened to be the one he chose?

Lying on one of the canopy beds mounted in the sand, the white cotton sheets draping over the top and down the sides of each post flapping in the wind, comforted her. Removing her pants, Nikki motioned for the waiter. "I'd like your signature mojito, please, with two sugarcane sticks."

Sugarcane fields deep in the South. Bogalusa, Louisiana. Nikki closed her eyes, remembering the days her grandfather would go out into those fields, whack down canes with a sickle knife, then peel away the stems with his pocketknife and hand her and her two sisters a slice of what Grandpa called "Heaven's sugar." No preservatives. No additives. She missed her grandparents, her parents, and her sisters too. They were all alive, and presumably well, living what they considered Christian lives. They'd disassociated themselves from her, saying she was destined to go to hell. Well, that was okay with Nikki, because to live any life other than the one she wanted would be a lie. And God, who was a forgiving God, would never want her to be unhappy. She opened her eyes.

There were a few tables with chairs at Nikki Beach, but most guests came to experience being served food and drinks in a bed while tanning on the beach in the sun. Easing on her sunglasses, she reclined under the 80-degree heat as the bartender set her beverage on a tray at the foot of her bed beside her feet.

Reaching for her phone, Nikki answered Lexington's call. "Hey, baby. How are you?"

"I'm good, and you?" he said seductively.

"I had so much fun at the club. We on again next Saturday?" she asked, smiling while biting her bottom lip.

Hesitantly Lexington said, "Let me think about that. I'll let you know."

"There's nothing for me to think about. I'll be there. The question was intended for you," Nikki said. "Call me later. Bye."

Nikki wondered why she took everything she'd done seriously except being married. Ten years in, it was safer and cheaper to stay legally obligated to Herschel. Marrying him in the first place was her mistake. In retrospect, it wasn't a good idea inviting him to her home for a private party she hosted for her thirty-four neighbors on The Island. How was she to know Herschel would befriend her neighbor Anthony? What was she thinking? She wasn't. Nikki was simply enjoying her life when she'd met Herschel. And when they first met, he was a ton of fun. Everybody at the party that night, including Lexington, liked Herschel.

Nikki's waterfront property on Biscayne Bay, her yacht, her Lamborghini, which she seldom drove because she was always traveling, her infinity pool, her outdoor and indoor Jacuzzis, and her tennis court were comparable to what Lexington and Brian owned. The difference was Nikki had purchased her property before getting married. They each lived approximately two blocks' walking distance away from one another. The barriers of tall palm trees, larval and nectar plants that attracted beautiful butterflies, bird-of-paradise, bougainvillea, and other exotic tropical plants provided added privacy for each neighbor.

A woman with her own shit didn't need a dick to validate her, but Nikki's traditional Southern churchgoing parents didn't see things her way. They felt Herschel was sent by God. Having a husband was an investment in the future of their family, whenever Nikki did decide to settle down and have the babies Nikki never wanted. She was one of four girls (if she counted the daughter her father had out of wedlock) and her parents desperately wanted lots of, as they'd say, "grandbabies."

Nikki's parents' emotions had ruled over her senses when Herschel proposed to her on national television during one of her cooking shows. Why had she invited him on as her guest? That was the first and last time she'd made that mistake. Of all the places Herschel could've gotten down on both knees, pulled a decent diamond ring out of his pocket, and popped the question, why did he have to do it when millions of people were watching her show live? Watching him on two knees begging, instead of being on one knee proposing, Nikki didn't want to embarrass him; and she did like him, so why not marry him? It would make her Christian parents happy.

Before and after marrying Herschel, fucking Lexington kept Nikki happy. The more she became emotionally attached to Lexington, the less she visited Donna and the more she tolerated Herschel. The only thing she had to get under control was Herschel's raging temper. His aggressiveness in the bedroom had grown increasingly dangerous. At first, she was cool with a little light physical interaction. But not anymore. Herschel's hands had gotten too heavy. What if one time he went too far and choked her to death? Maybe that was his intent, so he could inherit her millions and her property and share it with his baby mama. Unbeknownst to Herschel, everything Nikki owned was willed to her girlfriend Venus. Sometimes friends were closer than family.

Men weren't as smart as women. Until today, Herschel thought Nikki didn't know anything about his so-called private lifestyle. To the contrary, she knew Ivory was a well-kept mistress who didn't work. The truth was, Nikki was glad Ivory had given Herschel a son. Now Herschel could shut up and stop pressuring Nikki about having his baby.

Nikki knew about the house that Herschel had bought with her money for his mistress and their son, but she didn't care. As long as he stuck to their agreement and lived off the interest of her money and his salary, Nikki didn't care what Herschel spent money on.

When she had less money, she wanted to please her husband more. Now that she had more money, she wanted to please herself more. She couldn't take any of the money to her grave, and the money she made allowed her to live a lifestyle most men would die trying to attain. Nikki didn't really care about Herschel being bisexual, because she was too. Venus was more than just a friend.

Nikki's business was blossoming, and yes, her husband did look great on her arm and they were the envy of many couples when they attended celebrity functions. Herschel tried hard to model himself after Brian and elevate his status by proclaiming they were a power couple too, but the media saw right through Herschel's desperate attempts to stay in front of the cameras in hopes of making himself a star. The only real attention Herschel would get would be if he came out of the closet or if she divorced him. Then the media would grant him a few moments of fame before everyone, including the media, would forget he ever existed, until a conversation of down-low brothas and the sistahs who shouldn't have married them came up.

Nikki removed her pants, stretched her body on the white cotton sheet, sipped her mojito, closed her eyes, and relaxed in the sunshine. Mentally channeling her energy throughout her body, she visualized Lexington's strong hands pressing her breasts together. His tongue circled her areolas before suctioning her protruding nipples. She felt his mouth on her mouth, slowly trailing kisses to her clit—licking, then sucking, then gently kissing her pearl. Nikki closed her eyes tighter as his hard dickhead pressed against her shaft, making her pussy pulsate with his throbs. Sliding back her hood, exposing her clitoris, Lexington teased her clit. His lips surrounded her clit while his tongue flicked up and up and up again. Nikki squeezed her thighs, butt, and vagina, thrusting her shaft in his mouth as she came repeatedly.

Life for Nikki Henderson was good. Real good.

CHAPTER 5

Brian

Houston, Texas. Home of the most beautiful—inside and out—women in America. Business wasn't always before pleasure. Last night, Brian struck gold with a tall, long-legged, Creole, slender, supersexy woman, with flowing chestnut-brown hair and dreamy hazel eyes. No doubt if he weren't already married, he could've taken her home to meet his parents. She had the perfect fitting name that meant fair-skinned. Zahra almost made him break his rule of never sexing the same woman twice.

Zahra was so strikingly gorgeous men gawked at her. Women stared with envy, rolling their eyes at her. She was so beautiful he refused to take her directly to any hotel. Chest thrust forward, head stretched to the heavens, Brian dined her at the Grand Lux Café on Westheimer Road, treated her to the lingerie of her liking from Victoria's Secret at the Galleria

Mall, reimbursed her double what she'd paid for the suite at the JW, spent the night at the hotel with her, had breakfast at Empire Café, then reluctantly dropped her off at her home on Sherman Oaks Drive.

He was tempted to accept her invitation ("Come inside for a moment") but reluctantly declined. "I'd better get going. The game starts at four."

"Please, Malik. It's two o'clock, you're not that far away from the arena, and I promise it'll only take a minute. I have to show you something," she insisted, sitting in the passenger seat, with the door opened.

Her feet were flat on the asphalt, but her ass was still in his car. Obviously, she wasn't giving up. He couldn't push her out of the car. That would be rude. The time they'd wasted going back and forth, he could've seen whatever it was she desperately wanted to show him.

Brian removed the key from the ignition, locked the car, then followed her to her front door. Crossing the threshold, he stood in the foyer. His eyes roamed in amazement. Everything in her spacious living room and foyer was white. The wallpaper, the sofa fabric, chairs, decorative pillows, the picture frames, candles, lamps, ceiling, hardwood flooring. He'd never seen a house so bright.

"Come see my bedroom," she said, holding his hand.

What the fuck! Everything in her bedroom was black. The carpet, drapes, ceiling, comforter, chaise lounge, armoire, nightstands, and dresser. Standing beside her, surrounded by the sunshine beaming through the skylight over her bed, Brian asked, "Are you OCD?"

"Don't be silly. We just spent the night together. I sucked your dick, licked your asshole, and I let you fuck me in the ass. If I were OCD, you'd know it. I just like sleeping in the dark and awakening to natural sunlight, not an alarm blaring in my ear. I'm an angel. I have one more room to show you; then you can leave."

Her self-proclaiming she was an angel was debatable and not clearly defined. Did she mean "angel" as in "sweet" or "angel" as in an "escapee from Heaven"? Either way, Brian was getting the fuck outta her eerie house.

"I'm good," Brian said, moonwalking to keep his eyes on her. Thank God he didn't have any hair for her to snatch off his head or pubic area. His mother warned him as a child that Creole women knew voodoo, but he'd never met one and he prayed Zahra wasn't going to cast any spells on him. She'd drawn him in enough last night.

"It'll only take a minute," she insisted.

"I've already been here a minute. Thanks for your Southern hospitality," he said, swiftly heading toward the front door. He'd seen more than enough of her "mistress of the dark and light" museum.

"Brian Malik Flaw," she said, with a tone only his wife had used when she was pissed at him.

Oh, fuck! Brian stopped three feet short of the threshold, looked at her, then asked, "What did you call me?"

"I know exactly who you are, silly. Our meeting was no accident. I was paid by this person to follow you to Starbucks for some joke show," she said. "I thought you knew. I didn't expect you to take me out. I've been your biggest fan since you played ball in high school in New Orleans. You're the agent that's recruiting Marcus Monty. You're married. You live in South Beach. You have two kids. You played professional basketball overseas, then here. You used to coach the team you played for. Now you're an agent. I love you. Can I have your autograph?"

Okay, this bitch is crazy, he thought, swallowing the lump in his throat. Zahra was the first light-skinned chick he'd fucked who knew all about him. His father hadn't warned him about her kind that would follow him his entire career. Zahra was stiffening his spine with a crisp winter chill in the middle of summer. Brian hurried out of the house, got in his car, locked the door, backed the hell up out of her driveway, and left.

"Shit! What the fuck is that?" Brian said, glancing over to the side. A black flat envelope appeared in the passenger seat. Obviously, she'd left it there. But what the fuck was in it? Should he open it or toss it out of the window? Brian decided to do neither. He kept driving until he arrived at the arena.

Picking up the envelope, Brian nervously exhaled. "Best I find out what ole girl is up to." He peeled away the tab. He eased his hand inside, then removed a few sheets of paper printed from Wikipedia.com. One sheet documented his early life, the other his playing career, coaching career, and personal life. Last, there was a 4 x 6 photo on 8 ½ by 11 paper of him shaking hands with Marcus. Did Marcus know Zahra?

Placing the papers back inside the envelope, Brian rubbed his head, then ground his back teeth as he entered the arena. He was glad Zahra didn't have his phone number. Backtracking, he tried to recall any peculiar behavior. They'd met at Starbucks, walked over to Grand Lux, walked to the mall, crossed the street, went to Walgreens for Magnums, crossed the street to the hotel, spent the night, and woke up. She'd reentered the room as he opened the bathroom door. "That's it," he said, sliding the papers from the envelope. Brian's lips tightened as he read the date and time on each page. She'd printed the papers that morning. But how did she know his real name?

His thoughts of Zahra faded to screaming fans that gradually quieted under the dimming lights. Silence proceeded as *"O say, can you see, by the dawn's early light"* resonated from the basketball court to the ceiling of the arena. *"O'er the land of the free"* echoed simultaneously with piercing screams from anxious fans that vibrated in his ears.

Free? Not really, Brian thought, watching Marcus bounce on his toes. Waving his fist high above his head, Marcus Monty was ready for the game that Brian hoped would make Marcus the number-one draft pick and him the top sports agent in the country.

"Oh, shit!" Brian said, turning to acknowledge the tap on his shoulder. He relaxed when he heard, "What's up, man? I didn't mean to startle you. You all right?"

Exhaling, Brian said to his number-one competitor and longtime friend, Brandon, "Well, I'll be damned. Man, where've you been?"

"Trying to stay two steps ahead of you, man. That's why I'm here. 'Cause I knew your ass would be here trying to sign Marcus. How's Michelle?" he asked.

"She's good. The kids are good. And how's your wife and kids?" Brian asked.

"Divorced, man. Said she couldn't take me being gone all the time. Claimed she was a married woman living the life of a single mom and checked this shit out. Can you believe she called me a single husband? What the fuck is that, some new feminist terminology? Anyway, she's with some other man now and I hope he makes her happy, since I apparently screwed up the best years of her life," Brandon said, biting his bottom lip.

Brian watched his friend's lip quiver, moving Brandon to tears that he refused to let fall. Damn, that was fucked-up! Watching a grown man cry over a woman. That shit would never happen to him.

"The problem was, she didn't have a life of her own, man. That's not your fault. You had to do what you had to do to support your family. These women start out wanting a rich man, with lots of money. Then when you marry them, they want you to stay home. How the fuck you supposed to make paper sitting on your ass all the time? I'm glad Michelle travels too. Would your wife, I mean ex-wife, rather you be at home all the time and struggling financially, or on the road providing a grand lifestyle for her and the kids?"

"She's fucking gone, man. She left me. I think that answers your questions," Brandon said angrily.

"Whoa, I didn't divorce you. You still my nigga. Let me buy you a drink after the game," Brian offered, since he didn't have a fuck buddy to cuddle up with for the night. Tripping off the mysterious Zahra, Brian had his own issues. Zahra never said who paid her. Shit, he could use a drink just as much as—if not more than—Brandon.

"Sure thing. Spencer's steak house inside the Hilton Americas?" Brandon said, sounding better already. "I have a taste for one of their double pork chops."

"One better. Skyline Bar and Grill on the top floor," Brian said.

Michelle texted Brian. *BJ is crying for you. I know you're busy but can you call your mother's and talk to him for a minute?*

Brian texted back, *Of course, baby. I love you.*

"Excuse me, man, I gotta make a call right quick," Brian said, exiting into the lobby. Not wanting to upset Brandon further, Brian omitted mentioning his wife or his son.

Damn, that was fucked-up. Brandon's wife seriously told him that shit. After all Brandon had done to give her a luxury home, top-of-the-line foreign automobiles, live-in nannies—whatever Brandon's wife wanted, he bought her—and she still left him. That was seriously fucked-up. Would she rather have a man sitting up under her ass all day, or a husband out working his ass off for her and the kids? Enough about Brandon, Brian had better figure out if that Zahra chick was lying, telling the truth, or if she had intentions on stalking him. What difference did she make? Whatever she wanted from him, she could forget it.

Brian dialed his mother's number to speak with his son.

His mother answered the phone immediately, then said, "I don't know what's wrong with BJ. He won't stop crying."

"Put him on the phone, Ma," Brian said, eyeing a woman at the margarita stand. Her titties were huge, waist small, complexion fair, and hair was long, just the way he liked. He imagined pouring that margarita all over her pussy hairs, teasing her nipples with the lime, then licking the tequila off her clit until she screamed his name, "Oh, Malik!"

"Daddy, I miss you. Come get me," BJ cried into the phone.

"I miss you too, son, but Daddy is too far away from home to come and get you right now," Brian said loud enough for the woman to hear. Slowly she stuck out her tongue, swiped a dash of salt into her mouth, then sipped her drink. She knew what she was doing. "Daddy is going to call you back right after my meeting tonight. Stop crying. Tell Grandma to let you stay up until I call you back."

"Okay, Daddy," BJ said, sniffling. Brian felt the faint smile in his son's voice when he said, "I love you, Daddy."

"I love you too, son. Daddy has got to go watch the game. I'll call you later," Brian said, ending their call.

BJ was Brian's biggest manipulator. He'd learned that if he talked his grandmother into calling his mother, Michelle would text Brian, and Brian would let him stay up late.

Brian wasn't hungry, but the beautiful woman occupying his eyes and his mind made his dick and his tongue thirsty for some juicy pussy. What the fuck was wrong with him? Nothing. Being sexually attracted to attractive light-skinned women was as natural as breathing.

"Let me get that for you," he said, curling her long red acrylic fingernails around her twenty-dollar bill. Her hand felt like satin. "Let me have a, um . . ." A hot dog was out of the question. He didn't want a pretzel. All he really wanted was the woman in front of him, sitting naked on his face. "A Sprite," he said.

"Are you here with someone?" she asked.

"No, but I do have to watch the game closely. Can I buy you a drink later tonight? After the game perhaps? Can I get your number?"

Tucking her hair behind her ear, she casually asked, "What's your name?"

How rude of him. Glancing over his shoulder to make certain no one he knew was within ear range, he was so excited about fucking her later he hadn't thought to tell her. "My name is Brother Malik."

Frowning, she asked, "Are you Muslim?"

"I'll answer that later," he lied. What difference did it make if he were Muslim, married, or single? She should've asked if he was a serial killer or a con artist. That would've made sense. He wanted to fuck her. She obviously wanted to fuck him or she would've left by now. "I've *got* to get back inside."

"Save my number in your phone. Seven seven three," she said, pausing for him to program all of her digits. "Call me right after the game."

"Chicago, huh?" Brian thought, pressing the corresponding numbers. Area codes didn't mean much nowadays. Memorizing each digit, he backspaced, deleting the numbers he'd pressed on his phone. If he couldn't remember a woman's number, he wasn't interested enough in her. Of all the numbers he knew, he didn't know Zahra's number, but he did know where she lived.

Memorizing numbers kept his telephone history clear of

all potential allegations from females plotting to entrap him in a scandal. He didn't have to hide his phone from his wife. There was nothing incriminating for her to find. Before he returned home from his road trips, Brian placed his clothes in the laundry bag at the hotel for overnight dry cleaning to make sure he didn't return to Michelle with any parts of him smelling like another woman.

Brian loved traveling. As much as he loved his wife and kids, he couldn't imagine being home with them seven days a week, fifty-two weeks out of the year. How did couples that ate together, slept together, and worked together too, not tire of seeing one another? That would drive Brian fucking nuts. What did they talk about? Were their daily conversations monotonous, like tuning in to reruns of *Good Times* or *Girlfriends*? Brian often grew impatient holding the phone, waiting for Michelle to say something. His preferred communication was face to pussy. Not texting and definitely not talking on the cell phone. Before and after marrying Michelle, he made certain he had obligations other than being home under her all the time.

Brian made it back to his seat in time to see Marcus Monty tip off his last college conference championship game. Becoming a sports agent allowed Brian to remain anonymous most of the time. Most groupies were excited about the current players, not the former players or the agents. He doubted that the woman he'd just met in the lobby had any idea who he was, and he'd plan to keep it that way. A few what looked like teenage girls waved at him. Brian waved back, then quickly looked away. Entertaining young girls was never a consideration.

Anxiously Brian wanted to sign Marcus before Brandon made his final pitch. If he got Brandon intoxicated until he passed out, Brandon would miss his opportunity to meet with Marcus. Brian could return home tomorrow night, but he might stay in Texas a few extra days to find out something about Zahra. Did she live alone? Did she have any siblings? A husband? Who were her parents? A man could tell a lot about a woman if he knew her mother and her father.

If it weren't for his mother keeping the kids, Brian's marriage would be totally different; he might be getting divorced along with Brandon. Brian would insist that Michelle quit her job or reduce her hours to stay at home with the kids, like his mother had done for him. Unlike penguins, where the males cared for their young, rearing kids was inherently a female's primary responsibility.

Brian enjoyed taking his family on vacations, like his dad had done with him. As Brian grew older, his father began taking him on business trips, which were pleasurable. That's when Brian witnessed his father having affairs and one-night stands. His dad was a good man and his role model.

Sitting in the aisle seat on the last row of the first level, Brian witnessed an incredible game. Monty's stock increased when he got MVP of the conference. Brian scurried down the steps, courtside, to congratulate Marcus and Ms. Monty for doing an awesome job single-parenting Marcus; then he left the arena.

Making his way to his downtown hotel, he used the pay phone in the lobby to call the woman he'd met at the concession stand. "Hey, I can meet you in two hours," he said.

"That's fine. Where're you staying?" she asked.

"I have to meet a client. Can you reserve the room and I'll give you the cash when I get there?" Brian recommended the hotel he was already at.

"Call me back in exactly two hours. I'll be there," she said.

"Cool," Brain said, ending the call. Women who couldn't afford to rent a hotel room for a night were not worthy of him fucking.

The elevator ride to the bar on the twenty-fourth floor was smooth and fast. He sat at the bar, ordered a vodka martini with pineapple juice and a splash of coconut rum. Appreciating the panoramic views of downtown Houston, he felt Michelle's spiritual energy flow through his body. Four drinks and two hours later . . . no Brandon.

Brian had a nice buzz flowing. He returned to the lobby, then used his calling card to phone his fuck buddy. She'd already checked into room 18411. Brian programmed his cell phone to sound an hour after he'd arrived at her hotel room. One hour was plenty of time to bust a nut or two.

She opened the door; he handed her $200 for the room. She looked more delicious than when he'd met her. Her lips were red, sweet, and sticky, like watermelon. Her pussy was nice and plump. In seconds, his mouth was all over her body. Turning her body facedown, he strummed her pussy with his finger, slowly wiggling one of his other fingers into her asshole. Rolling a condom over its head and down his shaft, Brian put the head of his dick in her ass. She protested, moving away from him.

"Uh-uh, hell no. I don't do that shit," she said.

"Don't or won't?" he asked, resting on his knees.

"Same thing. You are not putting that big ole thing in my butt."

"Relax, it doesn't hurt. I promise I'll be gentle," he said.

She glanced over her shoulder, watching him. Brian removed the small bottle of lubrication from his pocket, squirted the gel over her asshole. Slowly he put the head inside her. She moaned. He eased in a little more. She moved away. Maintaining his dick's position, he followed her movements, trying to penetrate her deeper.

"Stop! Move, I gotta go to the bathroom. I gotta shit," she said.

"No, you don't. That's natural," he reassured her, thrusting a little deeper.

"I don't want to do this," she said, crawling away from him.

"Damn." Brian clenched his teeth, praying she'd shut up. The walls were thin. He heard the couple next door talking. That meant they could hear her protesting.

"Be quiet," he said, snatching off the condom.

Easing his dick into her mouth, she gave him the best blow job he'd had in two weeks. Her mouth felt incredible.

Stroking her deeper, he pulled out, then came in a towel. He wrapped the condom, the condom wrapper, and the lubrication in the towel, folded the towel, then placed it in his pocket. His alarm sounded. Brian dressed, picked up his phone, and said, "That's my client. I gotta go. I'll call you later," he lied, watching her completely naked body sprawled across the bed.

For the first time, he didn't care about making a woman come. He was done and he was gone.

CHAPTER 6

Herschel

Salvation meant different things to many people.

Most men were chronic idiots when it came to dealing with women and relationships. Herschel Henderson couldn't vouch for other men. Now that he was older, he had to try and understand how his childhood adversely impacted his adulthood. Some of the reasons he didn't trust or love Nikki the way he should have had absolutely nothing to do with his wife.

Reared by his single mother, abandoned by a deadbeat absentee dad, Herschel was confused and angry. How was he supposed to treat his woman, his lover, his wife, and his kid? He had no mentors or anyone in his life that cared enough to teach him how to be a man. His life had not come equipped with an automatic pilot for successful relationships.

What he did have growing up was religion; not beliefs, but principles. King James. Ecclesiastes. From Genesis to Revelation, to the First and Second Chronicles, Corinthians, Peter, and John. From sunrise service to fellowshipping as a child every Sunday afternoon, Herschel was too young to realize his mother's salvation was not his, until he'd moved out of her house and temporarily stopped going to church. Sitting in church eight hours on Sundays, praising the Lord's name to the top of his baritone voice, being baptized at the age of five—well before he understood why—hadn't made him a saint. No amount of Bible study, ushering, or participation in church plays could save him or the congregation from sin or deliver them from evil . . . a chasing after the wind.

Repentance.

What was the point in asking, seeking, or praying for forgiveness yet not changing one's ways? Or taking on bad habits that were sinful. Everything was meaningless. Nothing much mattered to Herschel when he was a child, except survival. His mother convinced him they had to fast three days a week, when in reality they didn't have a choice. There was no bread to break. There wasn't enough food for her to feed them seven days a week. The clothes on his back, the shoes on his feet, were hand-me-downs from his older brother.

Growing up in the Wild Magnolia, or what some New Orleanians called the Nolia, taking his first trip on his tenth birthday to the Audubon Park Zoo with his mother and two siblings—no father—walking to Booker T. Washington High School four years straight in tennis shoes with worn soles, Herschel knew he had to escape poverty, or die trying. As a young boy, what he didn't know was how. How dare those who hadn't known him stand righteous in judgment of him.

"Suck my dick, kid, I'll give you twenty bucks," a stranger in the French Quarters had propositioned him. No one was watching. No one would know. And his brother and sister could eat seven days that week. So he did what he wasn't proud of to help his mother. "Let man lay with man" wasn't God's plan. That wasn't Herschel's plan either.

He never told her or anyone else what he'd come to do more often than he'd wanted. The money was more than a motivator; it was his and his family's salvation. New clothes. New underwear. New shoes. Would God punish him for putting food on his family's table? That was a chance Herschel willingly took every weekend when he ventured to the back alleyways of "the Quarters."

Since the age of twelve, Herschel had worked out five days a week so he'd be able to hold his own if he got into a fight. Staying physically fit and playing football in high school allowed him to escape the backseats of NOPD police cars, avoid long nights of sitting on project steps drinking, gambling, telling lies, selling weed, or getting some teenage girl pregnant. In high school, having a better body meant he attracted older women, who owned their own homes in places like New Orleans East, Gretna, Uptown, or Metairie. He traded in sucking dicks for cash for sucking clits in exchange for a well-lighted, warm, quiet place to lay his head at night.

Being kept by a woman was better than sharing the ragged bunk beds that he'd outgrown before graduating from F. P. Ricard Elementary School—named after a notable professor who, in the early 1900s, at the YMCA on Dryades Street, instructed boys and men on the fundamentals and skills needed for gainful employment.

High-school graduation day at the Municipal Auditorium, Herschel had a diploma in one hand and a one-way ticket to Miami in the other in search of gainful employment opportunities. He'd heard South Beach had great weather year-round and incredible-looking women, so he hugged his mother good-bye, promising her he'd do good for himself, move her out of the projects, and make her proud of him.

Herschel's first real job—working for the largest cruise line in the nation—may not have meant much to some, but considering where he'd come from, it meant a lot to him. He'd worked his way up from clerk to management, bought his mom a shotgun house off Napoleon Avenue, above Claiborne Avenue in a good neighborhood, before proposing to Nikki. His wife wasn't impressed with how nice he treated his mother, nor had she cared about what she considered his menial occupation.

His great looks and big dick attracted her like she was game fish and his dick was the jerk bait that hooked her. There was so much more to him than the bedroom skills he mastered as a teenager or his ability to make every woman and man he'd sex have multiple orgasms. Herschel had an invisible bleeding heart. Emotionally wounded and all. Sometimes he believed Nikki married him because she felt sorry for him. She shouldn't. No one should. He'd kept his promise to his mother and made her proud, and unconditional love temporarily stopped his bleeding. His recollection of his father was vague. All Herschel knew was he didn't want to be the type of father or man that his dad had been. That was, if he could call his father a man. Apples didn't fall far.

Fucking and fucking over someone was easy. Without a Global Positioning System, a compass, a road map, role model, or father figure, Herschel had to blindly navigate how to love and make love. He knew infidelity was a sin. He'd spent enough days listening to sermons preached by married and unmarried sinning preachers, who'd slept with members of the congregation, to know that sodomy and fornication were equally detested in the Bible . . . damnation. What he didn't understand was how could something as blissful as sex be sinful, and why didn't the pastors practice what they'd preached to him? Regardless of what others thought or taught, as long as Herschel was alive, he'd continue to share his body with whomever he desired. No one else could die for him, so why should he live his life for them?

A physically fit, well-dressed, intellectual, working black man was a blessing and a curse. Women who didn't know his last name was Henderson lustfully stared at him, like his dick was stamped USDA Prime beef. They wanted to fuck him. Suck his dick with A1 Steak Sauce. Take him home to their mothers. Buy him expensive gifts. Marry him. Men propositioned him with the same things too.

Herschel's tight ass, thunder thighs, and six-pack abs didn't translate into him treating the better-looking men and women whom he attracted any better than he'd treated his wife, his mistress, or his male lover.

Parking his car in downtown Miami at the athletic club,

Herschel hurried inside, hoping the awesome abs class wasn't full. Afterward, he'd stay in the same room for the Brazilian beat class. One day soon, he was taking his dream trip to Rio to showcase his body and his salsa skills. His tight body, impressive dance moves, and deep pockets would guarantee him first pick of the sexiest women in the world. He'd read the book by Jewel Woods, *Don't Blame It on Rio,* but nothing could be further from Herschel's truth. His premeditated, promiscuous fuck-a-thon would all be blamed in the name of Rio de Janeiro. The main reason Herschel participated in the abdominal class was most of the women in the class were maintaining, not attaining, gorgeous bodies.

Placing his mat on the floor next to the woman he'd invited to his house the night Nikki showed her ass up at home early, he greeted her, "So where've you been? How've you been? What's up?"

Herschel had no reason to display anger toward her for him getting caught by Nikki. That was his fault. They wouldn't get caught again, not in his house. The woman's pussy was good, but the fuck wasn't worth the relentless fight with his wife.

Spreading her legs wide, like she'd done while fucking him, she smiled, then said, "Looking for you. I'm glad you came." She winked, then asked, "What are you doing after class? Is your wife home? My pussy could use another one of your big-dick tune-ups."

Herschel frowned, scanning the room to see if anyone had overheard her. Nodding, he replied, "Why wait until after class?"

She stood, rolled up her blue mat, tucked it under her arm,

then cheerfully said, "Ready when you are," waiting for him to get up.

Damn, was she that easy all the time? He was joking. She was serious. She positioned her pussy directly in front of his face. He grabbed his mat, tossed it on the stack of other mats. "Leave your car here, I'll drive. Meet me out front in fifteen minutes. I need to take a quick shower."

"I'll park—"

"No, leave your car here. I'll drive," he said, shaking his head. Women sure made it easy for married men to cheat.

Herschel entered the locker room filled with naked and half-naked men. Herschel sneaked peeks at a few big, succulent dicks. Staring at another man's dick was not tolerated. A few memberships were revoked for complaints about homosexual activities in the steam room and Jacuzzi. Fortunately, he wasn't one of the guys management had caught. Herschel removed his hygiene products from his assigned locker, showered, brushed his teeth, then hurried to put on his black wifebeater, baggy shorts, and sandals.

Parking in front of the Financial Center, Herschel waited for his sex mate. He couldn't call her a friend. He barely knew her. But what he did know was she was incredible in bed, and that was enough information about her for him to fuck her again.

Miami was a great place for him to work and play. No business or personal income tax. No state personal income tax. And corporate tax was only 5.5 percent of net income, which was why Nikki had declared herself a corporation as opposed to a sole proprietorship. Herschel was 100 percent certain if Nikki could, she'd list him as a dependent.

Scrolling through his phone, Herschel called a nearby hotel, made a reservation for a king-sized suite, then said, "Deliver a bottle of champagne to the room, chill it on ice, and leave two flutes. Oh, and add a half-dozen chocolate-covered strawberries." After regrettably inviting the woman to his lavish home on The Island, there was no way he'd downgrade by taking her to a cheap hotel. He was no fool. The classier the hotel, the better his dick got sucked.

"Hey," she said, smiling and sitting in the passenger seat. "This is a great deviation from doing that abs class. I'ma start out on the bottom and curve my pussy up into your dick to get my workout in. Them I'ma get on top and grind my pussy into your dick, so I can work my gluteus . . . whew! I can't wait. So where're we going? Your place or mine? Oh, excuse me, your mansion or my condo?"

"You really are bold. You'd actually go back to my house after what happened last week?" he asked.

"Sure. She can't beat my ass. She's your wife, not mine. Besides, you're the one who said she's never home," the woman said.

"No, I'm not taking you to my house. Not today. I have business in the city, so I don't want to drive back over to this area," he lied, driving a short distance to the hotel.

"Wow! Are you serious? This place is absolutely phenomenal!" she said, opening her door before the valet attendant was close enough to open it for her.

Yes! Herschel's incredible blow job was only a few floors away. Herschel didn't want to do a lot of talking. Maybe if he'd shut up, she'd shut up. He checked in, got one room key, and headed straight to their suite on the thirty-second floor. He slid the credit-card-style key in the slot, then held the door for her.

What was it about a man's dick that made him drop everything he was doing to ejaculate? Was his radical, animalistic, predatory behavior embedded in his DNA? Was bisexuality hereditary? Was Herschel treating women the same way his father had disrespected his mother? Had his father ever been fucked by or had fucked a man? If not, what made Herschel attracted to both men and women?

The woman standing naked before him had a choice. She chose him. She could've kept her mouth and legs shut. She could keep her clothes on and leave. She could drop to her knees and suck his dick. Hopefully, thoughts of sucking his dick were on her mind.

She smelled sweet, looked edible. Her brushed-back dark brown hair tucked behind her ears highlighted her mouth. The chocolate lip gloss drew his attention to her lips. He wasn't familiar enough with her to lick her pussy, so he kissed her. Touched her breasts, caressed her clit, then eased his finger under her shorts, sticking his finger inside her pulsating vagina.

"Ou, yeah," she moaned, squirming onto his finger.

Inside, her pussy was warm and creamy.

He'd done those things to get her in the mood to go down on him with those luscious, shiny lips. He watched her slowly strip out of her drawstring shorts and spandex top, pull back the comforter, then sit on the edge of the mattress. The bed wasn't where he wanted to fuck her. He wanted to pound her in the living area, with her big, spankable ass spread wide in front of him.

"Over here," he said, motioning a come-hither with his finger. "Get on your knees and suck my dick the way you did at my house." He stood tall beside the sofa, staring down on her. "You give the best fucking head I've ever had," he complimented, hoping to encourage her to do better this time.

Closing his eyes, Herschel relived how incredibly amazing his bulging dickhead felt when sandwiched between her fleshy jaws, gliding along her slightly abrasive tongue. "Wait," he said, taking off his shorts. Removing the magazines from the coffee table, he tossed them to the floor, then reclined on the sofa. His ass was cradled in the cushion. He slid his feet apart, settling them flat on the floor, then said, "Get on your knees on the table and bow onto my dick. Look up at me when you suck this big dick." He held his stiff erection straight up, waiting for her mouth to cover his head.

"Sure. Whatever you want, as long as you eat my pussy real good," she said, kneeling on the table. "Your wife got home before I got my pussy licked, and you ain't leaving here without doing me, 'cause I love having my clit sucked, nice and slow, and have no problem giving you step-by-step instructions."

As she braced her palms on his knees, her hands slipped off his thighs. *Damn!* She fell face-first into his dick, fucking up his orgasm and his dick.

"Oops," she said.

"Oops, my ass. Never mind," Herschel said, putting on his shorts. Rethinking his next move, he said, "Sit next to me."

He watched her as she sat on the sofa beside him. She

placed her hand atop his limp dick. "I'm sorry, Daddy," she said, gently massaging his dick before easing the elastic band underneath his balls. She gripped his dick with one hand, then leaned into his lap. "Um," she moaned, sliding her saliva up and down his shaft.

That was more like it. "Pump my dick," Herschel moaned. "Faster. I wanna get this shot out the way, so I can fuck the shit out of you doggie-style."

Herschel thought about drilling her asshole the way his boy Brian talked about fucking women in the ass. That way he was guaranteed he wouldn't end up with another kid outside of his marriage. Herschel liked the feel of pussy way too much to switch it up. Besides, ass-fucking a woman would mean being unfaithful to his man.

"Damn, you taste so good. What do you eat?" she asked, sucking harder.

Whatever his wife ate. Herschel didn't want to talk. Thrusting his dick deep into her mouth, he was on the verge of coming. "Yes, damn, it's right there."

"Ou, yeah. I taste it," she mumbled.

"You ready for this . . . ah! Ah! Yes!" he yelled, squirting deep in her throat. His head was so deep, she didn't have an option. She swallowed.

Coming in a woman's mouth was a male dominating tactic. Like a dog pissing territorial pheromones to claim his territory, Herschel came in a woman's mouth to feel empowered over her. His boys felt the same way. Once a man ejaculated in a woman's mouth, every time he saw her, with or without another man, he felt a sense of ownership, as though he could make her suck his dick anytime he wanted. Even if that power wasn't true, Herschel felt that way.

Why she'd let him come in her mouth was his pleasure, not his concern. Thankful he had a son, not a daughter, Herschel wondered if his father had treated his mother the same way. Herschel hated that Nikki consistently spat his sperm back onto his dick, or pulled his dick out of her mouth right before he'd come, spilling his seeds onto his stomach.

"Here, kneel on the sofa," Herschel said, holding the condom packet in his hand. He slid his dick inside her, feeling her hot, juicy pussy before he rolled on the condom.

She didn't hesitate to tilt her ass in the air and spread her lips for him. He liked that shit. "Yeah, play with that sweet pussy," he said, rubbing his forehead on her clit, stuffing his nose inside her pussy. He wanted to smell her pussy juices engulfing his nostrils. He teased her for a moment before sliding his bald head over her vagina. Feeling the warmth of a woman's pussy juices smearing the crown of his scalp was his private fetish, especially if she had coarse pubic hairs.

"Aw, yeah," Herschel grunted, closing his eyes. Nothing in the world felt better than pussy. Holding her butt cheeks in his hands, he slid his dickhead inside her pussy, then fucked her nice and slow.

"Stop playing with my shit and fuck this pussy like you want it," she commanded.

Bracing her hands on the back of the sofa, she pushed her pussy onto his dick and started stroking her clit. "Damn," she whispered. "Your dick must be dipped in platinum. I'm creamin' all over that motherfucker already. Ah-ha . . . that's my shit!" she announced several times, riding him like she couldn't get enough. "Pull my hair! Spank my ass!"

"Pa-yow!" he said, slapping her ass hard.

"Yes, do that shit again," she commanded.

"Pa-yow!" he said, smacking her two more times.

"Oh, that feels so fucking good," she said, rubbing her clit.

If Herschel couldn't please Nikki, he'd do his best to pleasure every person he fucked. "Get on your knees on the floor and crawl like a dog." He wanted to say "bitch," but he feared that might change her mood.

"Whew! You're a pit bull," she said, crawling in front of him. Collapsing onto the carpet, laughing, then rolling over, she stuck out her tongue like a puppy, spreading her pussy lips. "My turn. You ready to taste the best pussy in the world?"

Herschel frowned. Hell no. He wasn't lapping up her cum. "Let's shower," he insisted. "I'll go first." He locked the bathroom door, then scrubbed his body under the hot water.

A man wasn't interested in eating, chilling, cuddling, or conversing with a woman he considered easy, sleazy, or a jump-off. This chick was definitely a jump-off. She'd done her job. She'd gotten him ready to go fuck his male lover. Herschel would fuck her again, but he wouldn't make plans to hook up with her. Just like when he'd first met her and taken her home, then today; that was how his relationship with her would always be. Impromptu pussy. But she seemed to be okay with that. More women were becoming like men every day. Soon the scripts would change and men would be reduced to—not lovers—dick mills. Women would force men to come without giving any restitution. No home-cooked meal. No alcoholic beverage or water. No warm place to lay their heads overnight.

Herschel scrubbed his dick and balls twice, using the shower gel instead of the soap. His male lover easily sniffed the scent of hotel soap. Shower gel was what Herschel used at the gym.

Drying off, Herschel wondered, what could he do to win back his wife? Had they reached a point of no return? Herschel tried to determine if he ever had Nikki's heart. Now that he seriously thought back on how and why he proposed, probably not. Finally he admitted to himself that he'd married Nikki for her money. He wondered if his father had left his mother because his mother was poor. Herschel would give Nikki back every dime of her money that he'd spent on Ivory in exchange for Nikki's heart.

Stepping out of the bathroom, completely dressed, Herschel said, "Lay down on the bed." He spat on her pussy, then began massaging her clit, in tiny circular motions, with his middle finger. First clockwise, then counterclockwise. Stroking her shaft up and down between his thumb and pointing fingers, he held back her hood and began teasing her clit again. He watched the juices ooze from her clit.

"Oh, damn, that feels so good." She thrust her hips toward him.

Herschel massaged her clit with the tip of his finger until she screamed, "I'm coming!"

He wanted to lick her clit with his stiff tongue, but Anthony would detect the taste of pussy in his mouth. Since the room was in his name, he couldn't chance leaving her in the shower, so he waited for her to get dressed. Herschel left the hotel, dropped the woman off downtown at the gym, then drove to the condo he shared with Anthony. Knowing Nikki wasn't home, he wasn't ready to go back to an empty house.

Using his key to enter the home he felt most comfortable in, Herschel sat in front of the flat-screen television. He watched LeBron's interview, wondering why LeBron's son was seated at the press conference table, looking confused as to what he was supposed to do while his father answered questions from the media.

Anthony opened his bedroom door and asked, "You okay? I didn't hear you come in and you didn't knock on my door." Sitting beside him on the sofa, Anthony rubbed Herschel's thigh.

"I'm good," Herschel answered, trying to force Nikki's rejection of him out of his mind. But he couldn't. His suppressed anger had manifested into a hate so deep, his love for Anthony and Ivory was tarnished.

Herschel couldn't rationalize openly being in a relationship with a man. There was no social justification. If he wanted to salvage his marriage, he had to choose. Did he want Ivory? Anthony? Or his wife? He didn't want to risk losing them all.

"Herschel, what is bothering you? Is it your boss? Nikki? She still refusing to sign the divorce papers?" Anthony asked. "We could just live here together until our divorces are final."

"You know you are not divorcing your wife," Herschel said.

"I will if you will," Anthony countered. "I love you, not her."

What kind of father would Herschel be if he moved in with Anthony? Would he cheat on Ivory with another woman? Would he become frustrated or impatient with his son if his son couldn't understand that his father wasn't gay? Herschel was bisexual. What if Herschel moved in with Ivory? Would he be a full-time dad or an absentee father?

Anthony pinched Herschel on the arm, knelt, looked up at him, then said, "Let me suck your dick. You'll feel better."

Oh, shit. Standing with his shorts circling his ankles, Herschel gripped the back of Anthony's head when Anthony's mouth opened.

Herschel's eyes scrolled upward. "Damn, that feels good."

Anthony stroked his shaft, thrusting the head into his mouth. He sucked in the head, applying pressure along the ridge. In and out. In and out.

Herschel felt the passion each time Anthony sucked him in. Unable to hold on to his orgasm, Herschel let go of his sperm but couldn't let go of his heart. Loving a man was wrong.

CHAPTER 7

Lexington

Donna! Get the fuck off me," Lexington shouted.

"You are not leaving this house again tonight. I'm sick and tired of *my husband* leaving me every damn night to go out and get what you have at home," Donna cried, clinging to his shirt.

Suddenly he was her husband? After lying dormant next to him, his wife had awaken from her emotional coma to realize she was married, and he was magically supposed to be the rabbit she pulled out after stirring her hand around in an empty top hat for three years. Hell no. Donna could put her prolonged, unconscious, coldhearted, born-again-virgin pussy to sleep for ten more years.

Lexington lamented, "You're not interested in me. You're furious that I don't care anymore. I don't care that you think withholding sex from me is some sort of punishment. I'm not your fucking child. Your kids are upstairs. And thanks to you, they're probably awake. Let me go!"

Donna uncurled her fingers, then reached for his head wrap. Blocking her hand, Lexington scrambled out of the house, got in his car, and locked the doors.

"Get out the car! Lexington, do not drive off."

Looking in his rearview mirror, he saw Donna in their driveway, crying. Her bunny slippers were hideous. But seeing his wife wearing one of his button-up shirts was a first, but he liked it. His shirt was sexy on her. Now, if she'd do something with her hair and her damn attitude, maybe he'd give her the respect she deserved and listen to what she really wanted to say. Until then, it was Saturday night and she knew he wouldn't be back until sunrise. One day, he might not go home again. He should buy a second home and separate from Donna.

"I can't stop loving you. I can't help myself. And I can't get over you. No matter what I tell myself, baby" resonated from the speakers in his SUV, reminding him of last Saturday night when Nikki showed up at the club, all dressed up just for him. Cruising into the lot at the swingers club, Lexington self-parked his car, then continued listening to Kemistry sing the words that Lexington felt in his heart for Nikki.

Why did he love Nikki more than Donna? If he had lived with Nikki for ten years, would he feel the same about her? Why did he marry Donna? He couldn't recall. Oh, that was it. He'd watched Nikki accept Herschel's proposal on national television. That, and the fact that Donna was extremely accommodating. Willingly she'd relocated to a city she'd never visited, South Beach, to support him emotionally. She sold her New Orleans cuisine restaurant, downtown on Tchoupitoulas Street, to become his housewife and cook. Donna should've stayed in New Orleans and continued servicing her almost five-thousand monthly repeat and tourist customers if all she was going to give him was verbal lip service.

Changing his mind about self-parking, Lexington shifted into reverse, then drove a short distance to valet. He was excited his usual Saturday-night-live script was in motion. Handing the club monitor a new bottle of tequila, Lexington read the sign on the double doors before entering, circled his finger in the air, then handed the bartender a $50 tip.

Tonight, Lexington wanted intoxicating euphoria and escapism from being an entrepreneur. No meetings. No responding to text messages or e-mails. No returning calls. Unbuttoning his shirt in transit to the community dressing room, he motioned for the attendant to get on his job and open a locker. Quickly he removed, then placed his clothes, shoes, and wallet in the locker. Why in the fuck had he invited Nikki to his spot last week? Listening to her tell him she couldn't wait to come back pissed him off. She could forget that. He had not invited her back.

Entering the room with a glass door, Lexington motioned for the two women standing in the hallway to come join him. Plopping on the sofa, he spread his thighs wide. Lexington was in the midst of getting his dick sucked while chilling with his face marinating in some sweet pussy juices until the couple on the bed next to him and his crew suddenly stopped fucking.

Looking up from licking the woman's pussy, Lexington said, "Oh, hell no. What is she doing here?" He knew this fucking shit was going to happen; it was all his fault.

Nikki stood on the other side of the glass door. He wondered how long her voyeurism had honed in on his promiscuity. Scanning Nikki from her feet to her head, he saw she had on black gladiator-style strap-up shoes, a black thong, a black lace-up bustier, and a platinum ass-length wig.

Damn! Lexington thought, rising from his knees. "Excuse me, ladies, I'll be right back. Y'all play with one another to keep my pussies wet."

Exiting the semiprivate room, Lexington wrapped his towel around his waist, gripped Nikki's hand, led her to the dance floor, then scolded her. "Nikki, what's up? You need to take your ass home. I don't mind you coming to my spot when I invite you, but only when I invite you. Herschel is on his way, and he's going to flip the fuck out if he finds out you're here. And for the record, if he gets here before you leave, you are *not* with me, okay?"

Lexington had invited Nikki as a onetime adventure, but he didn't want her to start showing up on Saturdays like a regular. She didn't even have the decency to tell him she was coming.

"And what about Donna? You saying you have permission to be here every Saturday night? What if I bring her here next Saturday? We could have a foursome. Or better yet, why wait? How about I go get her and bring her here tonight? Oh, you don't think I saw her in the driveway with her damn slippers on, begging you not to leave. I do me, Lexington, 'cause all you married men are the same. Fucked up in the heads," Nikki said, pointing at his wrapped locks, then his dick.

Hearing Nikki talk down to him deflated his ego in more than one way. Lexington's dick slumped, and she saw it happen as the bulge under his towel disappeared. Was Nikki spying on him? The only possible way for her to see Donna standing in his driveway was Nikki either had binoculars, a telescope, or both.

Nikki continued, "And need I remind you, just like you, I'm the moneymaker in my house, not Herschel. I wish he would show his ass up here. He'll be sleeping at your damn house."

What had gotten into his friend? Was she straight tripping? It didn't matter how much money Nikki made, she would forever be a woman, and that was not his fault. Lexington's jaws tightened as he backed away from Nikki. He felt distant, like those two women who'd danced last week without touching one another. He'd known Nikki too long for their friendship to end over sexual encounters, because he was definitely fucking a few women tonight, but Nikki was not on his list. Not tonight. He seriously regretted introducing her to his favorite swingers club.

"Oh, shit," Lexington said, staring toward the front entrance.

A group of three sexy-ass women known as the "Queens of Ecstasy" walked in. Superfreaky shit was about to jump off with a vengeance in a blazing minute. Lexington untied his locks, tossing the head wrap over a rail that partially surrounded the dance floor, in case he had to put one of them in bondage. Lexington tried to figure out how to get rid of Nikki without pissing her off. His dick went from limp to standing hard, firm, and tall.

One of the Queens walked up to him, bowed before him, removed his towel from his waist. *Smack!* She slapped his ass hard, held his dick in her hand, and started pumping his dick like she was an air pump and he was the inner tube, then said, "Ladies, we've got a foot-long colossal dick over here. I'm gonna need some pussy power reinforcement for this anaconda motherfucker."

Aw, shit. No man ever chose the Queens of Ecstasy. Whatever man they wanted, they got, and every other man gawked on the sideline with envy. This was Lexington's third time being selected in six months, and he was not missing out on this opportunity by thinking about Nikki or Donna.

Beckoning for her other Queens to join her, she squatted to the floor, spread her thighs, stroked her pussy, then started licking his balls. Motioning with her free hand, she curled her finger at the guy across the room. He scurried over, damn near slipping on the hardwood dance floor.

"Lay your ass down underneath me and eat my pussy while I teabag these casaba nuts," she said.

That motherfucker slid under her pussy like he was a fucking mechanic and started eating her pussy like he was trying to unplug a serious leak.

Holding Lexington's dick away from her mouth, she stared down at the guy eating her pussy, then said, "I am not a bitch. Stop licking my pussy like you're a dog. Switch that shit up. Suck. Lick. Flick. Now kiss. That's better. Keep that rotation going." The Queen resumed sucking Lexington's dick.

I sure hope that dude don't fuck it up for everybody, Lexington thought.

The other Queen extended her long lizard tongue, flicked it up and down from Lexington's nipples, his armpit, then down to his ass. He felt her hot tongue penetrating his butt cheeks; then she stood, grinding her pussy on his ass. Motioning for a guy standing on the sideline, she told him, "Come fuck this good pussy, you dirty-ass bastard, before I beat your naughty ass."

He already had his swollen dick in his hand before he stepped onto the dance floor. "Yes, my queen," he said, putting on a condom before standing behind her.

"Get your slow, inexperienced ass back over there and wait until I call you again. I may call you in two minutes or two years, but when a Queen calls you to service her pussy, motherfucker, you come correct or your ass won't come at all," she said, beckoning for his replacement.

The third Queen joined them, suctioning Lexington's dick deep inside her mouth. When she scanned the room, Lexington wanted to laugh but couldn't. Men were raising their hands like kindergarteners. She found her Puerto Rican man, then winked at him. He swiftly appeared as if Scotty had beamed his ass over to the Queen's pussy throne.

"Lick my pussy until it's nice and wet; then I want you," she whispered, "to fuck the shit out of me."

The man underneath the first Queen was flat on the floor. He slid his face between Lexington's feet, far up enough for the first Queen to ride his dick like she was a jockey on a thoroughbred, coming in first place a head in front of the other two Queens.

Closing his eyes, Lexington shook his head, hoping whenever he regained consciousness Nikki would have gotten up out of the chair she'd dragged onto the dance floor and was on her way home. Lexington had lied to Nikki. Herschel was never coming, nor had he ever stepped foot in the swingers club while Lexington was there. He had to say something to get Nikki to leave.

Opening his eyes, he saw the chair on the dance floor was gone. Nikki was gone. Or so he thought, until he spotted her across the room bent over a table with some dude fucking her from behind. Lexington squinted, trying to see if the dude was fucking his woman in the ass. *Damn, Nikki could take it like that?*

"On the count of three, ladies," the first Queen announced, and Lexington, along with the other two guys, screamed like bitches.

Lexington felt the cum being sucked out of his dick like it was a thick milkshake. He imagined the same shit was happening with the other guys, except the other two Queens used their pussies instead of their mouths. Shaking his head to erase the X-rated thought of helping ole boy please Nikki, Lexington was now willing to fuck Nikki in whatever hole wasn't occupied.

His dick hung limp in disagreement. His nuts were drained. Lexington walked away from the dance floor, bypassed the restrooms, and asked the locker room attendant, "Man, can you open up my locker for me?"

Stroking on a few dabs of cologne, Lexington prayed by the time he made his way back to the front, Nikki would be gone. Fuck that, he wasn't worrying about Nikki's ass. He was not going to the front area. He wrapped a fresh towel around his waist and headed to the Freak-a-Zone in the back, where everything went down except dicks on dicks. Lexington was glad none of that gay activity was permitted. The one thing he never wanted to see or experience was a man fucking or sucking another man. A man who lusted after Lexington's dick would get his ass kicked.

Strolling thorough the Zone to see what else was happening, and which regulars had slipped in while he had his eyes closed on the dance floor, Lexington nodded his head at a few of the guys he knew.

A guy he didn't know, or hadn't seen at the club before, said, "You my fucking hero, nigga! My dick would have paid big-time to trade places with you out on that dance floor. Goddamn!"

"That's what's up," Lexington said, bypassing him.

All five of the beds in the Zone were packed with women and men sitting on the edge, getting their clits licked or dicks sucked. A few women were bent over the sides getting fucked doggie-style.

Aw, damn, Lexington thought as he spotted the finest woman in the Zone sitting alone at the bar, checking out everyone else. What was up with her? Or what was wrong with her that she appeared comfortable being antisocial? Lexington welcomed the challenge to break her barrier and eat her pussy.

She looked classy, sophisticated, and very much in control of her hormones. "For sure. That's the one I'm fucking next," Lexington mumbled. She was obviously new to the club environment, reminding him of his first swingers experience in Atlanta.

Lexington preferred the swingers club in Atlanta over the one in Fort Lauderdale. When he went to the ATL, he'd travel throughout the community rooms, where beds were lined up under canopies draped with sheer linens flowing down each post, which reminded him of the beds at Nikki Beach. He'd stroll between the three Jacuzzis and the pool. The smell of chlorinated water gave him the feeling of sliding naked into the pool at Hedonism II in Negril.

In another room, he could join in or watch or steal away into one of the eight private rooms. He could chill and play a few games of pool or sit at the bar and watch men leaning back on sofas with their hands clamped behind their heads while naked females with nice bodies and booties were lined up on coffee tables bobbing for lollicocks—as if the one who could make her man come first would win some sort of prize.

Other than Nikki, he couldn't say he cared about any of the females he'd fucked at sex clubs. Lexington envied his boy Brian and the way Brian adored Michelle. Why couldn't Lexington feel the same way about Donna? It wasn't that Brian hadn't done shit on the side. Brian's preference was to fuck every woman he could, but never fuck any of them more than once. As long as Nikki was alive, that "hit it, then quit" philosophy wouldn't work for Lexington.

Brian differed from Lexington and Herschel in that he genuinely loved Michelle and kept her first. And Michelle loved Brian so much, she'd never leave him. Brian boasted about how his wife would never take another woman's word over his, so basically Brian didn't give a fuck if a chick ever threatened to tell his wife about their affair. One day, that shit was going to backfire on his ass like Mike. Then what?

Lexington wished like hell he could love his wife, but Donna was a straight bitch. She verbally humiliated him in front of her friends, his friends, their kids, and their family every time she had a captive audience. So why should he give a damn about what Donna felt?

Making his way to the woman who was sitting alone at the bar, Lexington extended his hand, saying, "Join me in a community room. I'll make it worth your while."

At first, he couldn't believe the club in Fort Lauderdale didn't have one completely private room with a lockable door. After a while, he got used to it, and when he wanted more privacy, he'd hop a flight to Atlanta. At least until the new swingers club opened its doors in Fort Lauderdale.

"Sit with me for a moment and I'll decide if you're worth my time," she said, licking her lips.

Lexington sat on the stool next to her. "What's up?"

"I'm not from around here. This is my first time to a sex club, so instead of joining in, I decided to watch tonight. But you just might convince me to change my mind."

"What's your name?" Lexington asked, watching her nipples peep over the towel halfway covering her breasts. Yeah, she was new. All of the other women strolling throughout the Zone were completely naked.

"Irresistible is my name."

"Don't give me no fake-ass name," Lexington said. "What's your real name?"

"That's what my mama named me. I didn't make it up. What's yours?" she asked.

Lowering the towel, he caressed her nipples before easing one of them into his mouth; then he looked up at her and said, "Lexington. Hey, let's go. I wanna taste your pussy." He firmly gripped her hand.

Irresistible stood. *Damn!* Her sweet ass rolled off that stool, wiggling side to side underneath that towel. Lexington anxiously led her into the single semiprivate room. While he tried to ease the towel from around her body, she gripped it tighter. Sitting on the bed, she began sucking his limp dick.

Tearing the edge of the condom packet, Lexington scooted back on the bed, tugging on her towel, but Irresistible wouldn't let go of his emerging erection or her towel.

Damn, is she that shy? he wondered.

Her mouth was tight and juicy and felt so fucking good, he wanted to come but couldn't. He probably didn't have very many sperms to ejaculate after his big O with the Queen. With the exception of the Queen, no matter how long a woman sucked his dick, rode his dick, or stroked his dick, Lexington didn't come until he was ready.

"Whew, baby, you gon' have to ease up off him so I can put this hat on his head before it starts raining in your mouth." This woman had superpowers, mechanical jaws, something. No woman had ever sucked his dick that strong, making him that hard right after he'd exploded a full load. He feared he might be wrong, twice in one night.

"You like the way I suck this big-ass dick, Daddy?" she said, getting a bit aggressive, sucking a lot harder.

Aw, fuck. What the hell? It's her mouth now, he thought. "If you don't back up, I'm about to bust a load." Lexington was enjoying this shit. That was until an uninvited guest stood in the doorway.

"Mind if I join you?" Nikki asked, entering their room without permission.

"Yes. Go away," Lexington said, holding back on blasting cum down Irresistible's throat.

Irresistible never looked up.

Nikki quietly approached Lexington, dropped the towel wrapped around her body, pushed him flat onto the mattress, straddled his face, and began fucking his mouth with her pussy.

"Nikki, cut this shit out," Lexington mumbled into her lips.

Irresistible started massaging his balls while steadily sucking his dick. "Ride him and don't stop until you come across the finish line, honey. Come in his mouth, god damn it," Irresistible said, cheering Nikki on.

"No, don't encourage her. You don't understand," Lexington mumbled.

"Aw, now who's acting new?" Irresistible moaned.

Nikki reached over Irresistible and started squeezing Lexington's dick. "Let's switch," Nikki insisted.

Irresistible sat on his face, facing Nikki. Her ass kept brushing upward into his nose. *Aw, fuck!* This was not how his Saturday night was supposed to go. Lexington ran his tongue over Irresistible's shaft, trying to suck her clit out of the socket, but she wouldn't keep still long enough for him to clamp her clit. He wanted to see what was happening between the two of them, but he couldn't. He had pussy lips in his eyes every two seconds. *What the hell,* he thought. Inserting his finger inside Irresistible's pussy, Lexington began frantically finger fucking the shit out of her G-spot, hoping she'd come, squirt, anything, then get the fuck out of his face.

"Oh, my God! Yes! Yes!" she screamed. "That's my spot, baby! Go harder!"

Lexington felt Nikki bear down on him raw as she began riding him, fast-bucking her hips forward. Grinding her pelvis into his dick, Nikki screamed, "Fuck you, Lex! Fucking those bitches in front of my face. You gon' come for me tonight! Come for me, motherfucker!"

Hearing Nikki curse him turned him the fuck on. Suddenly it dawned on Lexington that he was ejaculating inside of his boy's wife without a condom, and as big and long as Lexington's dick was, none of his sperm had to swim. He shot his soldiers straight into her eggs like fucking arrows. That's how he'd ended up with five kids. Suddenly, kid number six didn't appear so appealing.

"No, Nikki, don't do this to me. To us. Stop. Please, baby, get up," he pleaded a little too late.

"Ahhhh!" Irresistible yelled, squirting fluids all over his face like a pissing pony.

Nikki's pussy clenched his dick so hard, there was nothing Lexington could do except yell, "Arghhh! Arghhh! Arghhh!" as he shot his remaining load, coming harder than before when his dick was in the Queen's mouth. Nikki's pussy was fucking great, and his dick was all too familiar with her body.

Irresistible and Nikki had fucked up his mind control and his night out. Never before had he exploded inside of a woman unintentionally. All five of his children were planned.

Lexington knew Herschel was a dog, but Nikki was a straight bitch for this shit. No matter how doggish men were, the one unspoken rule between real friends was friends didn't get their friends' wives pregnant. Nikki had to keep this shit between them. And if any of his sperm penetrated one of her eggs, Nikki was getting an abortion.

"Irresistible, you need to get your 'I'm new at this' lying ass up off my face. You too, Nikki. Get off my dick."

"You two know each other?" Irresistible asked.

Shaking his head, Lexington walked out of the room, went to the lockers, got dressed, retrieved his car from valet, and headed home to his wife. What should've been a great night ended up all bad. As he stepped into his living room, Donna was sitting on the sofa, wearing another one of his shirts and those fucked-up slippers.

"It's five o'clock in the morning, Lexington! Where the hell have you been? Don't walk away from me. You hear me talking to you."

Not tonight. Lexington did his usual. He showered and went to bed.

"Lexington, I think we should go to marriage counseling," Donna said, rubbing his shoulders. "I want the man I married back. I want my husband back."

The fact that counseling was her idea meant he should agree? Lexington would say anything to shut Donna up. Dozing, he mumbled, "Okay, Nikki. Whatever you want." No sooner than he'd said Nikki's name, Lexington realized he'd fucked up; he prayed Donna hadn't heard him.

Smack! Donna's palm landed against the back of his head. He ignored her—she'd be wise not to hit him again.

CHAPTER 8

Nikki

Nikki, call me immediately when you get this message. You've got some explaining to do. And you call yourself my friend. Don't let me catch you jogging while I'm driving."

Delete.

"Nikki, I know you're avoiding me. Don't make me come over to your house."

Delete.

"Nikki, you've got five minutes to call me back or else."

Deleting Donna's tenth message, Nikki knew fucking Donna's husband was wrong, but it wasn't a mistake. What had Lexington done or said to his wife to make Donna repeatedly leave one minatory message after another? On the first two messages, Donna seemed calm; then she angrily shouted her words, ending her final two voice mails with sniffles.

Nikki stood in the warm, breezy kitchen of her famous client's yacht, docked at the New York Harbor. She was prepping for the celebration of the owner's new ninety-seven-foot mega charter. Thirty-four guests invited by the owner were scheduled to be on board in less than two hours, and none of her sex recipes or appetizer specialties were complete.

Nikki's cell phone chimed again. This time, she answered. "Lexington, what in the world is going on with Donna?"

"Where are you?" he asked.

"New York. Why?"

"Stay there. I'm taking the first available flight to La Guardia," he said.

"I can't stay here. I have to cater a party in South Beach tomorrow morning," Nikki said, then asked, "Donna? What's wrong with her?"

"What time does your flight get in?" Lexington asked.

"Three," Nikki said, refusing to ask him any more questions.

"I'll pick you up from Miami."

"Sure thing," Nikki said.

"Perfect. See you then," Lexington said, ending their call.

The kitchen table was covered with large organic ruby-red strawberries with forest green stems, the finest shaved dark chocolate, ripe red avocados, and succulent black and brown figs—all great aphrodisiacs for women. Freshly shucked oysters on the half shell were on ice in a cooler. Clams, mussels, king crab legs, whole lobsters, and beluga caviar were in separate coolers.

The wines, champagnes, and top-shelf liquors, recommended by the owner, were uniquely arranged on the wood-paneled salon bar, where they awaited the bartender's arrival. Hopefully, the men wouldn't drink themselves into an intoxicated state. More than two drinks for a man impeded his ability to separate lovemaking from fucking.

Excessive alcohol consumption by men was courage juice, ego boosters, and, in some cases, performance busters instantly creating erectile dysfunction. Consuming alcohol decreased a male's testosterone level, thereby decreasing his sex drive. A man's desire to fuck increased tremendously after a few drinks, but the inebriating effect fooled men into believing they could knock the bottom out of a pussy when they could barely touch their noses—let alone find a woman's pussy hole without sabotaging her clit.

The opposite was true for women. A woman's testosterone level increased with alcohol consumption, increasing her desire to have sex and her ability to perform. In many cases, Nikki's sexcipes were simply delicious low-to-no-carbohydrate foods that energized her clients as opposed to making them feel sluggish and sleepy.

Walking away from the bounty of delicacies, Nikki watched nearby yachts sail toward Ellis Island. Standing at the helm in the captain's position, she realized she'd never failed at anything. Her parents encouraged her to excel, saying, "Nikki, be passionate about your life, always do extra, willingly work harder, and never, ever quit anything that you start. Do those four things, sweetheart, and you'll be successful. You won't ever have to depend on a man to support you financially, and you'll be happy. Don't ever let anyone tell you money doesn't bring happiness. It definitely does."

The party sailing by Nikki sure seemed happy—popping corks off champagne bottles, hugging, kissing, smiling, and laughing. Wow! Admiring the sunrise. When was the last time she'd truly enjoyed herself that way? Besides preparing food that made others happy, hosting her television show, sexing her friend's husband more than her own, and a few rendezvous with professional women, there was still something missing.

Her parents' philosophy was "Generate wealth. There are people in the world with lots of money; your job is to provide a service those people are willing to pay for. Everybody has to eat. Figure out what people like and how much they're willing to pay you to prepare their meals. Don't create debt. If you can't pay off what you borrow within thirty days, let whoever owns whatever it is that you want to keep these possessions until you have enough cash to own what you want. Especially a home. Interest on a home will cost you a minimum of three times the amount of the loan, and it'll take a lifetime to get the title." Her parents made it clear that debt was created to keep people indebted, and people in debt went to work every day for someone else, not themselves.

A melancholy half-smile crossed Nikki's face as she recalled memories of the way she and Lexington were as teenagers. Life was simple. They didn't have a lot of money. Their love was genuine. And they were happy. When had they drifted apart? Not Lexington. Nikki still loved him. Her parents. She missed talking with them.

"Hmm,"—Nikki exhaled—"I'd better light a torch under my ass." She had one hour to make thirty-five excited, influential individuals become ecstatic.

She stood overlooking crystal-blue salty waters. Blue. Salty. Waters. Could Nikki in her weakest moment be strong and call her mom? Could she stop dwelling on whether she'd terminated her friendship with Donna? If she'd stayed at home, instead of going to the sex club, Donna wouldn't be calling her. How would Nikki have felt if Lexington unexpectedly showed up at one of her events expecting her to cater to him? What had gotten into her? Fucking Lexington without using a condom? Did she want to have a baby with Lexington instead of her husband? Nikki had been jealous. She didn't want those "Queen" tramps all over *her* dick, sucking and rubbing Lexington like they owned him, so she fucked him raw.

The probability of her being pregnant was slim but possible, because she'd just completed the antibiotics her dentist prescribed before performing her upcoming root canal. She was intelligent. "Damn, you know better," she scolded herself aloud. She clearly understood the pharmacist when she'd said, "If you're sexually active and are taking oral contraceptives, make sure you use protection because antibiotics reduce the effectiveness of birth control pills." Contraceptives also decreased a woman's sex drive, but the foods Nikki ate kept her libido high.

Nikki didn't need the pharmacist to tell her what she'd already known. What Nikki didn't know was whether or not she wanted a baby. Some days she did. Other times, like when she was flying and a screaming kid wouldn't shut up, she wanted to have her tubes tied and burned. If she was with child, could she abort it? Tightening her lips, Nikki forced back her tears. There'd be no love in the appetizers she'd managed to somehow piece together. Hopefully, her clients would generously partake more in the libations and eat less.

Returning belowdecks to the dining area, Nikki neatly arranged the fruit, placing dark chocolate roses around the platters' perimeters. She placed the fresh strawberries in the center, then sprinkled edible chocolate rosebuds between the strawberries. A white-chocolate replica of the yacht drifted on five gallons of chilled blue curaçao in a medallion-shaped crystal bowl.

"Please don't sink," she whispered, carefully placing a miniature fluffy red-velvet cake replica of the owner's bed atop the back of the white-chocolate yacht. "Perfect." Floating real freshwater pearls in the blue liquor around the yacht display, Nikki was almost done.

"Whew, I don't know how I pulled this one off," she said as her phone rang. Donna's number appeared again.

Reluctantly she answered, "Hello."

"Hey, Nikki. This is Donna. We need to talk."

"Let me call you back," Nikki said, ending the call before Donna replied. Best if she waited until Lexington picked her up from the airport to fill her in on what the heck was going on.

"Nikki, this is marvelous. I love it!" the owner belted out. "You, my love, are worth your weight in diamonds. My guests are going to love me."

Oh, shit! Breathing deeply to calm her racing heart, she hadn't heard him come aboard. His overwhelming approval was all she needed.

"Thanks, I hate to run, but I have to catch my flight back

to Miami to prepare for my client tomorrow. If you have any questions, call me on my cell," Nikki said, then left.

The flight into Miami got Nikki in on time. Wearing wide-framed sunglasses and a white halter-top ankle-length sundress, she exited the plane. Dashing into the restroom, Nikki refreshed her red glossy lipstick, then hurried to baggage claim, where Lexington stood next to her suitcase.

"Hurry" was all he'd said before he whisked her off to his limo.

Relaxing in the backseat, Nikki quietly reclined in Lexington's arms. Pressuring him to talk would make him shut down completely. She'd wait until he was ready. They arrived at their favorite destination. Lexington flashed his VIP Black Card Membership and they were escorted to their reserved canopy bed mounted in the white crystal sand of South Beach.

Nikki untied her halter, exposing her breasts to the dissipating sunshine as she watched Lexington's white linen pants taper over his bulging dick. His beautiful locks flowed over his shoulders toward his tight ass. Lexington was gorgeous—more so on the inside, to her. Nikki wondered but refused to ask what had happened in his marriage to make him stop making love to Donna for years. After all, Donna was the mother of his children. Some questions were better left unanswered.

"I don't want to talk about Donna. I just need to be with you," he said, as if reading her thoughts.

Lexington leaned against the huge white pillow and Nikki comfortably nestled into his arms. Her lips caressed his.

Watching the sunset, Nikki softly kissed Lexington again and again. Passionately she pressed her outer lips against his, holding them there for a sacred moment. Partially opening her mouth, Nikki rolled the soft inner parts of her lips over the outer part of his lips. Gently she eased the tip of her tongue into his mouth, savoring his taste buds like his tongue was the sugar sticks in her mojito.

"Why am I so damn crazy over you? Umm, you taste so succulent," Nikki whispered into Lexington's mouth as his tongue delicately swapped places with hers. Lexington's tongue traced her outer lips, her inner lips, then eased over her taste buds. His hand roamed over her breasts. The ocean breeze swept inside her nostrils, causing her to gasp with pleasure. He caressed her hair. Should she have married Lexington instead of marrying Herschel? Lexington and Nikki would've definitely been a power couple, like Brian and Michelle. But Nikki—no matter how hard she'd tried—could never be as devoted to any man as Michelle was to Brian. Or maybe like Nikki, Michelle kept her private life private too.

As the sun began to set into a blend of pink and mauve hues dancing upon the shimmering ocean, Lexington said, "Let's go to your condo. I need to taste your pussy."

He didn't have to ask twice. Nikki's hideaway was a short walking distance, one block away from Nikki Beach. Lexington knew to wait fifteen minutes before making his way to her place, giving her time to pleasantly surprise him. Now, if Herschel were really smart, he'd know that his wife owned several properties, one in South Beach, two in Hawaii, one in New York, another in San Juan, and a few others. With the exception of her condo in South Beach, Nikki comped her other places to her top clients. But that wasn't Herschel's business, and her real estate sure as hell wasn't bought with his money.

Lexington tapped on the unlocked door to her condo, then entered. Nikki was so excited—instead of showering without him, she eagerly awaited her man. Hungrily her open mouth greeted his. Unbuttoning his shirt, Nikki showered kisses all over his chest. They stumbled to the bathroom, where Lexington's pants soon sat on the floor with each leg forming perfect circles.

Nikki turned on the shower, then stepped inside. Her body was drenched with warm water as Lexington teased her nipples. Lifting her thigh beside his hip, Nikki said, "Pick me up." She glided her hand to caress his hard dick, slipped his shaft inside her creamy pussy, then moaned, "Just what I fuckin' needed."

"Me or my dick?" Lexington asked, fucking Nikki and slamming his nuts into the crevice of her butt.

"Both," Nikki said, hugging his neck. "But if you go any deeper, these sperms won't have to swim to my eggs either. You're fucking like you want me to have your baby."

"Nikki, you are so crazy. I don't want to pull out, baby, but you're right. I should get a condom," he said. Penetrating her deeper, Lexington did not want to pull his dick out of her pussy, but he would if Nikki insisted.

"This big-ass dick is so fucking good . . . I think we'll be okay. Just pull out before you come." *Slap!* Before Nikki realized what she'd done, her palm landed against Lexington's face.

"Damn, baby. Chill on that shit. That's you and Herschel doing that aggressive role-playing. I don't get down like that. You gon' make me put my dick in reverse if you do that again."

"It's just so good, I wanna fucking cry!" Nikki screamed, bouncing her ass onto his shaft. Her wet breasts slid back and forth from Lexington's mouth to his hairy chest.

"I know, baby. I know. I know this pussy. My dick print is all over you. He craves you. This is my pussy. I can hit this sweet, creamy ass backward and forward, but I don't want to come inside you again without a condom. Get down and suck my dick," Lexington said, sitting her on the built-in shower bench.

Nikki sat on the bench under the flowing water and began kissing Lexington's head. She smeared the precum onto her mouth like lipstick. Wrapping her hand around the base of his shaft, she palm-rolled his dick like dough, then sucked the head.

"Get up," Lexington said. "I don't wanna come in the shower. Let's go out on the balcony."

Stepping out of the shower, Nikki reached for a towel. Lexington covered her hand, then said, "Leave it." He picked up the jojoba oil, slicked her body all over, then did the same to his. Leading her through the bedroom, bypassing the bed, Lexington opened the patio door.

"Relax in the hammock," he said.

Nikki leaned back and waited. The warm breeze blowing from the ocean made Nikki tingle all over. Lexington began massaging her feet.

"Did you notice?" he asked, staring up into her eyes.

"What?" Nikki asked, trying to sit up and get a glance at his dick.

"Lay down," he said, smiling. Looking up at the sky, he pointed.

"Aw, yes. I see. You know that's the beauty of living in South Beach," Nikki said.

The half moon illuminated the sky, but no matter how brightly the moon glowed, the moon could never outshine the North Star. How romantic and powerful. Resembling a starfish in the sky, the North Star, like Nikki, seemingly stood alone. Her husband was not married to her. Her childhood sweetheart was married to Donna.

Lexington sucked her pinky toe, then slowly licked each of her toes until his mouth surrounded her big toe. Nikki shivered with pleasure. Gently gliding her toe in and out of his mouth, Lexington caressed the arch of her foot, then said, "I should've married you instead of marrying Donna. What happened to us, Nikki? We were so good for one another. To one another." Lexington kissed her ankles, then lifted her legs. His tongue danced behind her knee, softly suctioning the crevice.

Nikki trembled. "We happened to us, remember?" Looking down at Lexington, she continued speaking. "You wanted a baby; I didn't. Neither of us was ready to start a family right after high school. You wanted to get married; I didn't. You were fucking too many other girls. If I had married you, I'd be Donna."

Lexington countered, "You would never be Donna. You're too much like a man."

"Whatever," Nikki said. "Before we got it together, we went to college, became successful, and we married other people. You have two kids, and I don't have any."

"Nikki, I've thought about what happened at the club. If you are pregnant with my child, I want you to have my baby," Lexington said, easing on top of her.

The hammock swayed. Nikki shook her head. "It's too late. For a baby. For us. We're both married. We both have demanding careers. Not to mention insatiable sexual appetites."

"That's exactly why we should have a baby. I wish Donna was like you," Lexington said, kissing Nikki's lips.

Nikki brushed his soft locks against her abs, then said, "Don't say that. Donna is a good woman. She takes excellent care of your kids. What happened between you two? Why is she calling me?"

"And . . . what about Herschel? Does he take excellent care of his son?"

"You didn't have to go there with me. This is about what you want."

"What we want. Can you look me in my eyes and honestly tell me what I want isn't the same as what you want?"

Nikki looked up at the North Star. "Just make love to me, Lexington. That's what I want. I want you, because you know exactly how to make love to me."

Lexington kissed away the tears silently streaming from the corners of her eyes. His lips traced a necklace of kisses along her collarbone. The wetness of his tongue streaked from her throat between her breasts, which he held in each hand, and down to her navel. He kissed each side of her pelvis, then kissed the top of her shaft. His tongue glided between her labia, along the right side, then eased over to the left side. The tip of his tongue pressed against Nikki's sensitive spot in the upper left crevice between her shaft and outer lip.

Nikki's body trembled.

Nikki reminisced about fucking Lexington in the semiprivate room at the swingers club the other night. She could have had a threesome with two guys or an orgy with any of those couples, but the truth was as freaky as Nikki was, she was selfish about Lexington. He was, and forever would be, her first love.

Slipping his finger inside her pussy, Lexington pulled it out, then traced tiny clockwise circles over her clit. He dipped his finger inside her again, then gently made small counter-clockwise circles on top of her clitoris.

Nikki moaned. "That feels so good. You just don't know."

"Trust me, I know," Lexington said.

He knew her body well, but he didn't know her as well as he believed. He knew exactly what pleased her in the bedroom. Outside the bedroom, Lexington was clueless.

Positioning her body sideways in the hammock, Lexington slowly entered the tight walls of Nikki's pulsating vagina. With each penetration, his dick throbbed in sync with her pussy. By the time his head reached a point where he could go no deeper, they both came hard. Holding one another tightly, Lexington whispered in Nikki's ear, "I love you."

Nikki exhaled. "I love you too."

Nikki wondered when was the last time Lexington spoke those words to his wife. More important, what did his words mean to her?

CHAPTER 9

Brian

Normalcy. Familiarity. Temporary fidelity. Loyalty. Good man. Occasionally unfaithful. Everything in life was subjective.

One sure thing was Brian was elated to get home to his wife. Hug her. Hold her. Kiss her. In transit from the airport, he called Michelle. "Get my pussy ready, baby. Your daddy's home."

Brian's dad had an intelligent answer to every question. He contemplated having his driver stop by his mom's so he could talk with his dad about Zahra. But once BJ saw him, his son would cry if he left without him. Taking BJ and his daughter home would mean postponing making love to his wife, and there was no way Brian wasn't diving headfirst into his wife's pussy, with his tongue ejected from his mouth. Talking with his father would have to wait.

Brian hadn't heard from Marcus Monty. He didn't want

to call too often, but another follow-up was necessary. As he waited for Monty to answer, Brian prayed he didn't get Monty's voice mail.

"Hey, B! What's up? I know why you calling, man. Listen, I'm close. Real close. I've narrowed my options to you or Brandon, man. Let's do dinner tonight."

Fuck! "I just got back to Miami a few minutes ago. I can be back in Houston first thing in the morning," Brian said, knowing he should've stayed one more day, but today was his special day with Michelle. Brian hadn't missed a single special day with his wife since they'd married.

"I'll be in Chicago tomorrow. I'll meet you there. Call me when you get in and we'll set a time and place then," Marcus insisted.

Cool. Brian exhaled, grateful he still had a chance to represent Marcus. "You got it. See you in Chicago. Peace," he said, ending the call. Now if Brian could resolve his uncertainties about Zahra, he'd clear his conscience. Until then . . .

Stepping out of the limo, Brian rolled his luggage into their bedroom, then licked his lips in anticipation, praying his wife had done what he'd asked. His lips spread wide as he looked in the bathroom. "That's my girl," he said, happy that Michelle had obeyed him. She was in the shower preparing his pussy for a cunnilingus treat. Closing the bathroom door, he removed his clothes, all except his underwear, then sat on the bed.

Wife first. Son second. Brian would keep his word to BJ and take him out on their yacht with six of his buddies. Guys' day out. That was tomorrow. Maybe Brian would invite his dad along, so his father could decode why Zahra had targeted him.

Brian listened at the bathroom door, making certain the shower was still running, then retrieved the envelope from his suitcase. Moving to the bench at the edge of their bed, he slowly removed the papers again.

Exhaling heavily, Brian slid the papers back inside, setting the envelope aside, then called his father. Waiting for his dad to answer, he stared at the envelope.

"Hey, son! You're back in town. BJ is so excited about his day out on the yacht with you tomorrow, he's gotten me excited too. Maybe I should join you, since it's just going to be the fellas, huh? What do you think? You want your ole man cruising around with you? Besides, it's time we have the family talk with BJ about girls. He's getting a little too attached to the sweet little chocolate girl next door."

This *was* a great idea. Not having the talk with BJ. There was no harm in him playing with the girl next door as long as BJ wasn't claiming her as his girlfriend. But it was better if Brian sought his dad's advice face to face rather than over the phone. Confined on the yacht, three generations of Flaw men could spend quality time together.

"Dad, I'd love to have you join us."

"Fine, it's done. I'll let BJ and your mother know. What's up?"

"It can wait," Brian said, dwelling on Zahra. "I have to meet Marcus in Chicago tomorrow," Brian said, edging toward telling his dad about Zahra. But he feared Michelle might overhear his conversation. Women had bionic hearing, strength, and every skill imaginable when it came to snooping on their husbands. "I'll see you in the morning. We can talk then," Brian said.

Could Zahra pose a threat to his marriage?

"Son, what's wrong with you? How are you going to keep your word to BJ and be in Chicago tomorrow?" his dad whispered.

"Damn, you're right. I can't afford to miss this meeting, Dad. I'll make it up to BJ later."

His heart tightened when Michelle asked, "What's that, baby?"

"Shit!" Brian hadn't heard his wife open the bathroom door.

"Son, what is going on with you?"

"Dad, let me call you back. Bye," Brian said, ending the call. Stuffing the papers inside the envelope, he closed it, placed it in his suitcase, then zipped his luggage. "Just some stats on a new guy. Nothing serious," he said. "Just got a call from Marcus. I have to fly to Chicago in the morning."

"Well, the look on your face sure says whatever is in that envelope is serious. The stats must be horrible. Mind if I take a look?" Michelle asked.

"I said it's not," Brian insisted, staring through Michelle.

"Fine. If you're going to lie, don't answer. But you need to check that attitude," Michelle said, tightening her lips.

Why did the woman he'd met at the arena suck his dick so fantastic, Brian wanted to hook up with her the next two nights he was in Houston? Stick with the rules and another woman would never show up at his front door. He hoped. After fucking Zahra, how could he make sure? Did anyone take pictures of them at the mall, the restaurant, arriving at or leaving the hotel together? *Fuck*. Would he end up on an episode of *Cheaters*?

Rubbing his forehead, Brian said, "Damn, woman, come here. I apologize, baby. I just want this contract with Marcus to be a done deal." He kissed his wife. "You are so sexy. Enough about work, you ready for me to please you?" he asked as Michelle stood in front of the mirror, then released the towel from her glistening body, dropping it to the floor.

His eyes trailed her to the bed. Brian watched his wife relax atop the sheets, the same as she'd done every first Saturday of the month since they'd exchanged wedding vows. It was yoni massage time. The one day of every month that he spiritually reconnected with his wife. Just like a car needed regularly scheduled tune-ups, his wife did too.

Michelle spread her thighs, nice and wide, then smiled at him.

Brian absolutely adored his wife. She was the mother of his two children, his very best friend, and his confidant. Brian told Michelle everything that he considered significant, but there were a few things not worth mentioning. Not if what he'd have to say would evoke sadness inside his home.

Red satin sheets covered their king-sized bed. A goddess of heavenly beauty stretched from the headboard toward the foot of the bed. The softest coco-buttered creamy skin he'd ever laid hands upon wrapped around his wife's flesh. Having Michelle as his eternal mate made Brian the happiest man alive.

Michelle's yoni was a precious space and a sacred temple. She'd taught him to love and respect her pussy before the first time they'd made love, before their wedding and before she gave birth to their children, saying to him, "Baby, it's my responsibility to teach you how to appreciate and pleasure my entire body. If you want to touch, taste, or feel your dick inside of this good pussy, you'll have to earn it. Don't worry. Mama's gonna show you exactly how to make and keep her happy."

The day Michelle let him watch her masturbate was etched in his mind forever, but it didn't have to be. The videotape was stored in their safe, along with the other XXX-rated home videos they'd done during their ten years of marriage. Brian knew Michelle was especially unique, because she was the only woman who had taught him how to make passionate love to her *without* fucking her. And no matter how many women he fucked outside their marriage, Brian would divorce Michelle if she ever gave *his* pussy away. The other women that he'd fucked didn't mean anything to him. What Michelle didn't know kept peace within their family.

Sitting on the bench at the foot of their bed, Brian buffed his fingernails as he admired his wife. She'd taught him that it was a man's responsibility to make certain his fingernails didn't cut or scratch a woman's delicate pussy, leaving her miserably sore with painful scars that would hurt her so much she'd resent him and regret having allowed him to touch her sacredness. Brian had learned so much from his wife. Admiring Michelle, he believed she was more beautiful today than the day they'd met.

Brian stood with his erection pointing toward the ceiling. Moving about their spacious bedroom, he lit twelve white floating candles, dripped a few drops of cinnamon oil (which Michelle had bought from their neighbor Donna) on the tall lamps beside the bed; then he walked over to their patio and opened the sliding glass door. The South Beach salty summer breeze engulfed their bedroom.

Standing over his wife, Brian leaned toward her, softly kissing her forehead. "Are you relaxed, baby?" he asked Michelle.

"Yes, baby. I'm relaxed and patiently awaiting my *wonderful* husband."

Brian whispered in Michelle's ear. "I'm here to please you, not just today but every day. Whatever I have to give, I freely give it unto you." That was true. Everything they possessed was jointly owned.

Delicately he fluffed, then placed a red satin pillow underneath his wife's head so she could comfortably watch him whenever she desired. Then he slid a pillow under her right knee and another under her left, separating her thighs for clear access to his pussy. The pillow Brian tucked under Michelle's curvaceous hips was sealed inside plastic, then covered with a satin pillowcase.

Seated at the foot of the bed, Brian whispered, "Spread your legs a little wider and bend your knees a little bit more so I can admire my pretty pussy."

Lowering his nose inches above her, Brian sniffed his wife's pussy. The scent of pink cotton candy stimulated his senses. "Inhale for me, baby," he said, backing away from his pussy. Together they inhaled deep into their bellies, then exhaled as much air as they could, like they'd done in Yoga classes on second Saturdays of each month.

"Inhale again," he said as they began to breathe deeply two more times.

Careful not to touch her yoni, Brian's strong yet smooth

hands journeyed up Michelle's thighs, passionately massaging her legs with his fingertips. Meandering up her thighs, he pressed his thumbs in the crevices between her outer labia and her thighs. Slowly he journeyed up to her abdomen, her breasts, then lightly teased the tips of her nipples. Picking up the bottle of WET, he squeezed a few drops of lubrication, then watched the moisture seep between the crevice of his wife's thighs and outer vaginal lips.

Slowly he caressed her pussy, starting from the outside, massaging her outer lips between his thumb and index finger. Gently twirling her outer vaginal lips all the way up, then all the way down, Brian took his time before he began massaging her inner lips, occasionally teasing the opening of her vagina. The time had not yet come to penetrate his wife.

Noticing Michelle's shallow breaths, Brian softly reminded her, "Breathe a little deeper, baby."

Their yoni massage ritual was a treat Brian never grew tired of doing for his wife. He wanted to make sure Michelle was always sexually pleased beyond her satisfaction. Brian's commitment to himself was to ensure Michelle never had the desire to or thought of being with another man. He glanced up at the framed wedding photo that Michelle's mother had given him, knowing he'd made Michelle's mom proud of how he'd treated her daughter.

No man could please Michelle better than Brian. And no matter how many women he fucked, no woman could please him better than his wife. Each third Saturday of the month, Michelle gave him a lingam massage. Imagining his wife's hands all over his body, Brian felt his dick go from limp to hard.

Keeping his thoughts inside the head on his shoulders, Brian knew it was best not to talk too much, although he wanted to say, "Baby, please let me slide my hard-ass dick inside your hot, juicy pussy. Just for a few minutes."

Michelle had taught him that excessive talking by either of them during her pussy massage would detract from maximizing her pleasure. Michelle's eyes rolled to the top of her head, exposing the whiteness of her eyeballs through the tiny slits in her lids. She'd told him that was the moment when she could feel his energy moving from her feet all the way up to the crown of her head.

That was the perfect timing for Brian to massage her precious pearl. Brian was slightly jealous when he'd learned a woman's clitoris was four times more sensitive than a male's glans, and that a woman could easily have five times more orgasms per session than a man. He recalled the day Michelle told him, "Look at me, Brian. I want to make myself clear. A woman's precious pearl has only one purpose—and don't you ever forget it—and that's to give her pleasure, pleasure, and more pleasure. So don't ever overlook touching, stroking, and kissing my clit."

Adding a little more lubrication, he stroked his wife's clitoris in tiny clockwise and counterclockwise circles, as if he were operating the controller of one of his son's video systems. Then he gently squeezed her clit between his thumb and index fingers, using various rhythms.

"Breathe, baby," he reminded her again.

Inserting his right middle finger into his wife's yoni, Brian lightly explored and massaged the inside of her vagina. Slowly stroking up, down, around, and sideways—varying the depth, speed, and pressure—he honed in on her G-spot then moved his middle finger silently, as if saying, "Come here, my pretty-ass pussy." Sliding in his ring finger, he stroked Michelle's G-spot to her liking and satisfaction. Putting his thumb to work, he massaged her clit in an up-and-down motion. Brian didn't stop there. Using the same hand, he slipped his pinky inside her anus.

Lifting her head, Michelle gazed into his eyes.

Brian softly said, "Thanks for letting me hold God's greatest 'gift' to mankind in the palm of my hand. I cherish your mind, body, and spirit." Then he caressed his wife's breasts with his left hand, pausing for a moment to feel her heartbeat.

Michelle's hips jerked. Her pussy squeezed his fingers. Tears streamed down her cheeks, as though it were their first time bonding. Brian closed his eyes and said, "Thank you, God, for trusting me with the most beautiful woman in the world. Baby, I love you."

Culminating the massage, slowly, gently, respectfully, and passionately, he eased his fingers out, one at a time, from inside his wife. He held his left hand against her heart until all of his fingers were removed. Then Brian lifted his left hand away from her body. Joining Michelle in the afterglow of her yoni massage, Brian cuddled in a spoon position with his wife in his arms, telling her, "Baby, I appreciate and respect you."

Michelle had greatly enriched Brian's life and there was no way he could repay her; therefore, no matter what happened in their lives, Brian would never divorce his wonderful wife, nor would he let her leave him.

CHAPTER 10

Herschel

Huh? What?" Herschel vigorously shook, then scratched his bald head, frowning at Ivory. All he heard was "Wonk, wonk, wonk, wonk."

"You know Kwan's birthday is coming up and he wants to go to Disney World with three of his friends," she said. "I prepared the budget and for three days it's going to cost five thousand two hundred for top accommodations for the six of us, or if we stay five days it'll cost a little under eight grand. That's all-inclusive airfare, hotel, six five-day passes, food, and souvenirs. What do you think? Which package do you want to pay for?"

The trip for their son's birthday was perfect—except there was no way Herschel was spending five days with a bunch of ten-year-olds. "Baby, please. Put it on mute for a second,"

Herschel insisted, sitting on the edge of the sofa, trying to concentrate on the basketball play-offs.

Ivory picked up the remote, silencing the television. Was she fucking crazy? His fingers wrapped around the cable remote. Snatching the controller back from her, he restored the volume.

"Not the television. Your mouth. Damn. Just shut up for a minute. I can't focus on what's happening. I can't hear the sports commentator or hear myself think, and I don't know what the hell you're talking about," he said, moving from the sofa to the reclining chair.

The fourth quarter had just started and the Hornets were on fire. She knew better than to come between him and basketball. She was the one who begged him to come over. *Fuck.* Herschel should've gone to his place with Anthony or the sports bar. Anyplace else would've been better. And why did she wait until the last quarter to bring this shit up? Did she think he'd agree with her to shut her up so he could concentrate on the game?

"Oh! That's what's up!" Herschel said, rocking in his seat. "That was the fucking play of the century! Baby, look. You've got to see the replay."

Ivory cried. Standing in front of him, she said, "This is important to Kwan. You promised him and I want you to keep your word. Why won't you talk to me? I can see you're excited about the game, but can't you get excited about your son too? We have to keep our word to Kwan this time. We have to." Tears glazed her eyes.

Ou, this bitch is pushing me to the fucking edge. If she don't move from in front of the television! Damn! She's ruined my best play-off moment.

It wasn't their word that had to be kept, it was *hers*. She dreamt of this grandiose Snow White, Mickey and Minnie, family vacation and birthday celebration package by her damn self. He never agreed to go to no amusement park. Besides, Kwan was a boy and should've been anxious to go to football camp. After ten years of him not taking Kwan anywhere, she knew he wasn't going, but somehow convinced herself that she could, what, change his mind? Oh, yeah. Herschel could see that happening, only in his damn dreams. Now she was fucking crying in the middle of the last quarter of the greatest play-off game ever for New Orleans.

Not this shit again, Herschel thought. Ivory cried more than Kwan. "Is this what I'm going to have to deal with if I marry your ass? I can't fucking tolerate your crying all the time. It's driving me fucking crazy. Get out of my way and shut the hell up. In that order!"

Damn, what was it that I saw in her lately?

Herschel picked up his Blackberry. Anthony had texted, *? u c da b2b play? Almost str8 pissed on myself. Need 2 c u. Miss & luv u.*

What? He missed a play? Amazing moments in sports happened in a split second. That's why Herschel had to have his eyes glued to the flat screen and not to Ivory's miserable ass.

Responding to Anthony, Herschel texted, *Meet me @ my place n exactly 3 hrs. Wear those blk spandex boxer briefs I bought you. I'ma tear that ass up!*

Anthony texted back, *Can't u meet me @ our condo? I'm already here.*

No, Nikki is gone and I want to fuck you in my bed tonight.

Well, aw'ight. It's ur dick. I'm just tryna bust a nut n ur gut, Anthony replied.

Herschel hit him back: *Oh, you won't have to try too hard when I dig in dat ass.*

His lover would chill at the condo for two hours. By the time Anthony would change into his jogging shorts, T-shirt, boxers, and cross-trainers, and make it to The Island, Herschel would be waiting. Anthony would pretend to jog by Herschel's mansion, fake to the left, then cut to right into the wide driveway. He'd jog along the dimly lit driveway until reaching the back entrance, which Herschel and Nikki never locked. Anthony would find Herschel on the porch with a couple of ice-cold beers and a hard dick.

Ivory sat on the arm of the sofa closest to him. "Herschel, what do you want from me? I can't plan our first family vacation without you getting angry. Obviously, you don't know how to be a father to Kwan, but it's time you learn. What about me? I need you to care about me, about us. This trip is important to Kwan."

It wasn't that he didn't want to be a father to Kwan; Ivory was right. Herschel didn't know how to father Kwan's openly gay ways. Was being gay genetic? Why did his son have to be gay? Wasn't paying Kwan's tuition, buying his colorful outfits, and giving him a weekly allowance enough?

"I already explained my situation to you. What are you, deaf? How many times do I have to remind you I'm married? I can't go on no fucking five-day vacation with you until after my divorce is final, and that's final."

"Herschel! You're the one who's deaf! We've been together

longer than you've been married. You don't take me anywhere anymore. You don't spend time with Kwan. You tell me to send him across the street to his cousins' house every time you come over, as if you're ashamed of our son being gay. What! You don't think he knows? Every time I complain, you throw Nikki in my face. I don't bring that bitch's name up. You do. You conveniently mention Nikki when you don't want to do the right things for us. 'I can't jeopardize Nikki's career. She's a celebrity. We've got to wait.' I've been waiting over a decade. For what? I'm tired of fucking waiting, Herschel. Where's that bitch right now? Probably fucking some other man, just like you come over here all the damn time to fuck me. If you believe she's not sucking another man's dick, you're crazy. You need to decide right here, right now. Do you want her? Do you want me? Or do you want me to get another man and leave your selfish, inconsiderate, confused ass alone?"

Did that bitch have amnesia? Not this shit again. No, she was not giving him an ultimatum in the house he'd bought her broke ass. Herschel stood quietly. He walked toward the door. "You can go get Kwan. But if you bring a man up in here. Up in my house. The house I'm paying for. Let me make myself HDTV clear. Pack your fucking bags, leave my damn furniture, and go live with that nigga. Let him take care of you and Kwan. I'm out."

Ivory raced toward him, slammed her body against the door, grabbed his shirt, then cried, "I'm sorry. Don't leave. Please stay the night with me. I don't want to be alone."

Oh, *his* fault. She didn't have amnesia. Ivory was fucking bipolar, borderline schizophrenic. Staying the night was not an option. Herschel had plans that didn't include raging estrogen, out-of-control hormones, or endless fake-ass tears.

"Move out of my way," he said. Fucking around with her ass, he'd miss the postgame highlights.

Ivory slid to the floor, cradling her crying face in her palms. Biting his bottom lip, Herschel tapped his foot.

Damn. "Fine. I'll stay the night," he lied, "if you stop stressing me the hell out." Retreating to the kitchen for a cool glass of cranberry juice, Herschel asked, "You want some?"

"Sure," Ivory said, drying her eyes.

What she really wanted was for him to fuck the shit out of her.

Sitting on the bar stool at the island that doubled as a dining area when they ate together, she quietly sipped her juice. Herschel reached into the fruit bowl and picked up a ripe mango. Opening his mouth, he sank his teeth into the peel, biting a chunk of the fruit. "Damn, this is good shit right here," he said. "You've gotta taste it. Come here, baby."

Ivory smiled.

Yeah, her ass is bipolar, he thought. The minute Ivory got what she wanted, she was all happy and shit. Cupping her hand over his, she raised the mango to her lips. When she opened her mouth, Herschel shoved the fruit, trying to put the seed and all in Ivory's mouth.

"Don't ever give me a fucking ultimatum again, or you'll find yourself homeless. You got that!" he yelled.

Backing away, Ivory ran to the opposite side of the island. Herschel raced behind her. Bracing his hands on her hips, he hoisted Ivory high in the air, then slammed her hips on the island. Lifting her dress, he ripped off her leopard thong, then slid his finger inside her pussy.

"This is my pussy, you hear me. Mine!" he said.

"Okay," Ivory whimpered, surrendering to him.

Once she'd given in, Herschel peeled the mango with his teeth. He spat the rind onto the tile floor. Rubbing the mango on his bald head, he stretched Ivory's thighs as wide as he could. He lowered his head, then massaged the juices that were on his head onto her pussy.

Herschel squeezed the mango. The fruit gushed between his fingers, dripping juices onto Ivory's pussy. Removing her bra, he gently stroked the mushy mango between her breasts, circled it around her areolas, scrubbed her body with it, then sucked her sweet, tangy nipples into firm erections before licking her all over.

"Mmm," Ivory moaned, scooting backward onto the island. She locked her fingers in her hair, then tugged.

Stroking the mango between her pussy lips, Herschel braced her legs over his shoulders, then buried his face between her thighs. Since he couldn't figure out what Nikki ate to make her taste so good, he just rubbed whatever he felt like eating all over Ivory.

"Damn, you taste so fucking incredibly delicious. Whose pussy is this?" he asked, firmly pressing his tongue against her clit, the way she liked. "Don't move," he said, making his way to the refrigerator.

He retrieved an ice cube, melted it down a little in his mouth, pressed his cool lips against her clit, then slipped the ice cube inside her ass right along with his middle finger as he began to finger fuck her in the ass while sucking her clit.

Herschel enjoyed eating familiar pussy as much as he liked sucking his lover's dick. He buried his face deeper into Ivory's pussy until she came so hard he had to catch her before she slipped off the island and onto the floor. Maybe he should've let her fall. It would've been a justifiable accident.

It was a good thing women couldn't tell exactly what men were thinking. A man's actions spoke louder than his words, but nothing spoke louder than the emotions a man never shared.

"Baby," Herschel pleaded, holding Ivory in his arms, "don't ever leave me. I need you. Just give me a little longer. Everything is gonna be all right." Gently letting her go, he said, "I'll call you later."

Ivory frowned, then cried, "You're leaving? You promised."

Not soon enough. Damn, shut up. "I've got to. I'll call you later," he repeated, walking toward the door.

Trailing him, Ivory asked, "You've been leaving a lot lately. Are you seeing another woman? Just be honest with me. I want you to stay with me."

And what, listen to her cry again? Or badger him over the brain with Kwan's birthday trip, until he fell asleep. No fucking way. "No, I'm not seeing another woman. I gotta go. I'll see you at church Sunday."

"Sunday? Sunday is three days away."

"And? What's your point?"

Shaking her head, Ivory said, "Nothing. I'll see you Sunday."

Herschel didn't like the way Ivory had said "Nothing," but he couldn't keep Anthony waiting.

CHAPTER 11

Lexington

When a man loved a woman . . . he'd do any and everything for her.

Make love to her all night. Take out the trash. Eat her pussy until she begged him to stop. Inquire about her day with genuine concern. Plan vacations with her. Satisfy her sexual desires first. Send her flowers without her having to ask. Cook, clean, and keep her company. Suck her toes. Entertain the kids and insist she hang out with her girlfriends for the weekend. Give her a relaxing body massage. Tell her, "I love you" so often, she'd never have to wonder or ask, "Do you love me?" All the things a man in love did for his woman, he did them willingly, not under duress or protest.

"Lexington, I'm not going to pretend or ignore the fact that you laid in my bed and confessed you're having an affair with Nikki."

"Your bed?" Lexington repeated, refusing to look up at Donna, while he struggled to tune her out, eat a late lunch, and watch the Hornets.

"Are you having an affair with Nikki?" Donna asked.

"Confessed?" Lexington said, raising his eyebrows, keeping his—thanks to Donna—divided attention on the game. "Did you say I *confessed*?" He should've accepted Brian's offer to watch the game at his house.

Donna yelled, "Answer the damn question. Are you having an affair with Nikki or not?"

"Nikki who?" Lexington replied.

"Nikki who? Nikki who? Ou, if you answer one more question with a question . . . ," Donna lamented, raising her voice.

"What? You gon' leave me? You gon' get out of my house? Is that it?" Lexington asked. "If you had a life of your own, instead of depending on me to satisfy your every need, we wouldn't be having this conversation."

"I did have a life of my own. Remember? A very lucrative life and business, mind you, until you came along with your long list of convincing promises, and like a fool, I sold my business, married you, gave you two kids, and this is the thanks I get. You owe me. And one way or another, you will repay me for the time I've invested in you and your kids," Donna said, bracing her fists on her hips.

She was right. There was nothing to debate. Lexington sat in his theater chair, turning up the volume on the television to drown out Donna's annoying voice. Most of what she'd said made sense; it was her delivery that made him want to regurgitate his lunch in his wife's face. Why didn't she talk to him when *The Tyra Banks Show, Oprah, Judge Mathis,* or those drama-driven soap operas were on? Donna's timing was always off.

Donna stood in front of him with her pussy at eye level. "Maybe I should call Nikki back and ask her what's going on. She's feeding you those sex recipes, huh? Got your dick all hard for every woman except me."

"Donna! Move the fuck from in front of the TV! The Hornets are playing for the biggest opportunity ever, and your mouth is wider and louder than the fucking television. I don't want to stare at your pussy, or lick it, or fuck you. You let yourself go, not me. Now move."

"Oh, so you think Nikki is prettier? Is that it? My ass is wider than hers? I've given birth to two kids to her none," Donna said, holding up two fingers in his face, like Lexington didn't know how to count. "She doesn't have to hide from me. I'm not stupid. She's not woman enough to show her face over here anymore."

"That's because her business is thriving," Lexington said in Nikki's defense.

"Oh, now you can give me a direct response. I want her to come over here so I can talk to her, woman to woman. Let her see what I have to deal with every day, crying myself to sleep. She needs to see what kind of empty-promises man you really are. You want me to move? Is that it? Then you make me move," Donna said, edging closer to him.

"Haaaa," Lexington exhaled, then stood, nudging Donna

out of his way. He snatched his keys and wallet off the red-stained glass coffee table and walked outside.

"Oh, you think you going somewhere?" his wife heaved after him. "Not today, baby. Like it or not, you're staying home with me. It's time you make a change. It's time you concentrate on me," Donna said, marching behind him. "It takes separation to bring appreciation. Remember that song, Lexington? I'm warning you, if I leave your ass, you won't have to wonder where did we go wrong, because I promise you there will be no getting back together for us."

"You promise," Lexington said, standing in the driveway. Donna had parked her three cars, bumper to bumper, sideways, behind his. "What, Donna? What do you want from me? If I make you so unhappy, why don't you find somebody who loves you? That would make both of us happy."

"You mean the way you love Nikki? I need to find another husband because the man I married doesn't love me anymore?" Donna countered.

Lexington's trembling voice said, "Exactly. I love Nikki. There, satisfied? Is that what you wanted to hear me say? I said it. I'll say it again. And I'll keep saying it until you get the fuck out of my face! Yes, I do love Nikki. Always have. Always will. And she might be having my baby."

No sooner than he'd spoke, Lexington regretted every word. Not because what he'd said wasn't true. His wife didn't deserve to hear that. He watched the tears that filled Donna's squinted eyes. Not the sad ones. The angry "I wanna kill your trifling ass for telling me you love another woman" kind of tears. Thank goodness his girls were on an overnight camping trip with their friends and didn't have to witness Donna's incessant rage, and, luckily, their closest neighbors were too far away to hear Donna scream, "Fuck you, Lexington Lewis! You can have that bitch!"

Lexington hoped that if the girls were home, Donna wouldn't conduct herself in such a reckless manner. Each day, Donna grew more careless with her words. Shouting at him in front of the girls, making his girls cry. Each time the girls got upset, they clung to him, not his wife. The girls would make separating from Donna difficult. Nikki was too busy to watch his girls; he was too. Lexington had to make sure that if Donna left, the girls went with her. He'd provide for them, the same as he did for his son and two daughters in New Orleans.

He considered walking over to Nikki's to borrow one of her cars, but Herschel was home alone again, probably depressed like Donna. Maybe they should wife swap. Yeah, two depressed married people should be together. Hershel didn't deserve Nikki, and Donna sure as hell didn't deserve him. Herschel and Donna were both miserable and deserving of one another.

"Let me take a piss and I'll give you five minutes of my undivided attention," Lexington lied. "Wait right here."

"Don't do me any favors. You're going to be here more than five minutes," Donna said, tossing her ass on the sofa.

She'd already blocked his cars. If she didn't move them by morning, he'd have the Mercedes, Lexus, and Bentley he'd bought her towed to the Salvation Army. Lexington exited the rear of his home. His feet lightly stepped along wooden planks until he reached the dock. He got in his yacht, stood at the helm, and started the engine.

Donna came running onto the dock, yelling, "Don't come back here, you liar, you hear me!"

Get real, he thought, speeding away, watching water splash in her face, hoping the water would help cool Donna off.

Rocking with the currents, Lexington turned off his engine, floated on the bay, then powered on his television to watch the last few minutes of the game in peace. Disappointed the Hornets lost, he phoned Nikki, thankful she'd answered on the first ring. "I'm ready to talk. You got a minute."

"I'm sorry about the other night at the club. I shouldn't have fucked you like that, but I was jealous of those Queens," Nikki said softly in his ear. She knew how to calm him. Nikki never yelled, or cursed, or disrespected his feelings even when she had cause.

"It's okay, baby. It's not your fault. It was mine. I shouldn't have disrespected you. That's why I just wanted to hold you in my arms the last time we were together. Whatever the situation is, even if we're pregnant, we'll get through this together. Just don't communicate with Donna. She knows about our affair," he admitted.

"Lexington, no. You didn't. Please tell me you didn't tell her. What about me? What about Herschel? What if she tells my husband?"

"We can't worry about that right now. Neither one of us is happy with either one of them, so Donna will do both of us a favor if she tells Herschel."

Lexington didn't want to fight the Lewis versus Henderson

battle alone. He didn't want to have to do anything without Nikki by his side. Removing all of his clothes, letting the sun warm his naked body, he asked, "Where are you?"

"At my hotel, downtown New Orleans. I'm catering a private affair on the *Queen Mary* tomorrow. Shit. Not the *Queen Mary,* that's a tourist ocean liner in Long Beach, California. I meant the *Cotton Blossom*. See how confused I am."

Hearing Nikki say the word "Queen" made his dick harden. The Queens were still in his fantasy repertoire. Lexington had to get Nikki focused on him, not his promiscuous behavior or her husband. Could he give up going to swingers clubs for Nikki? Would she want him to?

"Where are you?" she asked.

"On my yacht. Drifting mentally and physically as far away as possible from Donna. Nikki, I love you. I have every letter, e-mail, and birthday card you sent me while we were in college."

"You never told me that," she said.

Lexington heard the smile in her voice. "There's a few things I haven't told you that you need to know."

Nikki's voice trembled. "Like what? I thought we shared everything."

"The most important thing is, I love you. I'll tell you when I see you. Don't worry. It's nothing that'll change my love for you."

"Isn't it funny how we've always been crazy about each other, would do anything for one another, but never married one another. Why didn't you propose to me?" Nikki asked.

"You were always so self-assured, seemed like you didn't need me for more than having a good time. I accepted that," Lexington said, relaxing on the foredeck.

"But I wanted you. I wanted you to ask me to marry you. You know I come from a matriarchal family that strongly believes a woman should never ask a man to marry her. To do so is to take the kiss of death at the altar. I believe that's true."

"So you're saying, if I would've asked, you would've married me?"

"No. Not then. But that's exactly what I'm feeling now. But it wouldn't work. Baby, you know you don't want to stay married to Donna, but at the same time, you can't admit that you don't want her to leave you. Why?"

"When do you get back?" Lexington asked.

"Tomorrow," Nikki answered. "Why?"

"Don't come home tomorrow. I'm going to meet you at your hotel. I'll take the first available flight out. Tonight or in the morning. I'll be there."

"You are so crazy. That's why I love you," Nikki said.

Smiling on the inside, Lexington confirmed, "I am crazy. About you. So what are you wearing?"

Nikki moaned. "I have on a black lace thong."

"And?" he asked, massaging his dick.

"Nothing else. That's it. It's pressing against my clit. You're getting me wet," Nikki moaned in his ear.

"Take it off and spread my pussy for me," Lexington said, teasing his head.

Exhaling, Nikki purred, "They're dangling on the tip of my toes."

"Put the phone between your legs so I can hear you spank my pussy."

Smack! Smack! Smack! Smack! "Like that?" she said loudly.

"Ou, damn. I wanna fuck you so bad, Nikki. My dick is so hard," Lexington said, watching the sun fade. The late-evening temperature was a warm 80 degrees. The blue sky softly blended with clouded gray streaks. "Stick your finger in your pussy, then put it in your mouth."

"Um-um, yes," Nikki moaned, then said, "Baby, you wanna taste my pussy?"

"Fuck yes. I want you to sit your sweet pearl on my face," Lexington said, opening his mouth. He inhaled, picturing Nikki squatting above his mouth when they were at the sex club. Lexington could never take Donna to a sex club.

"Squeeze your dickhead until the precum oozes to the tip; then I want you to rub it on my watering mouth," Nikki moaned. "I wanna taste my dick. Then I want you to push me against the rail of your yacht and fuck this pussy—nice, deep, and slow—until I cream all over your big-ass dick, baby."

Sweat beaded all over his glistening body. Releasing his dick, which stood at attention, Lexington tied his locks into a bundle, then stroked his shaft.

"Damn, baby. Hold on tight. You making my dick drip cum. It's rolling down my shaft. I need to let go, baby. Is it okay if I blast off deep inside your wet, hot pussy?" Lexington asked, closing his eyes.

Stroking his shaft felt so good. He pressed his finger alongside the frenulum, about one inch below his head. Just like the left side of Nikki's pussy, between her labia and her shaft, was one of her favorite hot spots, massaging that same left area on the underside of his dick made him come quicker.

"Come with me, baby. Come all over my pussy. Fuck me,

Lexington. Fuck this pussy. Lexington. Lexington," Nikki moaned.

He loved the way she called his name.

"Lexington! You hear me calling you!"

Opening his eyes, he saw Donna standing on their dock watching him. *Fuck!* Marinating in his moment with Nikki, he had allowed the damn boat to drift back home. Lexington dropped his phone on the foredeck, then hurried to the helm. By the time he revved up the engine, Donna leapt onto the back of the yacht with a high jump that would've earned her a gold medal. She did a fireman's tuck and roll when he started the engine. Wrestling him at the helm, she turned off the motor.

"You got your naked ass out here stroking your dick for who? That bitch Nikki."

So now Nikki was a bitch again. Why? Because Nikki knew how to treat him and his wife didn't.

Slap! Slap! Angrily Donna hit him repeatedly on his back. His dick hung low, praying she'd leave him alone. What was Donna proving? Would her physically hurting him make him want her more?

Slap! His hand landed across Donna's cheek.

"Ahhh! Are you crazy? Why did you hit me?" she screamed, stumbling toward the floor. Donna picked up his phone and hurled it into the bay.

Lexington quietly stepped off the yacht, went inside, put on his blue linen slacks, buttoned up his shirt, stepped into his blue sandals, then swaggered straight to the guard shack at the entrance of The Island.

"Man, let me call my driver," Lexington said.

The security guard handed him the cordless phone without asking questions. Donna was crazy, but she had sense enough not to act a fool in front of security. The last time she'd followed him, security called the police on her.

In ten minutes, Lexington was en route to his office, then Miami International Airport for a late-night flight to New Orleans to lay his head in the arms of the one woman, other than his mother, who loved him unconditionally.

Chapter 12

Nikki

Draped in a vibrant tangerine strapless dress that barely covered her curvaceous hips, Nikki motioned for the bartender at Drago's, then ordered a French martini—vodka, Chambord raspberry liqueur, pineapple juice, and sweet-and-sour mix.

Ruminating on her conversation with Lexington, listening to him complain about Donna on his driver's cell phone while in transit to his office, Nikki knew it was time for her to have a more in-depth discussion with Lexington about his marriage. Everything bad in his marriage wasn't Donna's fault. Nikki had heard Donna scream in the background, right before a splash, then silence; Lexington verified his wife had intentionally disposed of his phone, hurling it into the bay. The slapping Nikki had heard made her wonder if Lexington was beating Donna. Nikki hoped not. An abusive man did not discriminate. If Lexington abused Donna, he'd eventually abuse her too.

"Compliments of the gentlemen seated at the high table by the window," the bartender said, setting two drinks on the counter in front of her.

New Orleans was one of the few cities Nikki visited where she could legally order alcohol twenty-four hours a day, seven days a week. Restaurants, like the one Donna used to own, operated like the po-boy shop We Never Close. No curfews on clubs closing or people partying. Why did the people in and of New Orleans drink all day and all night? Perhaps they wanted to forget the city's history.

True to her nickname, "the City that Care Forgot" was home to the largest slave trade. Raped from the Motherland, Negro, colored, black, African-American women were repeatedly raped of their womanhood; their men were taken, and their children were stripped away from their breasts the second the umbilical cord was severed. So were the family ties. Black men cared more about the economic depression than the black woman's postslavery depression . . . Society too.

Human cargo auctioned off to pass into repass, never to see their families again. Birthing from her belly jazz, blues, and to-die-for food—some say cuisine—the millions of spirits in New Orleans, Vieux Carré could cast a spell on any and all souls venturing or dwelling within her city limits, influencing them to generously consume alcohol, festively communicate with the unknown, and openly have sex with strangers they may not meet again in hopes of forgetting her pain and her disdain from the slave trades to the raised graves above sea level where blacks were buried with forcible separation from families. Memories of what whites celebrated lingered, so that subconsciously even when blacks were together, they never had a healthy union as husband and wives. The Motherland allowed an African man to be a man and support as many wives as he could, but the black man has never claimed his place as an African. He lives as an American. Whatever that is.

Nikki kept her eyes on the front door of her favorite seafood restaurant, eagerly awaiting her girlfriend. In a couple of hours, Nikki and her girlfriend were going to The Lounge. If her girlfriend approved, the twin guys who'd bought Nikki's drinks would be invited to join them for an unforgettable night of dining and fucking.

Crisscrossing her long legs at the knees, Nikki leaned back, holding both of her martinis in the air, smiled at the two guys, then mouthed, "Thanks, gentlemen." Stroking a man's ego made stroking his dick easier, especially if Nikki liked him . . . them.

"Hey, lady!" her girlfriend said, sashaying toward her with open arms.

Venus strutted in, modeling a red-yellow-and-green dress with a plunging neckline that exposed her diamond saint's symbol navel ring, a green head wrap to keep strangers at the sex club from touching what New Orleanians called "good hair," and red "come fuck me" stilettos. Her emerald contacts looked amazingly natural.

Rocking side to side, Nikki hugged Venus long and tight, then said, "Hey, back at you, Miss Diva."

"You look good enough to eat, Mama," Venus said, play-kissing Nikki's lips, careful not to ruin either of their lip gloss.

The bartender interrupted. "Excuse me, ladies. The gentlemen over there would like to buy both of you as many drinks as you'd like."

Nikki finished her first French martini, then said to the bartender, "I'm good. I still have one to sip on," then asked Venus, "What are you drinking tonight?"

Venus told the bartender, "I'll have two real dirty martinis and all of her drinks."

"You are scandalous," Nikki said.

"You're the one who's been gone too long from home. You know we do not turn down or toss out alcohol," Venus said.

"You down for inviting the guys who bought the drinks to hang?" Nikki asked.

"The twins?" Venus said, smiling, then answered Nikki's nod, "Without a doubt. If they pick up the dinner tab, they get invited to eat our pussies for dessert. If they don't, we leave their asses right here."

"But of course," Nikki said, thinking about Lexington. He'd be in her bed at some point before sunrise. Maybe she'd let the twins prep her pussy for Lexington.

Sometimes it was better for a woman not to tell a man too much. Lexington's invitation to his spot was new to her, but Nikki had frequented sex clubs since her twenty-first birthday, when she was legally old enough to purchase memberships. Lexington had no idea then, and she sure as hell wasn't telling him now. Lexington was strong, sexy, and successful, but his ego was marked *Fragile, handle with care.*

Nikki walked over to the gentlemen's table, then extended her hand. "Hi, I'm Nefertiti and that's my girl, Emerald. Would you gentlemen like to join us? We're being seated at a table for dinner." Their wide smiles were good indicators, but Nikki waited for a verbal response.

"Of course, we'd love to," they replied in unison, then paused before one continued, "I'm Vinson and that's my brother." Nikki held her breath until he said, "Victor"; then she exhaled.

She was glad he didn't say something rhyming, like Crimson. "Let's go," Nikki said, leading the way.

Nikki approached Venus, winked, then said, "Emerald, this is Victor and Vinson."

"Hello, Emerald," they greeted in unison.

Responding at the same time could prove beneficial later— if they had big dicks, Nikki thought, ordering two dozen of Drago's famous charbroiled oysters on the half shell.

"Do we need so many oysters?" Victor asked.

Venus answered, "If you're hanging with us, yes. If not, no."

"Where?" they asked.

"Y'all have to stop doing that," Nikki said. "It's a late-night club nearby. Walking distance."

Their smiles were wider than before. Victor said, "That's why we're in 'the Big Easy', to party all night."

Three dozen oysters and eight drinks later, Victor and Vinson debated over which one of them was paying the bill. "I've got it," Victor said, picking up the tab.

"No, I've got it," Vinson insisted, placing his credit card in Victor's hand.

"I've got the perfect high going, and I don't have all night. Split the bill and let's go," Nikki said, following Venus out of the restaurant.

Victor and Vinson caught up with them near Harrah's casino. Every night at the sex club where they were headed, ladies were admitted free. If the guys were going to the club without them, Victor and Vinson would have to pay $90 each; with them, they'd pay $50 each; if it was Saturday, they couldn't get in at all unless a woman accompanied them. Ladies ruled at sex clubs. A short walk down Gravier and a half block past Carondelet Street and they were at their destination.

Nikki showed her ID, then waited for Vinson to pay for all of them. They'd consumed enough alcohol at the restaurant and didn't need to bring their own bottles of liquor. Venus bypassed the bars and led the guys straight to the lounge area. The guys' eyes widened, their chins hung toward their chests.

Vinson said, "Damn, we've been to New Orleans several times, but we had no idea y'all party like this."

"Are you serious? Then obviously you don't know the history," Nikki said, pressing her lips against Vinson's mouth. She placed his hand on her breasts, massaged his dick through his pants, then said, "Touch my pussy."

Placing Vinson's hand between her legs, Nikki eyed Victor and Venus.

Venus's ass wiggled in front of Victor's face. Nikki bent over in front of her girlfriend. Venus proceeded to spread Nikki's ass and lick her pussy, saying, "I knew you looked sweet enough to eat. I've got to get closer to this praline pussy. Lay down," Venus said.

Nikki removed Vinson's pants, stretched her body across the armless chaise, then motioned for Vinson to straddle her face. Lubing her hand with saliva, Nikki stroked Vinson's dick, twisting her hand up and down his shaft.

She felt Venus's warm mouth gently sucking her pussy. "Damn, that's what I needed. Female and male energy at the same time." Nikki was moaning, tilting her hips toward Venus.

"Fuck me slow and deep," Venus instructed Victor, handing him a condom.

"Damn, y'all come prepared," Victor said, eagerly tearing open the packet. He knelt behind Venus, rubbed his dick over her opening, eased inside, then humped her doggie-style.

Venus found Nikki's pearl; like she was delicately shucking an oyster, she parted the muscle in the middle and sucked the jewel right from its hiding place. The tip of Venus's tongue slid around Nikki's pearl. Vinson teased Nikki's nipples, while Victor massaged her ass, holding her in place for Venus.

Nikki's juices trickled into Venus's mouth.

Vinson said, "I want to watch this."

"Not yet," Venus said, massaging his ass.

Nikki stroked Vinson's dick, slower and stronger. They knew what was about to happen to Vinson, but he had no idea his unofficial prostate exam and orgasm were seconds away. Venus slipped her finger in his asshole. Closing her eyes, Nikki massaged him harder.

Vinson trembled like a leaf. His knees got weak. His thick cum squirted above Nikki's head, right before his body collapsed on the edge of the chaise.

"Damn" was all he said as he stared at the couples on the bed across from him.

Maybe the twins weren't connected. Victor proceeded to dig his dick deeper into Venus's pussy. "This is fucking stupendous," he said. "My brother, man, you can't hang. You looked pussy-whupped."

Victor had no idea what was about to clench him.

"Aw, shit!" Victor yelled.

Everyone in the room applauded. Venus, nicknamed "Venus Flytrap" at the sex clubs, had trapped Victor's dick with her pussy and she wasn't letting go until she'd drained him of every seed her pussy walls could muster out of his nuts.

Nikki was sure Venus's mother named her after the Roman goddess of love and hadn't thought about her daughter perfecting a pussy technique that made men instantly fall in love with her.

"That's what you get," Vinson said, trying to get up.

"I have no complaints, my brother. None," Victor said. "Emerald, you can keep my dick in your pussy as long, and as often, as you'd like."

Venus's muscles ejected his dick out of her pussy.

"Damn, I didn't mean for you to spit him out right now," Victor said, shaking his head.

"I need to get closer to my girl's pussy. Vinson, I want you to kiss and caress Nefertiti's right breast, and, Victor, you do the same with her left breast. Don't start sucking her nipples until I tell you. I want you to start off sucking her nipples soft, then gradually add pressure, and don't stop until she comes in my mouth."

"Damn, Emerald. What are you? Some sort of professional genitalia therapist for the clit and the dick?" Victor asked.

"Get on your job, Victor," Venus commanded, going down on Nikki.

Nikki closed her eyes, focusing more on Venus gently sucking her shaft than on the twins kissing her breasts. Mirroring her intimate relationship with Lexington, Nikki loved Venus. They were friends in junior high school and lovers since high school. Nikki and Venus didn't see a stigma of two women being in love with one another and being friends. They enjoyed being in each other's company.

Nikki's entire body trembled with pleasure as she relaxed and enjoyed Vinson and Victor trying to watch Venus as they sucked her titties.

Venus whispered, "Now."

The twins were in sync with her twins, as if they'd done this before with a woman, but Nikki doubted it. Their palms circled her breasts like they were holding a bottle. Sucking in unison, they followed instructions well, applying lots of pressure to her nipples.

Nikki's body was on fire. Venus slipped her finger inside Nikki's pussy and began stroking her G-spot while isolating her clit in her mouth. The flickers of Venus's tongue and finger, coupled with the firm suction of Vinson and Victor on her breasts, caused Nikki to scream the loudest "Yes!" imaginable, like a spirit had escaped her body, stealing away her last breath.

Panting heavily, Nikki sat up. Her eyes fixated on Venus. Neither of them said a word. If Nikki could openly have Venus as her female energy partner and Lexington as her alpha male, her love life would be perfect. But Lexington would be intimidated by the fact that Venus could eat Nikki's pussy better. And Venus would have penis envy when she stared at Lexington's big, beautiful dick, knowing her strap-on could never measure up. Nikki wouldn't want to choose one over the other, so she'd keep sexing both of them.

Why shouldn't a woman have her cake and eat them two?

CHAPTER 13

Brian

"Man, I've never broken my wedding vows, nor have I been unfaithful during my marriage," Brian said to Lexington as he sipped on a vodka and pineapple, with a splash of coconut rum, martini at a small, quaint hotel in downtown Chicago. Adjusting his Bluetooth, Brian listened to Lexington complain about Donna, while Lexington waited to board a flight to New Orleans.

Being on the road all the time made Brian feel lonely at times. Now his occasional loneliness was exacerbated by his guilt for having fucked the wrong woman. It was a guilt he'd have to suppress a little longer. Brian wasn't ready to confide in his father. Tabling discussing his personal situation with his dad, Brian concluded "why bother?" Maybe if he ignored Zahra, she'd forget about him. Brian feared if he had said the wrong thing and pissed off his dad, his mother might get up-set too. Brian loved his mother too much to disappoint her.

Talking with his wife every day. Checking in with his parents to make sure the kids were okay. Hearing his kids tell him how much they wished he could stay home more often. Those were the things that created voids in his life when he wasn't home with them. Brian couldn't have gotten a better wife, better kids, or a better life—unless he'd written the script.

If Brian could map his future without any repercussions, he'd change a few things. He'd have an open marriage. He'd share everything he did outside his marriage with his wife. He'd have Michelle give up her career and travel with him. That way, he wouldn't secretly lie in the arms of other women to satisfy his sexual appetite. And he'd be allowed to freely explore his fantasies of having threesomes and foursomes with his wife included, sometimes.

"Man, you need to stop lying to yourself," Lexington said. "You cheat on Michelle just as much as I do on Donna."

"I keep telling you, I never signed up for fidelity. That word is not in my wedding vows. I've never been monogamous and don't plan on starting now. The difference between us," Brian said, "is you're fucking playing Russian roulette, dicking-down Herschel's wife on the regular. There's too much pussy out here, man. Stick with the sex clubs, if that's your thing, but stop fucking Nikki."

There was no way Brian would fuck his neighbors' or any of his boys' wives. That was the type of foolishness that made people homicidal and suicidal, then plead temporary insanity.

"Man, Nikki was my first piece of pussy, my first virgin,

and my first love. No way I'ma stop making love to her. Besides, if Herschel was handling his business, I wouldn't have to keep Nikki happy. He should thank me."

A person's judgment could easily be altered if all they remembered was the immediate gratification they'd get from having things their way. What about the long-term effects? That's what Brian kept clear, at all times. No piece of ass was worth his cash or his marriage. Pussy was free and plentiful, he hoped . . . thinking about Zahra.

"What about keeping Donna happy?" Brian asked. "Damn, man, spend some quality time with your wife and kids. Even if you don't want to have sex with her, take your family out."

"Fuck Donna. She brought this shit on herself. I work too fucking hard to provide for her, for her to disrespect me in my own damn house. I was done with Donna years ago. You're the one in denial. Fucking around on Michelle. Now, Michelle is a good woman. If I were married to your wife, I'd be faithful."

Whateva. Lexington must've forgotten whom he was talking to. Lexington could try to convince somebody else of that bullshit, but Brian had known Lexington since they were in kindergarten when Lexington kept two or three girlfriends, and Nikki was one of them. That's why she never married his ass. Throughout their entire relationship in high school and college, Nikki was number-one, but Lexington always had a number-two and a number-three chick on the side.

"Yeah, nigga, you'd be faithful. Just like me. I gotta go—this *badd,* big-booty Latina just walked into the bar. She's got on a slightly see-through top. You should see her pretty titties, man. Her hard nipples just made my dick hard. And she's got that 'I know I'm all that' happy strut going on. I'ma be all up in that ass before the end of the night," Brian said.

Lexington replied, "You gon' fuck the wrong chick in the ass and end up like ole boy when she go running off to the hospital on your ass."

"Man, unlike other fools ramming their dick in a woman's ass, I'm a professional anal penetrator. I know how to hit that G-spot from the ass and make women come in a way they didn't know they could come. They like that shit when you hit it just right. Besides, fucking these women in the ass assures me I will not have any woman trying to contact me, talking about she's having my baby."

"Shit, you really think those chicks can't find your ass once you're gone?" Lexington asked.

Confidently Brian answered, "Got that right. That's why I call them from a calling card, never my cell. I never give them my phone number, e-mail, nothing where they can track my ass down. I don't even give them my real name."

"Yeah, yeah. Here we go with that shit again. Go on with all that Brother Malik bullshit," Lexington said, laughing.

"Keep 'em guessing, man." Kicking in his African accent, Brian said, "They believe I'm from Africa and in the Nation. I give them as much misleading information as possible, and if you were smart, you would too. Stop fucking Nikki, man. Peace," Brian said, ending his call with Lexington.

Brian's mouth watered and his tongue hardened as he watched the Latina woman hoist her booty in the air to sit on the bar stool. Her pear-shaped ass was so nice. She smiled at him, then swung her long, dark, wavy hair behind her shoulders. She leaned toward the bartender and opened her mouth.

Brian interrupted. With his African accent, he said, "Let me get that for you," moving to occupy the empty stool beside her. Damn, she smelled tasty.

Her mesmerizing brown eyes darted from his dick to his lips. "But you have no idea what I want," she said, with the most amazing smile. Her breath smelled fresh and refreshing at the same time, making him want to grab the back of her head, pull her lips into his mouth, and tongue kiss her so he could taste what she tasted.

His offer wasn't about what she wanted. It was all about what he wanted. Brian mentally undressed her, imagining her pussy was smoothly waxed. The hairs between her butt cheeks were waxed too. Her asshole was silky soft and tight. Her shaft was nice and short and her pussy was sweet and juicy.

The woman rubbed her leg against his underneath the bar table, then eased her hand up his thigh to his dick and said, "I'll have a slow screw with Goose."

His dick throbbed in the palm of her hand.

She was so damn cute—with sparkles on her arms and enticing, kissable lips. She had a wide mouth he wanted to stick his dick in, and her small waist made him want to hold her sides and bounce her pussy on his dick right at the bar. If no one was watching, he'd fuck her right now. She smelled like a bouquet of roses. Grazing her tongue over her upper lip, pausing the tip of her tongue in the corner of her mouth, she smiled, then circled her finger atop the glass that the bartender had poured her drink into. His dick got harder.

"So, are you staying at this hotel?" she asked.

"Are you?"

She nodded, then smiled again. Her teeth were white; her tongue nice, clean, and pink. Her mouth was so fucking inviting. "I'm Carmelita. I'm here for three days. Room 1018. You?"

"My flight leaves early in the morning," he lied. "I'm staying downtown on West Michigan," he lied again. His hotel was near O'Hare International Airport.

Brian refused to give her accurate information. Definitely not enough info for her to track him down after he'd tapped her ass. Oh, he was determined to get into her hotel room tonight.

"Married?" she asked, sticking the tip of her tongue inside the rim of her glass, scooping out the cherry.

Brian shook his head and smiled.

"What's your name?"

"Malik. Brother Malik," Brian said.

"Well, Malik, if you'd like, we can take another round of drinks and this conversation to my room for a nightcap."

Hell yes! "Ten-eighteen," Brian repeated, motioning to the bartender for another round of drinks.

"Bring the drinks and that big-ass African dick to my room, will you?" she seductively asked, standing and putting her titties in front of his mouth before he could answer.

With so many beautiful women walking around with succulent pussies, there was no way Brian could keep his dick and tongue away from all of them. Michelle's pussy was his favorite, but throughout his marriage, he had to taste other women in order to appreciate his wife. Actually, he'd never stop fucking other women. What was the point?

Brian waited for his soon-to-be titty-flopping, ass-bouncing date for the night to step onto the elevator before adjusting his Bluetooth over his ear and dialing Michelle's cell phone. When she answered, he said, "I miss you, baby. How'd your meeting go?"

"It went well. I'm so tired. Just made it home. I got off the phone with my mother a few minutes ago. The kids are asleep, so I didn't get to say good night to them. Did you talk with them?"

"No, I called you first. Why are they at your mother's house?" he asked quizzically.

"She is their grandmother too. Your mom keeps them all the time. My mom is giving her a break. I'm too exhausted and sleepy for you to make love to me over the phone, though I really, really want you to talk dirty to me and make me come." Michelle exhaled. "I'm about to shower and call it a night. How was your day, baby? Did you remember to take your vitamins?" she asked.

Watching the bartender set both drinks on the counter, Brian said, "Baby, hold on just a second while I take this call right quick. It's Lexington."

Touching the mute button, Brian glanced at the forty-eight-dollar tab, handed the bartender $60, then said, "I'm good. The rest is for you."

"Where'd your date go?" he asked in an overfriendly tone.

Defensively Brian answered, "She's not my date."

"No need to get defensive with me. Aren't you—"

"No, I'm not," Brian spit out between his teeth, realizing he'd dropped his accent when he called his wife.

"You sure look like . . ." the bartender said, snapping his fingers and squinting his eyes. "What happened to the accent you had a few minutes ago when you were talking to that hottie?"

Picking up the tray, Brian moved to a table far away from the bar, near the elevator. The Latina pussy that got on the elevator and went upstairs should be showered, fresh, clean, and waiting for him to fellate with his tongue. Pressing the mute button again, Brian said, "Baby, sorry about that. You know how long-winded Lexington can be."

"I don't like the way he treats Donna," Michelle protested. "She could do a lot better, you know. I think I'm going to ask Nikki to bake Donna some of her special brownies and sprinkle them with extra lovemaking chocolate and we can take them to Donna this weekend and tell her to feed them to Lexington. I'm not condoning her cheating on him. She should try to work things out, but if her husband isn't treating her right, she needs to get with a man who's going to treat her the way she deserves to be treated. And if that man isn't her husband, she needs to divorce him."

"Baby, you are tired. Michelle, do not call Donna or Nikki. Stay out of it. They're not the problem, or *our* problem. Donna knows what she signed up for."

"Baby, I just want you to know if you ever treat me the way Lexington disrespects Donna, I'll divorce you in a hot second. I know exactly how to handle infidelity. Don't ever let me find you cheating. It's the blatant disrespect and pathological lying that I wouldn't accept. I'm glad you're just as faithful to me, baby, as I am to you too."

Wrinkles formed across Brian's forehead. Silence settled

between them. He knew Michelle was prompting him for confirmation that he was faithful. "Baby, don't go there. I'm happily married and I want us to be happy for a hundred-plus years. Let's not make their issue ours."

The elevator door opened and the Latina woman who was supposed to be in room 1018 waiting for him stepped off, wearing blue low-rise jeans, a tapered T-shirt clinging to her breasts, and sexy silver slip-on stilettos. Brian placed his finger over his lips, signaling for the woman to be quiet. Plopping her irresistible ass in the chair next to him, she picked up her drink and began sipping.

"That's Lexington calling again. Let me call you in the morning. Good night," Brian said, picking up his phone and ending the call without responding after his wife had professed her love for him.

Smiling, Carmelita looked into his eyes, then said, "You are a very good liar, Malik. I'm going to spank you for being a naughty, naughty man."

Brian could hardly wait to fuck the shit out of Carmelita. He'd call his wife later, letting her know he accidentally pressed the end call button before saying, "I love you too, baby."

It didn't take much to keep Michelle or any woman happy. Respect. Love. Affection. Investing quality time. And always keeping family first. These were the basics to his healthy and happy relationship. Most men fucked up because they didn't respect or show appreciation for their wives. Brian felt bad about abruptly ending the call with his wife, but he was glad Michelle wasn't the type of wife that would relentlessly call him back until he answered the phone.

"Now I see what took you so long," his fine-ass Latina woman said.

The freshness of her body lured him closer as he sipped on his martini.

"Why don't you go back to your room, put on something sexier, and, I promise you, I'll be there in less than ten minutes."

"Your English is *ver-ry* good, Brother Malik," she said, holding on to her drink.

Watching her walk away, Brian began having second thoughts about fucking Carmelita, but the arch in the thong hovering the V above her ass persuaded him to hit it fast and furious.

Damn, that's a nice ass, Brian thought, quickly finishing his drink. Soon as the elevator door closed, he called Michelle back to say, "The call ended before I could tell you, 'I love you, baby.' Now go back to sleep."

Ending the call, Brian made his way to the elevator. Exiting on the tenth floor, he tapped on 1018, hoping she'd had enough time to change into something sexy for him, but praying she still had on that thong. Brian wanted that thong and the ass in it spread across his face.

She opened the door and his jaw dropped witnessing the prettiest set of perfect breasts he'd ever seen. And all she was wearing was that black thong and a black beaded necklace.

"Get in here before somebody else sees me," she said, closing the door behind him.

"Damn, you look hot! I can't believe you're not married," Brian said, unbuckling his pants. His hard dick sprang forward.

"I never *said* I wasn't married," she said, kneeling before him and sucking his dick.

Brian moaned, "Aw, yes." Whatever her marital status was didn't matter to him, and the way she was sucking his balls, it obviously didn't matter to her either.

"Take off your shirt and relax. I want to show you something. I have a little fetish," she said, reaching into her over-sized purse, with *Who's Loving You* embroidered in gold on the front.

Women were far more promiscuous than men.

She pulled out a giant watermelon Blow Pop, slowly un-wrapped it, then stuck it in his mouth. How did she know watermelon was his favorite? He preferred watermelon Now and Later candies, but a watermelon Blow Pop was just as tasty.

Trying to impress her, he sucked it, pretending it was her clit as he fluttered his tongue on the top of the sucker. He couldn't wait to roll the sucker over her clit, then pop her clit in his mouth. He watched her ease the sucker out of his mouth, lick it all over, and then put it back in his mouth.

"I enjoy sharing," she said.

She dug into her purse, pulled out a small bottle of baby oil, and began massaging her titties. She teased her nipples. Lying on the bed, she said, "Stand in front of me. I want you to watch me play with my pussy, baby."

Spreading her labia, she dripped oil onto her shaft, her stomach, and her thighs. Rubbing the oil all over her body, she used both hands to open her pretty pussy nice and wide. Sucking the Blow Pop, he lusted to lick her protruding clit.

Brian started stroking his dick as he watched her shaft swell.

Never had his body been so fucking hot from watching a woman play with herself. He wanted to explode all over her pussy.

Toying with her necklace, she unhooked the small gadget that was attached and pressed a tiny black button at the top three times. "Come. Feel this," she said, dropping the short black weiner-shaped attachment in his hand.

"What the hell?" Brian said as the gadget vibrated in his palm. He felt the pulsation throughout his entire body.

"Give it to me. That's my handy bullet. I never leave home without one," she said, strumming the tip along the side of her slippery shaft.

Brian's heart pounded fast, thumping against his chest. Anxiously, he wanted in on the action as she rotated the bullet on the tip of her clit.

"Ah, ah, ou, yes, ah, I'm coming," she said, humping her hips upward toward the bullet.

Damn, that was fast, Brian thought, feeling he was going to come equally as fast inside her ass in less than one minute.

"Now that my pussy is all wet, it's time for you to get down to business and satisfy me," she said. "Five hundred."

Brian frowned. "Five hundred what?"

"Don't play dumb. You wanna come or what?" she asked.

She eased off the bed and took his dick out of his hand. Slowly sliding his erection into her mouth, she asked, "Like what you've seen so far?"

Brian sighed heavily.

Taking the sucker out of his mouth, she placed it in hers, then reached into her purse again. She pulled out three gold condom packets and a small blue packet of WET lube. She held the sucker in her mouth while opening the condom. Squeezing a few drops of lube inside the condom, she rolled the latex onto his rock-hard dick, then feverishly kissed his sticky lips, like they'd met someplace before.

"You don't have to say a word," she whispered in his ear. "Just put the money on the chair beside the bed and I'll do the rest." Crawling onto the mattress, she glanced over her shoulder. Softening her eyes, she squirted baby oil on her ass, smoothed the oil over her butt, then asked, "You ready to fuck me in my big, beautiful, lovable ass?"

Brian had never directly paid for pussy. Obviously, this woman was a prostitute, or one smart, beautiful lady. If he left, she could cry rape, and although there'd be no evidence, his wife would find out about him being with another woman. If he paid, he might get arrested. He'd take his chances on getting laid. Reluctantly he counted out 5 one-hundred-dollar bills, then crawled onto the bed behind her. Her asshole was nicely lubed and wide open. Moving her thong aside, he stuck his dickhead in.

"Aw, fuck," he moaned, leaning his head back.

He groped her oily ass. And what a pretty ass she had. He stroked a little deeper.

"Ah, yes. Take your time, baby, or you can bang this pussy real hard if you want to. I like whatever you like," she said, slapping her own ass.

She didn't have to offer it rough twice. He did want to fuck her hard. Grabbing her hair, Brian slid his dick all the way in her ass, pounding her ass. She slammed her ass onto his dick.

"Ou, yeah. Um. Yes. You're making my pussy so wet," she moaned, reaching for her bullet.

Turning on her gadget, she pressed it against her clit until she came really hard. Then she reached back with one hand, pulled his dick out of her ass, stroked it tight, then put it back in. She massaged his balls with the vibrator, making him come before he realized the condom was gone and he wasn't in her ass. He had exploded a full load inside her pussy.

Coming, Brian yelled, "Aw, fuck!" He was in too deep to stop the flow of his cum. By the time he pulled his dick out of her pussy, he was drained and pissed off. "What the fuck happened here?"

Looking over her shoulder, frowning, she asked, "What? What's wrong, baby? Didn't you like it? Didn't you come?"

"You know damn well I came! Why did you take off the fucking condom and stick my dick in your pussy?"

She started shaking her head. Tears flooded her face. "No, no." She inserted her finger inside her ass, pulled out the condom, and started crying harder. "My husband is going to kill us if I'm pregnant," she cried. "You gotta give me another five hundred dollars for an abortion."

"*Us? Husband? Pregnant? Abortion?* What the fuck are you talking about?" Brian asked, putting on his clothes.

Walking over to the chair to pick up his $500, he glanced at the notepad on the nightstand beside the bed, looked away, then back again. "What the fuck!" How did Carmelita know his wife's name and cell phone number?

"I'll be damned. Bitch, you're trying to set me up?"

Carmelita smiled up at him. "Make that ten thousand, or should I call and ask Michelle?"

CHAPTER 14

Herschel

Love. Lust. Lies.

Herschel stood outside his lover's bedroom door. They'd shared their beachfront condo almost as many years as he'd been married to Nikki. At the condo, Herschel spent quality time making love to Anthony, resonating in their moments of being away from their wives. Away from a world filled with judgmental people. Away from those who wouldn't try or care to understand how two men could genuinely love one another.

What difference did it make if a man sexed a male or female? Human companionship came in many forms. To Herschel, both men and women looked and felt great. Both were aesthetically and intellectually stimulating. Front door, back door, pussy, asshole, mouth—his erect penis penetrated exactly where his lovers craved.

The mental connections between Nikki, Ivory, and Anthony vastly differed. The orgasmic outcomes produced by the emotional attachment to each of them created the same explosive reactions from his nuts. Contrary to what some women believed, bisexual men were emotionally and physically attracted to one another. Herschel loved Anthony. The depths that two men related to one another was magnified times ten in comparison to the minuscule level of communication men had with women.

Attitude. Ranting. Crying. Making up their minds before the dyad ever began. Most women never genuinely tried to understand the inner struggle of their men. The women who thought they knew their men well probably drew reactionary insight from how the man treated her, not from how he'd felt about her or himself. Every man fought internally with how society viewed him, shielding all vulnerabilities that could strip away his manhood. Herschel shouldn't have married a woman like Nikki, who'd spit gasoline on his flaming insecurities with her careless, lethal tongue. Anthony had never degraded him the way Nikki had.

Opening his bedroom door, Anthony said, "How long you been standing there? Come in here, man." As he reached inside his cotton boxers, and adjusted his limp dick, Anthony commented, "You look a hot mess. You're not living right. You need to decide which family you want to be associated with."

Why? Herschel thought.

"You hungry?" Anthony asked. "I can whip you up something to eat."

"No, I don't have an appetite for food, but thanks." Herschel motioned for Anthony to come into their living room, then replied, "Stop acting like you're one hundred percent gay. You know you're not divorcing your wife either."

"Please, I haven't touched hers or any other woman's pussy in years," Anthony countered. "I have a marriage of convenience, 'cause I love living on The Island and neither one of us wants to downgrade our lifestyles. She does her thing and I do mine. You know that. You're the one who is still fucking Nikki once a month and your baby mama every time you feel like controlling somebody," Anthony exclaimed, massaging Herschel's shoulders. "Relax. I know what you're going through. Once I accepted the fact that I'm gay, I stopped pretending, and met you. You need to do the same so we can move forward."

Herschel slouched on the black leather sectional in their living room. Anthony stood behind him and continued massaging his neck and shoulders. Herschel stretched his neck left, then right.

"You know what it would take for me to get Nikki to give me a massage?"

"A handwritten demand note from God cemented on stone like the Ten Commandments," Anthony said jokingly. "And even then, she might take her chances on going to hell."

Herschel didn't share in Anthony's laughter. "You think she hates me? Am I that bad of a person?" Herschel asked. He needed answers to the multitude of questions plaguing him. Slowly he exhaled, figuring he'd go to his grave without understanding his wife.

"Stop avoiding my question," Anthony said, rubbing the nape of Herschel's neck.

"I'm not avoiding choosing sides. That's not it. I don't need to choose if we're going to be together or if I'm going to be with my wife. I have intentions on leaving Nikki, but she's the one who doesn't want me to go," Herschel lied, wondering why Nikki hadn't mentioned Anthony or Ivory again, then continued, "Besides, I don't want to downgrade my lifestyle any more than you do."

Anthony dug his fingertips deeper, saying, "What about Ivory? What's your excuse for still fucking her?" Walking over to the entertainment center, he turned on the sports channel so they could watch the basketball pregame show.

"What about Ivory? I'm never going to marry her. She's not the marrying kind," Herschel said.

"And Nikki was?" Anthony said rhetorically, then asked, "Aren't you considering moving in with Ivory?" Anthony stretched his body across the floor in front of the television.

Herschel then lay on the floor beside Anthony, reclining in his arms. "Hell no. And live full-time with a gay kid? Never. I'm cool with what Ivory and I have."

Sliding from underneath Herschel, Anthony braced himself on his elbow, then stared down at Herschel in disbelief of what he'd heard. "*A gay kid? That's your damn son, man. That's your seed. So you're lying to Ivory about being with her? You're fucking confused. You can't accept Kwan, 'cause you haven't accepted yourself,*" Anthony said, sitting up and bracing his back against the sofa.

"I'm not gay." Herschel sat up too. "I love Ivory in my spe-cial way, but she complains too much. I couldn't deal with that headache every day. She'd make me go off." Herschel wanted to stand and pace the floor, but he continued sitting next to Anthony.

"Can you blame her for being upset? She's not stupid. She probably senses something's up with you, but she can't imagine we—two masculine-looking men—would be sexing each other crazy. She has no idea you come here to kick it with me the same way you chill with her, except without all the drama. You invite me over to your place to hang and have sex whenever Nikki is gone. Correction, whenever you want me to suck your dick and you don't want to be alone."

Herschel shook his head. "Stop. You don't even know where you're going with all of this nonsense. You're all over the place. That last part isn't true, man, and you know it. Our shit is special. For real."

"Then why can't you tell me you love me?" Anthony asked, staring into Herschel's eyes.

Herschel's eyes drifted to the television. The truth was, Herschel didn't want to love Anthony. Loving Anthony was too permanent. Too gay. Just not right. Herschel was married. He had a mistress. A kid. Those were the people society dictated that he should love, not Anthony.

Herschel glanced at Anthony. His eyes darted back to the television. His thoughts were scattered. He felt Anthony staring at him. The silence made Herschel uncomfortable. Easing his hand onto Anthony's thigh, Herschel said, "I do care about you." Herschel massaged inside Anthony's thigh, inching his hand toward Anthony's dick. Anthony's erection sent a signal of approval. A stiff dick was always in search of a hole.

"Lie down and let me make love to you," Herschel said,

sliding Anthony's boxers over his butt. Anthony's dick sprang forward.

Herschel took his time enjoying and exploring Anthony's body as though it were their first time together, but he was searching for signs of infidelity. Anthony had to have somebody on the side. Herschel's fingers strummed over Anthony's chest, down to his abs. There was no need to rush the moment. They could catch the highlights of the basketball game at halftime.

His lips pressed against Anthony's pubic hairs. Lowering his mouth over Anthony's erection, Herschel extended his wet tongue, then glazed his saliva from Anthony's balls up his shaft to his head. He savored the slight saltiness that lingered in their exchanging moisture.

Stroking his own dick, Herschel gripped Anthony's dick, shoving the head deep into his throat until Herschel's lips pressed against his hand. Precum oozed from both of their dicks. "Stay right there," Herschel insisted, unwrapping a condom. He slid the condom over his dick, reached for the water-based lubrication, squirted it onto Anthony's swollen erection, and began massaging him.

Anthony exhaled. Herschel knew Anthony wanted to hear him say, "I love you," but he couldn't say it. Professing love during sex was bad timing. Sex clouded judgment. Orgasms eclipsed reality.

Herschel smeared more lube over Anthony's asshole, raised Anthony's legs missionary-style, slowly penetrating him. Herschel fucked Anthony hard, never raw. Their moments together were more than sexual; they were spiritual.

The more Anthony's dick rubbed against Herschel's stomach, the more excited they both became. "You ready?" Herschel asked, penetrating as deep as he could.

"Fuck yes," Anthony said, palming his strong masculine hands onto Herschel's ass. Passionately Anthony extended his tongue into Herschel's mouth.

Exploding like fireworks, Herschel released himself inside Anthony. Semen flowed from Anthony's dick onto their stomachs. Motionless, Herschel's body weighed heavily, relaxing on top of Anthony. Herschel was in a place where he didn't have to guess; he knew he was wanted. Anthony made him feel at peace. Herschel lay atop his lover and his friend, whispering inside his mind, *I love you, Anthony,* but the words never escaped his lips.

CHAPTER 15

Lexington

Laissez les bons temps rouler . . . Let the good times roll!

The Big Easy was oh so sleazy, and Lexington loved that shit!

He didn't give a fuck about Donna tossing his phone in the bay. All of his information was backed up. In anticipation of the accidental death or the premeditated murder of his personal property, Lexington stored in his safe at work a spare set of keys to his house, the condo Nikki owned, and all of his cars. He had two brand-new iPhones with separate phone numbers, one precharged and preprogrammed with all of his personal information ready for immediate use. One phone call and his main cell phone number would replace either of the current cellular numbers. He'd bought three laptops, four business suits, and five pair of shoes that were stored in his closet at work. Two travel suitcases—one for personal use, the other for business, both loaded with toiletries, casual attire, and underwear—were always ready for him to take flight with short notice. Those were the things Donna didn't need to know about him.

Lexington was sufficiently prepared for "Hurricane Donna" and any other hurricane, tornado, or tropical storm headed his way. He was always ahead of, yet never in the path of, the eye of the storm. Donna's anger had stirred for three-plus years, secretly gathering strength offshore in her fucked-up head. Finally, after whirling around and around, she'd gathered the courage to hit him, scratch him, slap him in his face, and she came assured with a vengeance to make him do the right things. What Donna had done to Lexington didn't mean much to her. But he was furiously fuming, and unlike Hurricane Katrina that destroyed people's lives and livelihoods in New Orleans, and adversely impacted the world, Donna would live to regret what she'd wrecked. Their marriage.

A lot of the important things every businessman should know and do, Lexington had learned from his boy Brian. Knowing basic shit helped Lexington keep his cool. Donna thought he was going to freak-the-fuck-out over a damn phone? Her mistake. Lexington would bet money that Donna didn't have a backup for anything, not even her list of clients' profiles and their orders. She'd probably thought saving information to a USB and keeping the data in the same location as her computer was brilliant.

Seated in first class, looking out the window over the "Crescent City," Lexington smiled. In less than an hour, he'd be holding Nikki in his arms. He'd checked out a few local swingers clubs online in case Nikki wanted to venture out. It wasn't Wednesday, so Lexington didn't have to dismiss going to the club on Gravier. It wasn't local night, where local resident couples were admitted free. He did not want any unexpected classmate reunions with a group of known voyeurs watching Nikki suck his dick.

Exiting Concourse C, taking the escalator to baggage claim, Lexington's driver greeted him. "Hey, man, what's up? You creeping in town before sunrise to get laid or here on unofficial business?"

There was no use in Lexington being professional with his local clients, with his family, his driver, or his friends in and from New Orleans. Nawlins natives spoke to everybody— from the preacher to the homeless—the same. Direct. Even the elderly would curse anybody out without hesitation. But New Orleans was also home to the kindest and most hospitable citizens in the world.

"This is all I have," Lexington said, giving his driver his suitcase.

Following him to the limo, Lexington settled in, poured himself a shot of his favorite tequila, then phoned Nikki. "I'll be there in fifteen minutes. Have my pussy ready and waiting. I need to taste you," he told her. "On second thought, get dressed. Let's take an after-midnight stroll along the Riverwalk and go to Café du Monde for some café au lait, beignets, and down-home conversation, like we did when we were kids."

Lexington wasn't ready for Nikki to see his back all scratched. He'd have to explain to her what Donna had done—

so Nikki wouldn't think some other woman had clawed him in the heat of passion. His eyes narrowed. *That's exactly what Donna wanted Nikki to believe.*

"Whew! That sounds great! See you in a few," Nikki said. *What was that "whew!" all about?*

Women. What man, other than his boy Brian, had figured out how to separate his emotions for his wife from his sexual encounters with so many women? When Lexington divorced Donna, if he didn't marry Nikki, he was never volunteering for a trip through hell wearing gasoline drawers with any other woman. Marriage to the wrong woman was torture. With the exception of a few desperate women, most women seemed loving and normal in the beginning, then turned to werewolves right before his eyes. From now on, Lexington preferred the crazy ones. At least he knew what he was getting into from the beginning.

Texting Nikki, *I'm here,* Lexington told his driver, "Wait a minute" as the bellman removed the suitcase from the trunk.

"I got it, man," Lexington said, taking his suitcase and rolling his bag to the elevators.

Nikki greeted him with a hug and a long, passionate kiss, then said, "How was your flight?" His scarred shoulders tensed as she let go.

"The trip was good. You just don't know how happy I am to see you," he said, staring at her.

"You okay?" she asked, frowning.

"Now that I'm here with you, I'm great. You okay?" he asked eyeing the green wrap on Nikki's head.

"Oh, this," she said, patting her head as if she'd forgotten she'd wrapped her head. "Yeah, I'm good. Just having a bad hair day," she said, tugging the wrap over her ears.

"Bad hair day, my ass. Whoever fucked the shit out of you, I don't want to know his name," Lexington said, leaving his suitcase in the foyer of Nikki's suite.

"Man, go on, we'll walk," Lexington told his driver as they exited the hotel.

Holding hands, they strolled past Harrah's casino over to Decatur Street, bypassing a few people along the Riverwalk. Thankfully, no major events, like Mardi Gras, the All-Star Game, or Essence, were happening in town, or downtown would have been packed with partiers this time of the morning. Pre-Katrina, every week some major organization had held its convention in New Orleans. After the devastation, some of them had returned slowly. It was kind of nice experiencing a quieter side of the city. The French Quarters, with the exception of new and newly renovated places, was barely impacted by the hurricane. Holding Nikki's hand and strolling through the Quarters reminded Lexington of his good days growing up.

"I can feel what you're thinking," Nikki said. "You know, we take so much for granted. Being here reminds me of how so many of our family and friends lost everything. Lexington, we have to live and not be so attached to material things. We have to accept life and death. Do you have any idea how many people were swept away in that river and never accounted for?"

"Nikki?"

"Yes."

Lexington took a deep breath, then said, "I want you to marry me. I'm asking. Please don't say no."

Nikki smiled, then said, "Come with me," leading him to the water. "Stand behind me." Easing her pink dress over her hips, she said, "Make love to me. Stick it in. I want to feel you make love to me like I'm your wife."

Instantly the tone of Nikki's beckoning voice made his dick hard. Glancing around, Lexington wasn't worried about the tourists. He feared Donna might jump out of a bush or come sailing out of a tree.

Glad Nikki had asked, Lexington stroked his enlarged dickhead over the opening of her pussy. The humidity clung to his sweaty body. His head gradually penetrated Nikki's hot, juicy, tight pussy. He figured the head wrap meant she'd been fucked already. He was wrong. Taking his time, he inched his shaft inside her.

Lexington kissed the back of Nikki's neck, while caressing her breasts. She shivered, then moaned, "Yes, baby. Don't ever stop loving me. One day, we will be together, baby. I will always love you."

Was there a reason why he should stop loving Nikki? None he could think of. "Nothing could make me stop loving you," he reassured her. "You still haven't answered my question."

"I will, baby. I promise. Stroke my clit for me," Nikki moaned, thrusting her ass toward him.

"Ou, yeah. Your clit is fat and wet. Damn, I need to taste you, Nikki. Turn around."

Facing him, Nikki spread her legs. Lexington knelt in front of her, grazing his tongue between her lips. Slowly he sucked her clit into his mouth. The sweet aroma of her pussy over-powered the stench of the muddy Mississippi River waters. Her dress fell to his face, forming a tent over his nose. His hands cupped her ass, pulling her in closer.

"Yes, baby," Nikki moaned, tilting her head backward.

Yes, what? She'd marry him? She was coming? What?

Lexington sucked in as much of her shaft as he could, held her precious pearl in his mouth, then danced his tongue on her clit. Alternating, he scrubbed his taste buds on her clit creating friction, sucked her nice and firm, then slowly danced the tip of his tongue on her clit until Nikki's juices flowed in his mouth. He wanted to penetrate her with his middle finger, but he hadn't washed his hands since he'd landed. In her best interest, he resisted.

"Fuck . . . you," Nikki grunted, stuffing her pussy in his mouth.

"That's my girl. Let it go," Lexington said. He patiently waited until Nikki was completely satisfied and she was the one backing away first.

"You should taste what I'm tasting. Your pussy is incredibly sweet all the damn time." Lexington stood, straightened her thong, smoothed her dress over her hips, and French-kissed Nikki, soft and long. The residue from the humidity made his body feel clammy.

Lexington said, "I'm hungry for some hot powder-covered beignets."

"Me too," Nikki agreed.

Continuing their stroll a short distance to underneath the green awning, Lexington pulled out one of the rod-iron chairs for Nikki, then sat beside her. "Two café au laits and two orders of beignets," he said to the server.

He wrapped his arm around Nikki's shoulders. "You are so beautiful. Every day for us should be this good. I want you to be mine."

"I'm not so sure I want to rush into getting married again after I divorce Herschel. You're not a woman, so you could never see things my way, but as wonderful as you are to me, men are selfish. For no rational reasons, men expect women to submit and accommodate them. Honestly, I think we would clash as wife and husband."

"Don't you mean husband and wife?" Lexington countered.

"My point exactly," Nikki said, looking up at a young man standing in front of their table. She whispered, "Well, I'll be damned."

"Hello," he said. "Excuse me, I don't mean to be rude, but I had to come over and speak. Hi, Dad."

Nikki stared at Lexington.

Whoa, of all the times and places he could run into his son, why now? "Hey, son. How's your mom?" Lexington said, not knowing what else to honestly say.

"She's good. We get your checks every month. Thanks," his son said, dragging a chair to their table.

Shifting his eyes toward Nikki, Lexington didn't want his son to stay. There went getting a yes to his proposal.

"So, is this what you wanted to tell me? I can look at him and tell he's yours, but when were you going to tell me?" Nikki asked, pretending she was calm. "How old are you, sweetheart?" Nikki asked him.

"Eighteen, ma'am," he politely answered.

"Eighteen?" she repeated, looking at Lexington. "High-school graduation present? If you can keep something this major from me, God only knows what other secrets you have. How could you do this?" Nikki asked, looking back toward his son. "What's your name?"

Damn, was she going to crash interview his son on the spot like that?

"My apologies. I should've introduced myself. My name is Lexington Lewis the second."

Nikki frowned. "The what?" Raising her brows, Nikki extended her hand. "Pleased to meet you, Lexington the second. I'm Nikki Henderson. Who's your mother—?"

"Son, don't answer that," Lexington interrupted.

"Dad, I apologize. I didn't mean to interrupt, but I was so happy to see you. Mom said you told her you can't make it to my graduation next week. I just wanted you to know I'm valedictorian and I earned a full scholarship to play football at USC." Tears fell from his son's eyes. "Dad, please. Can't you do this one thing for me? I know you're done with my mom, but what did I do to you? I'm your son. I need you in my life."

With tears streaming down her cheeks, mucus sliding out of her nostrils, Nikki stood, wiped her face with a napkin, then sadly said, "Nice meeting you, Lexington. Good-bye," then quietly walked away.

Her good-bye seemed intended for both of them.

CHAPTER 16

Nikki

Just when you think you know a man, God shows you that you don't know him at all. Nikki took Lexington's suitcase down to the concierge for him to pick up, went back to her room, and texted him, *Why?*

He had the audacity to ask her to marry him, and although she hadn't given him an answer, she was seriously considering saying, "Yes, Lexington. I will marry you." That was before she learned about his son.

Shit. She was better off keeping the dysfunctional husband she had. At least she knew about Herschel's son. Suddenly Nikki cried out loud, "I might be carrying Lexington's baby! Oh, hell no! This child will never see the light of day." She angrily paced the floor. "No way in hell would I have my child begging for his father to be man enough to show up at his or her high-school graduation."

Nikki yelled at her reflection in the mirror, "Fuck you, Lexington! You will never taste my pussy again! Pick your fucking suitcase up downstairs!"

Two seconds later, Lexington called her. Nikki refused to answer.

Her phone beeped with a message. *Nikki, please. I need to explain. It wasn't my fault. I do support him. Didn't you hear him say his mother gets their check?* Lexington texted.

Him? He has your fucking name! He's your damn son!

I'm sitting downstairs. I came to New Orleans just to see you. Please come down and get me and I promise I'll tell you anything you want to know.

Marching back and forth in her suite, Nikki was confused. What if Lexington did have a justifiable reason? Even if he didn't, she deserved an explanation. Who was his son's mother? Did she know the woman? Did they go to high school together?

He texted again, *I am going to his graduation.*

Don't try to impress me. What's up with the word "his"? You act like he's somebody else's child that you're sponsoring, Nikki fired back, wishing that were the case, but the child was a younger replica of Lexington and even had locks down his back.

You're right. That's why I need you in my life. You tell me exactly what I need to hear. Baby, please. Come get me. The doormen are staring at me.

Fine, Nikki texted back. *But only if you tell me everything and I mean everything.* This might be her last opportunity to search Lexington's eyes, and his heart, for the truth.

I promise, he replied.

Nikki texted, *Meet me at the elevators.*

Nikki reluctantly met Lexington downstairs, then escorted him to her suite. "Leave your bag in the foyer. You might not be here that long. Let's sit in the living room," she demanded.

"Whatever you say," Lexington agreed.

Damn those twins. Crossing her arms underneath her aching nipples, Nikki flatly said, "I'm listening."

"Don't get upset, but I have three kids outside my marriage. I was young, dumb, and full of cum. But I've always provided for each of my kids and their mothers. I bought them houses and cars. I pay their bills every month."

Nikki's lips tightened. "Three? So you have five kids?"

"I have five well-provided-for kids. And if you're having my baby, I'm going to be there for you, every step of our pregnancy."

"When did you have these kids? Why didn't I know about them? Who are the mothers? It'd better not be somebody I know. As much as I want a child, there's no way in hell I'd have a baby for you."

Lexington held her hand, then said, "Don't say that, Nikki. We've been together practically all our lives. We belong together. You don't think I ask every woman to marry me, do you?"

Nikki stood, tugged her dress over her head, stepped out of her thong, then said, "Shut up and fuck me."

Lexington's mouth opened.

"Close your damn mouth. I said, 'Shut up and fuck me.' Don't say another word."

Nikki decided she would utilize Lexington for what he was worth. A good fuck.

Walking through the double doors into the bedroom, Nikki said, "Lay your ass down."

Straddling Lexington, she snatched his dick, plunged it inside her wet pussy, and started bucking him raw. "Is this what you want? Pussy motherfucker," she said, slamming her pussy on his big dick. "Then that's what the fuck I'ma give you. This is *my* dick!" Nikki yelled. "Say it, motherfucker. Whose dick is this?"

"N-Nikki's," Lexington stuttered as his body flopped against the mattress like an inflatable doll.

"I can't fucking hear you. Say it louder."

"Nikki, please. What are you doing? I'm not Herschel. Stop it, baby, please."

"Didn't I tell you to shut the fuck up?" Nikki said, grinding on Lexington's dick. "Don't tell me what the fuck to do. I'm running this bitch tonight."

Nikki showed no mercy. She was angry with him. How dare Lexington not tell her about all his fucking babies? "Stroke my clit, goddamn it."

His finger bounced on and off her shaft, attempting to keep pace with her frantic rhythm.

"That's not it, motherfucker. I said stroke my clit, not my lips," Nikki insisted.

This time, he found her spot and held his hand there.

"Don't fucking move. I'm coming. Oh, yeah. That's it, you lying-ass bitch," Nikki said.

Conceding, Lexington flopped his hand to the bed.

Nikki got off him, stared down, then said, "Get the fuck outta my room."

His eyes drooped, but she didn't care. He was the one who didn't care enough about her to tell her the truth. Whoever his son's mother was, she'd obviously done an incredible job without Lexington. The same as Donna had done with his daughters.

Shaking her head, Nikki could only ask him, "Why?"

Lexington didn't respond. He stood, turning his back to her. Nikki stared at the striped bloodstains on the sheet, then at his back. *Oh, my God. Who did that to you?*

Pulling up his pants, Lexington walked toward the living room. Nikki stared at his back, ran into the bathroom, leaned over the toilet, and started throwing up. One minute later, she heard *Click.*

The door had closed, Lexington was gone—probably for good—and in that moment, she prayed she wasn't pregnant with his child.

CHAPTER 17

Brian

Will golf for group sex.

Hanging out with his boys was going to get wild and crazy. Brian welcomed a change of pace—an explosion of testosterone among men in the same house for two consecutive days without their wives. Yes, indeed. Maybe Brian could confess the weird shit that had happened to him with Zahra and Carmelita and get some feedback from his boys Lexington and Herschel.

Brian packed his suitcase: golfer's hats, shoes, polo shirts, socks, underwear, and swim trunks. His underwear and swim trunks were sexy and new, so he stuffed them at the bottom of his suitcase. He placed his designer golf clubs at the door for the driver to put in the car. He zipped up his suitcase, stood it on the four wheels, and placed it at the door.

"Brian, you seem awfully happy."

Oh, shit. He was trying to get out of the house before Michelle's mother showed up to pick up the kids. "Hey, you're looking good," Brian said, kissing her cheek.

"Not nearly as good as you. Where's Michelle?" she asked, perusing his luggage like she was a TSA employee.

"You want to see my passport too?" he asked.

"That won't be necessary. I've got your number," she said. "Go get my grandbabies for me."

What did she mean by that? *Gladly,* he thought, trotting upstairs. "Michelle, your mother is here," Brian yelled from the top of the stairs. "Let's go, kids. Grandma is here."

"I don't want to go with her. I want to go by Grandma and Grandpa Flaw," BJ protested.

"Next week, I promise," Brian said. "Now get your overnight bags."

"Daddy, why is it called an overnight bag if we're staying two nights?" his daughter asked, emphasizing the *s*.

"Good question. Ask your mother," he said, ushering them along.

Kissing his wife, Brian said, "Baby, I'll call you as soon as my plane lands in Atlanta. Take good care of your sister, BJ. And you, young lady, make sure you listen to your big brother." Looking at Michelle's mom, Brian said, "If you need anything—"

She interrupted, "I'll call my happily married daughter."

"Mother, stop it. Why do you give my husband such a hard time? I love my Brian," Michelle said. "Have fun, baby, you deserve it."

"Thanks, honey," Brian said, kissing his wife. "Good-bye. I love you too, baby."

Hurrying out the door, settling in the backseat of the limo, Brian's driver stopped by Herschel's mansion. Herschel was standing in the doorway, waiting. The driver loaded his bags in the car. They made one final stop in front of Lexington's place. Donna was in the doorway with her hands on her hips.

"Why you think she wears those hideous slippers?" Herschel asked.

"Better his wife than mine," Brian said. "I'd throw those things out."

"I'm sure he'd rather throw her out," Herschel said. "That's my boy. Hell, sometimes I want to put Nikki out."

"Nigga, you don't make enough to put Nikki out. What you mean is sometimes you want to pack your shit and get out, because your ass always gets left out. Damn, Nikki invites us to more events than she tells you about. You fucked up when you proposed. She hasn't invited you to a taping of her show since she married your ass," Brian said.

"Whatever. Until she grows a dick, I'm the man in my house," Herschel countered.

"You right. *In,* not *of,*" Brian said.

"Chill with all that, B. The minute Lexington gets in this car, no more mentioning of our wives," Herschel reminded him.

"I might have to break the rules, man," Brian said.

"Not you, Mr. Get Smart. Do I detect trouble in power couple paradise?"

"Never that," Brian said.

Tap. Tap.

"What the hell?" Herschel said, looking out the window.

Lexington was stooping outside the limousine door. "Open the door, man."

Brian opened the door and Lexington crawled in. "Nigga, this gives 'creeping' a whole new meaning."

"Close the door and drive off," Lexington said.

"Fuck you, Lexington! You sneaky bastard," Donna yelled, running toward the car.

"Let's go," Brian instructed the driver.

Lexington sat in the seat across from them. Brian and Herschel burst out laughing.

"I told you what you need to do, man," Brian said, laughing.

"That shit ain't funny, man. Donna has lost her damn mind. Stop by my office so I can get my luggage," Lexington said, pouring himself a drink.

"Pour one for everybody, man, so we can toast," Herschel said.

Lexington handed Brian and Herschel each a glass half-filled with silver tequila.

Brian announced, "A toast . . . to single husbands."

"I'll toast to that," Herschel said.

"For sho'," Lexington agreed.

"And I'm drinking to y'all because I'm very merrily married and in love," Brian added.

"Yeah, but what about Michelle? I bet you're so busy, you wouldn't notice she's fucking around too," Lexington said.

"Don't go there, Peter Cottontail," Brian said, bending his wrists like the ears on Donna's slippers. "Sorry about that shit, man. No more talk about our wives for real."

A knot formed in Brian's intestines. He hated the thought of any man penetrating his wife. Lexington had better not be dropping hints that he fucked Michelle. This weekend was supposed to be fun, so Brian opted for a double shot of tequila to wash away any negativity brewing in his mind.

Two drinks later, they checked in at First Class at the ticketing counter, retrieved their boarding passes, cleared security, and headed straight to the bar . . . for more alcohol.

"Let me have a Loose Goose, with pineapple and a splash of coconut rum," Brian said, chilling at the bar with the intent of getting his heads bad before they arrived in "Hotlanta."

Quietly Brian sipped on his nice, cold martini, watching the fine Puerto Rican women stroll by. "That's what's up right there," he said.

This was their seventh annual "ball out of control" single husbands' bash. The shit they were getting ready to do! "Ou, wee!" Herschel said, interlocking his thumb with Lexington's, gripping his fist tight, then bumping shoulders.

"Don't leave me out," Brian said, bumping chests with Lexington, then Herschel, as though they were all in the end zone and had scored the winning touchdown.

"You ready, B?" Lexington asked Brian. "Hit me with a double Patrón Silver. It's on," Lexington told the bartender. "This vodka ain't getting it."

"Make that double a deuce," Herschel said, joining in.

They all stood, shuffled their feet, danced at the bar,

then laughed like they were single men in college headed to Summerfest.

"Who we got, Lex man?" Herschel asked.

"Y'all ain't ready," Lexington said, smiling and covering his mouth.

Brian nodded his head, then said, "Hit me with your best."

"Don't worry, B. I hooked your ass up real sweet with double-dipping, white-chocolate, big-tittied, long-blond-haired, exotic babes from"—Lexington paused—"Rio. And not to worry, they're not identical, so you won't break your rule. How's that?"

Lexington was always on point. Brian smiled his approval. "You in the wrong profession, nigga—"

Herschel interrupted, "What about me?"

"Let's see . . . how about a big booty, tiny waist, triple-D, dark-skinned, down-to-earth, plus-sized sistah that can tie a knot in a cherry stem."

Herschel frowned. "That's cool, but who else I got, man."

"You mean *what* else." Lexington held up his hand, downed his double, then said, "With her pussy."

Herschel's eyes widened to the size of fifty-cent pieces. "Don't play. You the shit for that one, man."

Brian asked Lexington, "What your ass got?"

"That, my man, you have to see to believe, 'cause if I told you, you'd swear I was lying," Lexington said, crossing his feet at the ankles, spinning in a complete circle. "If I could clone them into life-sized blow-up dolls, I'd put Donna's ass out of my bed permanently. I'd get better results and the dolls wouldn't talk back."

Brian and Herschel held out their hands at the same time.

"Whateva, niggas. So now our policy is in place?" Lexington said, reaching in his pocket and removing a roll of hundred-dollar bills. He gave $100 to Brian and $100 to Herschel.

Their rule during single husbands' weekend was they were forbidden to mention anything about their wives, especially their wives' names, or they had to pay a fine each time.

"That's cool. Y'all know I'ma get my money back. Herschel, you might as well hand me back my money right now. You know you won't make it to Atlanta without saying her name at least three times."

"True that," Brian said. "Let's go. I'm ready to do some thangs I ain't never done befo'."

They partied hard in first class, all the way to Hotlanta, consuming a lot more alcohol while eagerly anticipating their fuck fest. Another hour in flight and all the alcohol in first class would've been gone. Brian let Herschel and Lexington walk ahead of him to baggage claim. They were all different, yet the same in many ways.

Herschel let Ivory raise Kwan alone. Brian would never abandon his kids.

Lexington reneged on going to his son's graduation to be with them in Atlanta. There was no way Brian would miss any of BJ's graduations.

Brian knew BJ didn't want to go to Michelle's mom's, but he sent him anyway.

All of them were successful, but none of them were rearing their children. Money. Material gain. Women. Sex. Fun. Success? They truly were single husbands. But this trip felt different for Brian. They were all getting older. One day, their dicks wouldn't get as hard. Their bodies wouldn't look as great. Their money wouldn't bring them the same kind of unadulterated pleasure. Then which women would they turn to for companionship? Brian would have a blast this weekend, but this was his last trip with his boys. Too many strange things had happened to him lately. If shit came in threes, Brian prayed this weekend was not his finale.

"You okay, B?" Lexington asked, looking at Brian. "You want another shot? You ain't there yet, man?"

"Nah, I'm cool. Probably had too many, man. Trying to clear my head. So much shit happening nowadays. But it's all good," Brian said.

"Well, I got what you need," Lexington said as the limo swerved into the circular driveway of their three-story rental estate in Buckhead. "We've each got our own floor, B, so if you don't want to see us after the pool party, you don't."

Nudging Herschel, Brian said, "Man, wake up. We are here."

"Damn, this is living, man," Herschel sleepily said, stretching his arms above his head, yawning.

"B, you got the third floor, because you make the least amount of noise. Herschel, you on second, and I'm on first. Hit the showers and be by the pool in fifteen minutes for the honeys' arrival," Lexington said.

Brian wasn't surprised. Lexington didn't waste a minute of time getting the party started. The driver delivered the luggage to each floor. Brian sat on the side of his bed, then phoned his wife.

"Hey," she answered, sounding real happy. "You made it there safely. I'm glad you called."

"Please turn off all cellular devices, electronics . . ." Brian heard the familiar announcement in the background.

"I thought you were working from home. Where are you going?" he asked.

"Baby, I'll call you when my flight lands," Michelle said, ending their call.

She could've told him she was leaving home. Was his wife seeing someone else? With the exception of penetration, he did satisfy her sexually before he'd left. Brian showered, brushed his teeth, lathered his body with sunblock so he wouldn't sunburn, put on his white swim trunks, his sunglasses, and headed downstairs.

Herschel was already lounging by the pool, drinking.

Before Brian sat in the lounge chair, the bartender handed him his favorite martini. "Thanks, man," Brian said.

"Enjoy," he said.

Lexington stood by the pool, stretched his arm toward the perfect blue sky, 75-degree sunshine, then loudly announced, "Ladies! DJ!"

The DJ on the patio turned up the music. Brian's twins entered first, but they weren't walking. Six guys carried them in. Herschel's girl was carried in behind them. And Lexington's quintuplets were hand-delivered poolside, wearing nothing but shoestring thongs and high heels.

"You wrong for that shit, man," Herschel said, amazed that all five of the women were identical. "Dick paradise."

"Believe that," Lexington said. "Y'all gon' have to roll my

dick up outta here after being with these bootylicious babes for two straight days."

The music silenced. A new song played and the curtains behind the ladies parted.

"Ah, yeah." Brian nodded with approval. "How do you come up with all of this, man?"

Three elegantly draped king-sized beds sat on platforms. One purple. One green. One gold. They did not need to guess who the golden bed was for, as it was a double-king with two sets of mattresses merged as one.

"Three black men, living on The Island, holding our shit down—we're royalty, fellas, and that's how we're about to get treated," Lexington said. "This is a take-it-to-your-grave weekend that we'll never forget."

The bartender, who doubled as waiter, opened the chafing dishes, then said, "On the menu for today, at station number one, we have pineapple buffalo hot wings, Kobe beef meatballs with orange marmalade, USDA Prime grilled steak kabobs, and Southern fried chicken. At station number two, we have chilled oysters on the half shell, cocktail prawns, and Alaskan king crab legs. Station number three is "choose the toppings for your dick sundae." We have toppings from, of course, whipped cream, warm fudge, cool caramel, which sticks to the dick, making you a human dickpop, strawberries, cherries, bananas, which can be dipped in chocolate, and we have coconut cream pie filling. Be careful with the sprinkles."

Every damn day should be this fucking good, Brian thought, heading over to his green bed. Purple was too dark and gold was already taken. Brian lay out in the sunshine, his arms and legs spread wide. "Make me the kitchen-sink sundae. I want it all, including the banana. Just don't put that banana anywhere close to my asshole and we good."

"I'm with you, B," Herschel said, following and flopping onto his purple bed. "The kitchen sink sounds good."

Lexington snapped his fingers. His ladies escorted him to his bed. "You," he said, pointing to the one closest to him, "your job this weekend is to feed me." He pointed at another. "Your job is to bathe me. The rest of you, your jobs are to take turns sucking my dick all weekend long. The word for this weekend is 'share.' I want my dick in a mouth or a pussy nonstop for the next forty-eight hours . . . starting now."

Brian's body was covered from the neck down with all the toppings. Cherry juice seeped between his toes.

One of the twins asked Brian, "Would you like for me to pop your cork?"

He wasn't quite ready for champagne, but it was cool. Brian answered, "Sure."

She scooped up a handful of whipped cream, smeared it all over her sister's titties. Her sister sat beside him, spread her legs, then slowly peeled a banana. Somehow Brian knew he wasn't getting any champagne.

She scooped another handful of thick cream, and this time smeared it all over her breasts, stomach, and pussy. Straddling him, she glided her creamy clit, nice and slow, up and down his shaft.

"Damn," Herschel said. "I want what he's having. Lexington, man, can I borrow one of your chicks?"

The DJ played, *"Come, girl, I'm tryna get your pussy wet . . ."* Lexington had a woman straddling his face, his stomach, and riding his dick like he was the main attraction at an amusement park. They rotated their pussies over his body in unison.

Herschel mumbled, "With all that pussy, he can't hear shit. I bet if I yelled 'fire,' he wouldn't move."

The twin straddling Brian scooped a handful of coconut cream, then rubbed her hands together. She circled her thumb and index fingers to form human cock rings, the tips of her fingers touched, forming O shapes.

Pop!

She tightly slid the first hand over Brian's dickhead.

Pop!

She slid her second hand over his head, joining the circles in the middle.

Alternating her hands, she maintained pressure, squeezing upward, popping over the ridge of his dickhead, swerving to the right with her right hand, and the left with her left, until she had his dick nice and hard. The coconut in the cream added a nice, natural abrasion.

Gradually, with each stroke, she moved a little closer and closer to the base of his dick until she pleasured him with long, tight, full, upward strokes—each time popping her O-shaped fingers over his ridge. Adding in her palms, she started gripping his shaft from the base to the head, quickly massaging his cork with her palm before working him from the base up.

Her hands flowed in a rhythmic motion that had Brian's mouth wide open. Her sister spread coconut cream on her titties, then put a nipple in Brian's mouth for him to suck on. Brian sucked her sister's breasts like he hadn't eaten all day.

"Damn, these are the best twins I've ever tasted," Brian said, rubbing her creamy breasts all over his face. "Put some of that coconut cream on my head. Then I want you to fuck the top of my head with your pussy."

Placing her O-shaped fingers at the base, the other sister focused on his dick. She trapped the blood inside his dickhead. Holding her right hand at the base, she spiraled his dick upward with her opposite hand until he screamed, "Fuck!" Then she circled both hands an inch below his head, swiftly alternating up and up and up and up, until his dick popped, shooting cum in the air like a freshly opened bottle of champagne.

"Oh, shit!" Brian yelled, spreading his arms and legs like a frog sprawled on its back.

"Come pop my cork!" Herschel yelled.

"It's up to you," Brian said, watching her smear his cum all over her beautiful, creamy body. "If I never come again this weekend, damn, I'm straight for the next two days," he said, closing his eyes.

CHAPTER 18

Herschel

Multiple orgasms were a beautiful thing.

Herschel was on an unbelievable high, having had his cork popped two days in a row. Brian had chilled out the rest of the weekend, trying to catch up with Michelle. Lexington rode his gravy train all day, both days. Passing out was his temporary sleep time.

Being back at home, Herschel felt great. His wife was home. His mistress was home, and Anthony was at the condo. Herschel had all the options he wanted—except Nikki hadn't spoken a word to him since he arrived home early this morning. Her ostracizing him crushed his weekend high.

Emasculation.

A melancholy glimpse of his wife sitting in the wicker chair on the patio porch outside their bedroom, sipping iced tea, reminded him of the love they once shared. Crackling. Vibrant. Happy. Crisp. Clear. Her silhouette of perfection, shadowing the glowing sunrise, appeared at peace. At ease. Without him beside her. She seemed content. What was she thinking? Why did he care?

The time had come for him to seriously entertain moving. Where? Move on? Move out? Move aside? How much longer could he live under the same roof with a woman who didn't want him? Which of his lovers would roll out a welcome mat for him? Ivory? Anthony? A man's stock was easily tradable when his demand was high. Sure, Nikki would continue tolerating him. Ivory would be happy with him, but for how long? Anthony adamantly refused to move off The Island permanently.

Nikki stood, exhaled, then walked inside. Her packed suitcase was at the back door awaiting her departure to . . . He'd stopped trying to keep track of his wife's destinations. What was the use? She didn't need him. Even worse, she didn't want him any day of the month. Herschel wondered if it was his mother who didn't want his father around. Perhaps his father wasn't a deadbeat dad, after all. What difference did his feelings about his parents make?

Call me when you get in, Herschel tried to say, but his lips remained shut as the words resounded in his head.

Herschel texted Anthony, *I really need to see you. Can you come by in an hour?*

Anthony texted back, *Of course. I know you. She's leaving again. Right?* Lately, Anthony knew whenever Nikki was leaving. He probably sensed the dejected tone of Herschel's text message.

Nikki's driver parked in the driveway, opened the door for her, then drove off.

No "Good-bye, call me" or "I'll call you." How could people live under the same roof, sleep in the same bed, and not speak?

Come right now, Herschel texted, standing in front of his home, watching the limo exit The Island. The distance between him and his neighbors varied, but Anthony was a short jog across the two streets that separated their estates.

Greeting Anthony at the back door, Herschel was already naked, with his dick in his hand.

"You happy to see me or what? I've told you, you need to make up your mind," Anthony said, sitting in the wicker chair where Nikki was less than an hour ago.

Having sex was Herschel's way of avoiding and coping with the issues he didn't want to address. An escapism. Coming was a sedative to numb his aching heart. "Suck my dick," he said, standing in front of Anthony.

"I'ma do you, but I want to hear all about your golfing weekend in Atlanta, because you didn't call or text me once," Anthony said, gripping Herschel's limp dick.

"Ah, that feels so damn wonderful," Herschel said, closing his eyes. His dick was soft, but the more Anthony sucked and stroked him, the harder he got.

"I'm the one who needs the tune-up," Anthony said, removing a condom from his pocket. "Do me."

"Don't stop. You make me feel so good. I'm coming already," Herschel said, ejaculating his newly rejuvenated seeds.

Depending on what release he sought, Herschel could come in a minute or in an hour. He felt the clear, waterlike fluids flowing from his prostate. The semen generated with his testicle orgasms were thicker, more like cream.

Anthony continued sucking him, then said, "Okay, my turn. And since you can't get another erection right now, I'ma do you."

Herschel didn't deny Anthony the pleasure as Anthony rolled a condom up his dick, dropped a wad of spit in his hand, lubed the condom, then slid his dick in Herschel's ass.

"Here, lean over the wall and back that ass up," Anthony said, pushing Herschel forward. "I miss you," Anthony whispered. "I love you," he said, slowly grinding deep inside Herschel.

"Hold me," Herschel said. "I need you to hold me."

Anthony had done more than penetrate his anus. His energy resonated throughout Herschel's entire body. Later he'd try to pop Anthony's cork. But for now, he enjoyed being in the moment with a person that he did love.

"I love you too," Herschel said.

Anthony didn't say word. He didn't have to. Anthony stood still and held him tighter. Nikki wouldn't have done that.

"What the hell are you two doing?" a female voice shouted. The woman ran toward them, then stood face-to-face with Herschel. "You two faggots," she screamed. "How could you do this? That's good for her ass. That's what she gets and I can't wait to tell her."

Herschel knew someday he'd get caught, but he never thought she would be the one to catch him with his lover coming in his ass. What should've been a special moment turned out to be a nightmare. Herschel wasn't worried about *her* finding out. He was concerned, knowing she'd definitely tell her husband, Lexington.

CHAPTER 19

Lexington

Can a man change his ways overnight?

Lexington hated to admit that Nikki was right, yet he was thankful. He wanted all of his children in his life. Sitting on the edge of his bed, he recalled looking into his son's eyes—eyes that mirrored his—that night they were at Café du Monde. Lexington was proud of his son, and disappointed in himself. His son was the one who'd called him after Lexington missed the graduation.

He couldn't claim his son's success after his son told him how his mother sacrificed to keep him on the right path, saying, "My mom told me not to expect you to show up at my graduation. I wanted to prove her wrong. I sat on stage praying that you were somewhere out there. That I'd somehow overlooked you or couldn't see you in the back. I prayed that when I made my valedictorian speech, acknowledging my parents, that my mother wouldn't be the only one standing, clapping, and cheering for me. You know, Lexington, I wouldn't be the man I am if it weren't for my mother. She put my needs ahead of hers. Lexington, I can't say that you've ever done that for me."

Damn, his son had called him "Lexington," not "Dad."

No need to argue, his son was right. The time had come for Lexington to become more than a payroll dad, thinking money was enough to fulfill all of his children's needs. Money was great, but there was no substitute for a father's love. Lexington the second's request to meet all of his siblings was one promise Lexington would keep. He'd contacted the mothers, glad they'd all agreed to send him his kids for a few days.

"Baby," Lexington said, calling out to Donna, "come here for a minute."

Lexington accepted partial responsibility for Donna's outrage; he acknowledged he'd driven her insane. What feelings did his babies' mothers harbor for him? Hate? Envy? Were they apathetic? Did his other children dislike him? Or were they like his son, longing to have him in their lives?

"Donna," Lexington said, then shouted, "Donna!"

She appeared in the bedroom doorway, her hands on her hips. "What?" she grunted.

"Come here," he said, patting the mattress.

"What?" Donna asked, sitting beside him.

"Thank you for agreeing to let me have all of my kids together, here in my home," Lexington said. "Go tell the girls to get dressed. You get dressed too. We're going out for the day," Lexington stated. "I'm going to pick up my kids from the airport. I'll be back in an hour. Be ready to leave when I get back."

Donna walked away quietly. What was her problem? Couldn't she give him credit for doing the right thing? Lexington stepped into his beige linen pants, button-up shirt, and tan leather sandals, then headed outside. Getting in the limo, Lexington reflected on his weekend with Brian and Herschel. That shit was crazy, and damn sure 'nuff worth doing again— sooner than later. He prayed his wife would do something more with her hair, but even if she didn't, she would still remain his wife, because Nikki turned down his proposals four times.

Donna was okay with him when he traveled out of town. She didn't call or text him—unless it was something urgent about his girls. But when he was home and left her at home, that was when she protested. If Lexington was going to make amends with his wife, he'd have to travel more often for business *and* his sexual pleasure.

The driver parked outside of baggage claim and opened Lexington's door. Lexington eagerly hurried inside the terminal.

"Here we are," his son said, waving.

Lexington greeted his son. Wrapping his arms around his son's shoulders, Lexington held him tight, professing, "I love you, son. I apologize for missing your graduation, but I promise you, I won't miss one of your football games and I'm going to visit you at times just so the two of us can hang out."

Letting go, Lexington watched tears form in his son's eyes.

"Don't make me any promises. It's okay you missed my graduation. I understand you had more important things to do."

Shaking his head, Lexington countered, "No, it's not. It's not okay."

"Well, maybe you can make it when I graduate from college and go pro. I'm just thankful for this moment to hang with you."

Lexington wanted the instant gratification and acknowledgments he wasn't getting, and clearly didn't deserve. Redirecting his attention to his two daughters, Lexington gave each of them a hug. Sixteen and seventeen, they were so gorgeous. "Hello," they said, standing with their hands at their sides.

Damn, had he fucked up so badly that his kids didn't know one another or him? Both of his girls stared at him.

"Give me some love. I know I haven't been there for you, but that's all about to change. This is your brother, Lexington the second. Lexington, these are your sisters Alexis and Alex."

"Well, pleased to finally meet you, Alexis and Alex," his son sarcastically said, hugging his sisters at the same time. "I want to get to know you guys. Will you give me your cell numbers?"

The girls laughed.

"Okay, so you've met already. Let's go," Lexington said, escorting them to the limo. "Leave your bags on the curb, the driver will get them."

"I'm moving to South Beach with you," Alexis said. "This is living."

Lexington got into the limo after his kids, and their ride to his house was hilarious. They laughed until their stomachs hurt. He didn't know his kids were so smart and humorous.

"Okay, no cracking jokes about my wife's appearance," Lexington said, leading them into the house.

"Wow, this is it!" his son said, staring around the house. "I'm going to live like this when I go pro. Can I check out your crib, Dad?" he asked.

"Sure, son. Knock yourself out, it's your home too."

Alexis and Alex followed Lexington into the living room.

"Where's your mom?" he asked Alexandria and Alexandrea.

The girls pointed behind him. "Whoa." Lexington could not believe his eyes. The woman he'd fallen for ten years ago stood before him looking ravishing. Donna's makeup was flawless. Her full lips glistened like sparkling raspberries. Her hair softly flowed over her shoulders. Her ankle-length dress, light, white, and tapered to her shapely body, made Lexington want to take his wife into the bedroom and make love to her. Donna was hiding her amazing body under oversized clothes and he'd grown so accustomed to not seeing his wife, he imagined her overweight and out of shape.

Oh, my God, he was wrong.

"Whoa, is that your yacht out back?" his son asked, hurrying into the living room.

"Our yacht," Lexington said.

"I wanna see," Alex and Alexis said.

"Daddy, can we show them?" Alexandrea asked.

"Sure, but be safe," Lexington said, still stricken by the sight of Donna. "You look amazing," he said. "Come here."

Lexington opened his heart first, then his arms. "I apologize for all that I've put you through. Can I have my wife back?"

"I'm not the one who left," Donna said.

"I think we'd better sit on the back patio and keep an eye on the kids. Thanks for letting me have all of my children together with us today," Lexington said, lounging on the cushioned patio chair. "Sit with me."

Donna clarified, "Your kids are my kids, and they were always welcome in our home. You were the one who didn't want to invite them."

Holding Donna in his arms, admiring the five brilliant kids he'd fathered, Lexington was proud.

"Can I tell you some things, and you promise you won't get mad?" Donna asked.

"After all you've tolerated from me, you can tell me anything and I promise I won't get mad," he said, cuddling her in his arms.

"I went over to Nikki's, thinking you were there with her, or in hopes of catching her home alone so I could talk with her, and . . ." Donna paused.

The time had come for Lexington to let Nikki go, emotionally and sexually. He'd hurt her too deeply and didn't want to cause Nikki any more pain. Admiring his kids, Lexington was glad his son had confronted him that night. If Lexington the second hadn't came over to his table, Lexington's wife would not be lying in his arms.

Donna continued, "And I saw our neighbor Anthony, from across the way, fucking Herschel in the ass. They were on the patio cuddling and fucking like a man and woman."

Lexington moved his body from underneath Donna's, saying, "You don't have to make up lies about Herschel to keep me away from her. Let's keep him out of this. I don't want to hear any more about Herschel being with a man. Trust me, Herschel is one-hundred-percent alpha male, just like me."

Darting her eyes toward him, Donna frowned. "Believe what you want, I know what I saw."

His kids roamed around the boat, going upstairs and downstairs. His only son was at the helm, pretending to navigate. Lexington smiled. "Anything else?"

"Yes, there's one more significant thing," Donna said, looking into his eyes and smiling with hers. "I bought my restaurant back from the guy I sold it to. I'm reopening in two weeks. I took out a full-page ad in the *Times-Picayune*, letting my customers know 'Donna's is back!' I'm moving home to New Orleans permanently. I bought a house, I'm leaving next week, and I'm taking the girls with me. I've already enrolled them in private school. I'm not asking you to come with us. In fact, I don't want you to come with us. Lexington, I want a divorce," Donna said.

"A what?" Lexington said.

"A divorce. You don't love me anymore and I'm tired of being miserable. Now you can be happy with Nikki or whoever else you want. I don't want your money. But I do expect you to provide for me and the girls the same way you take care of them," Donna said, pointing at his other kids.

Whoa! All this time he was out running around, he thought Donna was home being lazy and she was plotting every move. An educated woman was a silent killer.

"Come here. Let me show you something," Lexington said, holding Donna's hand.

"I don't care what you show me. I'm not changing my mind," she said, following him.

"I don't want you to," Lexington lied, leading Donna to their bedroom. He unlocked his safe, then handed Donna the title to a restaurant in South Beach. "I wanted you to be happy again. I bought this for you. It's yours. You can have two restaurants. Or you can sell this one in South Beach."

"What about my husband?" Donna asked. "Is he for sale too?"

Lexington raised Donna's dress over her head, eased off her white boy shorts, and kissed her. "Oh, wait one minute," he said, locking the bedroom door. "Don't want any surprises."

"But what if they knock?" Donna asked.

"We'll pretend we're not in here."

He kissed his wife's raspberry lips, then pressed his mouth to her collarbone, trickling wet kisses down to her breasts. She shivered as he softly nibbled on her nipple. He laid her atop the comforter, then slowly undressed in front of her. Turning around to toss his shirt on the chair, she gasped, "Oh, my gosh. I didn't realize I scratched you so—" She choked on her words, with tears in her eyes.

"I'm okay," he said, kneeling before her. "Let me make love to my wife."

His tongue fluttered on the tip of her clit, right before he suctioned her into his mouth. "I missed you," he whispered, leaning back to look at his wife's pussy. "I want my wife back."

"Don't talk. Make love to me, Lexington," Donna cried. "My body needs to feel a man's touch."

Wow. All the sexcapades Lexington had had with Nikki and other women on the regular, he never once thought about Donna's womanly needs, until now. Kissing her tears away, Lexington said, "I'm gonna make you happy. You'll never have to cry again."

Was Donna telling the truth? Was his boy Herschel bisexual?

CHAPTER 20

Nikki

Nikki opened her sleepy eyes. "Where am I? How did I get here?" she whispered, blankly staring at the ceiling. The pulsation beating against her forehead caused her to close her eyes, praying, "Please stop it."

The arduous demands of traveling extensively had cemented her worn body to the bed. She felt like a ton of bricks sinking into the mattress. Partying hard, staying out all night, fucking at the sex club, then fucking some more, she was tired and her pussy was exhausted.

"Herschel," she called out wearily. Lifting her head a few inches from her pillow, she looked around the room. "Okay, I am home," she confirmed, looking at the crystal ball embedded in the bedroom wall. She'd left it there as a reminder to her husband to keep his hands off her.

"Herschel," she called out again.

The breeze blew into her bedroom, pushing her head back against the pillow. "This is too much," Nikki said. "I'm sick again. I'm too tired to get up." She suppressed her urge to regurgitate all over the bed. After Lexington had left her hotel room, she'd emptied the contents of her wet bar into her stomach. Vodka. Gin. Tequila. Wine, red and white.

The pain of knowing Lexington over half of her lifetime, and he hadn't mentioned his son or his two other daughters once, wounded her. Nikki prayed she suffered from a terrible hangover and wasn't pregnant.

"Herschel! You hear me calling you! Ouch." Nikki pressed her palms against her temples.

Herschel was gone. She hadn't spoken with Lexington since her return from New Orleans. How could he propose to her, then not call her? Where in the hell were they? How did she get to and from the airports to her bed?

The bedroom clock displayed 8:00.

Nikki's cell phone rang. Clipping her Bluetooth over her ear, she answered, "Morning."

"Girl, it is not morning," Venus said cheerfully.

"It's not."

"Get your sweet-ass pussy up. You been in bed since I got you home yesterday? I'm still in town and I want to check out that sex club in Fort Lauderdale tonight."

"What day is it?" Nikki asked, managing to toss her feet to the floor while her head remained on the pillow.

"What difference does that make? I'm not accepting no for an answer," Venus said.

She might have to, if it was Saturday. Nikki could picture Venus's smile. "No, I can't go there again. That's Lexington's spot," Nikki said, gazing at the clock on the nightstand. "I can't believe I was twelve hours off. What's wrong with me?"

"You've overdosed on dick. And the best relief for a hangover, no pun intended, is more of the same thing that fucked you up in the first place. That means going to the club is ideal for you. Fuck Lexington. He doesn't own the damn place," Venus said with a serious attitude. "You are going with me, and that's final. I'll see you in a few, baby."

Oh, no. Please don't come, Nikki thought, collapsing to the floor. She hadn't been hungover since college.

This was one time Nikki wished Venus wasn't in town. She knew Venus well enough to take her seriously. Venus would be at her home shortly. Nikki picked up her cell phone and called Lexington.

"What do you want?" a woman asked.

"Huh? I must've dialed the wrong number," Nikki said, holding her stomach.

"You got that right. My husband is busy. I suggest you find somebody else's marriage to wreck," Donna said.

"No, Donna, wait. Let me explain. You don't—"

Donna ended their call.

Donna misunderstood Nikki. Nikki couldn't change that she'd fallen in love with Lexington *before* he married Donna. Or that she'd never fallen out of love with Lexington. Who was she to judge why Lexington hadn't spent time with his son? Nikki didn't like this newfound relationship. Had Donna said, "My husband is busy"? *Doing what?* Nikki wondered.

Hopefully, something Nikki had said to Lexington would make him a better father, but he wasn't a bad person and she wasn't trying to make him a better husband to Donna. Why was Nikki rationalizing Lexington's behavior?

"What? Oh, hell no," Nikki said, pulling herself up on the bed to redial Lexington's number. "Did that bitch hang up on me?" Before she redialed him, her phone rang, with his name and number showing.

"What the hell is wrong with you, Donna?" Nikki asked. "I didn't wreck your damn marriage, you did!"

"Nikki," Lexington said, "calm down. Look, we need to talk."

"About what? What is there to discuss?"

"Nikki, where's Herschel?" Lexington asked.

"Since when are you concerned about Herschel?" Nikki asked, staggering back and forth across the floor.

"Is he there?"

"No, and—"

"I'm on my way over," Lexington said, hanging up the phone.

Nikki halfway closed her eyes, walking toward her bathroom. Staring in the mirror, she saw her hair was a mess. Stepping into a cold shower, she lathered her exfoliating gloves, quickly washed her body, brushed her teeth, huffed into her palm, gargled with mouthwash, then rinsed her mouth. As she walked out to her patio for fresh air, Lexington was sitting in her favorite wicker chair.

"What was so important that you actually came to my house?" Nikki asked, sitting in the seat next to him.

"I have to know," he said.

Frowning Nikki asked, "Know what?"

"Are you pregnant, Nikki?"

"Maybe. Maybe not. What do you care? I have enough money to take care of a child on my own," Nikki said, holding her forehead with one hand and her stomach with the other.

"If you are, I want to do what is right," Lexington said. "Come with me."

Nikki's frown returned, causing her forehead to pound. "This is my house, not yours."

"Just come with me," Lexington insisted, leading her into the bedroom.

"What? You want to shower? Fuck? What, Lexington? What if Herschel comes home and finds us in the bathroom?" Nikki said.

Lexington handed her a box way too weird-shaped to have a ring in it.

Reading the box, then looking at Lexington, Nikki said, "This is a pregnancy test."

"I know what it is, I bought it. I want you to take it right now so we'll know."

His eyes didn't blink as he watched her hold the stick in the flow of her urine. Taking the stick from her, Lexington focused his eyes, awaiting the results. Slowly he stared at her.

"What? What? What is it?" Nikki asked, snatching the stick from him.

Lexington exhaled. "It's positive," he said.

"What's positive?" Venus and Herschel asked, standing in the doorway.

Nikki tossed the stick in the toilet, then quickly flushed.

CHAPTER 21

Brian

Summertime was a great time to stroll along South Beach. Visitors and natives alike strolled, seemingly in search of serenity. Reclining in a white plastic beach chaise, Brian glanced but didn't stare at the topless, light-skinned women bathing in the sun. A tan wasn't always a good thing. Skin cancer and excessive pigmentation were bad.

Interlocking his fingers behind his head, Brian wondered, how was he going to keep Carmelita and Zahra from contacting Michelle? How did Carmelita get his wife's number?

Brian considered lying to his wife and saying, "Baby, I don't know no Carmelita." In part, that was true.

He had refused to give Carmelita $10,000. Thinking back, he realized he should've negotiated paying her something. But giving her money was no guarantee she wouldn't call Michelle. He feared Carmelita would call his wife at some point. Why didn't he get her phone number? He desperately wanted to call that slimy, scamming, no-good Latina chick, but he couldn't. Probably best. Now he'd have to wait for her to make the next move. For how long?

Brian watched the waves pushing white sand upon the shore. What if she demanded some ridiculous amount of money? More than $10,000. What if she claimed she was having his baby? Either would dissolve his marriage if Michelle found out. There was no way Carmelita could be pregnant by him from a one-night stand. Could she? What was wrong with women? Were women that desperate for money that they'd selfishly ruin a good man's life and his marriage?

Brian glanced at his phone. No missed calls. That Carmelita chick still hadn't called him. Why? Reclining his head, Brian closed his eyes. His marriage was perfect. Would Michelle abandon a perfect marriage or stand by him? How deep and how long would his wife hurt if he confessed before Zahra or Carmelita contacted her?

The melody of "You Are So Beautiful" resounded from his cell phone, startling him.

"He-ey. Hey, baby. How are you?" Brian asked.

"I'm okay. What's wrong with you?" Michelle asked. "I hear trepidation in your voice. Don't tell me Marcus Monty signed with someone else?"

"No, naw. I have a good chance. He's narrowed it down to me or Brandon, saying he'd call me when he decided. I just dozed off and the phone woke me up by surprise. What's up?"

he asked, eyeing a woman in a thong. The string had disappeared into the crack of her creamy behind.

Keep your mind off women! You've got enough females dogging you.

"I need you to come home first thing in the morning. We need to talk before I leave," Michelle said.

Sitting up, Brian's voice trembled. "I'm on my way."

"You don't have to come home early. I have a few things to sort out, and the extra day will give me time."

Nervously Brian replied, "Oh, okay."

He'd made it back to South Beach earlier today but wasn't quite ready to take the ten-minute drive home. His driver was parked in front of the hotel. Not knowing Michelle's intentions, he'd wait until tomorrow—after he cleared his conscience and rehearsed his lies.

His eyes widened as he thought, *Ou, shit. She's beautiful.* Brian drifted into a fantasy of fucking her on the beach. Massaging his dick, he stared at the camel-toe imprint of her pussy. Why were women so fucking irresistible? *Down. Damn. Down.*

His dickhead crept along his thigh toward his knee. Brian wanted to come. He needed to fuck somebody. Brian exhaled, wondering, *Am I a sex addict? After that shit with Zahra and Carmelita, I should be through fucking around. I should make an appointment. Have myself checked out. Maybe telling the truth, then asking Michelle for forgiveness, better than seeing a sex therapist. Not a good idea at all, though, if she finds out about my golfing trip to Atlanta.*

"I'll call you back later," Michelle said.

Aw, damn. He'd forgotten she was on the phone. Scratching his bald head, Brian asked, "Are the kids okay? Are you okay? What's wrong?" Brian prayed to God that Carmelita hadn't called his wife.

"No worries. Right? I'll talk to you when you get here. Bye," Michelle said, ending the call. She'd never abruptly hung up on him with an attitude.

A woman dressed in a black tank top and white pants stopped, then asked him, "You okay?"

Brian nodded, thought, *Get your pussy out of my face,* then said, "Thanks."

"I can tell something is bothering you. You look like you could use a secret friend," she merrily said, smiling at him. "You know, it always helps me to talk things through with nice strangers. They don't know me. I don't know them. It's not at all like secret shopping or dining, where you wait for the person to make a mistake so you can rate them. My being your secret friend, you can say whatever is on your mind. Drink?" she asked, pointing toward the poolside bar. "I could use a stiff one myself."

Arching his foot, Brian's knee bounced rapidly. *Why not?* he thought. They were outdoors on the beach surrounded by strangers. Maybe talking to her would help him to get his lies straight.

Brian phoned his driver, then said, "You can leave. I'm going to stay here tonight."

"Certainly. Would you like me to pick you up tomorrow?" the driver asked.

"I'll call in the morning, if I need you. Bye." Brian ended the call, ordered his favorite drink, then motioned to the strange woman to order her drink.

"A strawberry colada, with an extra shot of rum, please," she said. "What's your name?" she asked, then immediately said, "Don't answer that. If you tell me, then you won't be a secret friend anymore. Have you ever made love on the beach in the middle of the night with the salty ocean breeze caressing your naked body?" she asked.

She'd managed to divert his attention to her. Brian tried imagining her naked. Watching her lips made his dick hard. "Sounds crazy, but actually, no, I haven't," Brian answered. "Have you?"

"No, but I'd like to," she said, licking the cherry. "What's bothering you?"

"No need to discuss it. Whatever it is, it is. Just having someone to talk to is good enough for me," he said, placing $30 on the bar. "Let's sit outside by the pool."

He led her beside the pool and he sat sideways on a lounge chair opposite hers, gazing up at the sky. The moon was half full. Stars bright. He sat confessing his dilemma to an attractive woman he'd rather fuck than talk to. Coming would temporarily take his mind off trying to figure out what Michelle had to say. Each wave gradually washed away the lavender and rose-colored sunshine. The darkness softly swished upon the sand, until he no longer saw the beach. With his sense of sight limited, his hearing became more keen as he listened to the waves softly crashing ashore, one behind the other. Just as daylight traded places with the moonlight, so could his life change drastically in one day.

Reaching for his phone, Brian said, "I need to take this," answering, "Hey, Marcus, what's up? Great hearing from you."

"You in," Marcus said.

"No shit?"

"I want you to represent me, B. I need you on the first plane back to Houston tomorrow, man. We need to talk face-to-face. Call me when you get in. Later," Marcus said, ending their call.

The woman positioned herself closer, sat on the edge of his chair, placed his legs across her lap, then began massaging his feet. She kneaded his arch. "Whoever it was, I'm glad to see they cheered you up. When was the last time you had a reflexology massage?" she asked.

"That's fucking great!" Brian yelled, smiling until his jaws ached. "That feels great," Brian said, downing his drink. Whatever she'd done to his feet made him hella sleepy superquick. Moaning, struggling to keep his eyelids from closing into a comfortable, much-needed sleep, Brian mumbled, "I got the big contract."

Slowly she unzipped his pants, taking him into her mouth. She sucked his dick, then licked his shaft from the base to the ridge, then sucked his head again. She licked him again. The wetness of her tongue, the softness of her mouth, made his dick harden, growing toward her throat.

"Relax," she said. "You'll be more comfortable if you remove your clothes. No one can see us out here now. They're gone and it's way too dark."

Helping him remove his shirt, then his pants and underwear, she placed his belongings on the lounge chair next to her purse.

"Huh, what? We shouldn't be doing this out . . ." His voice trailed off.

"Relax. Stop worrying. Whatever is done cannot be undone. Fixed, yes. Forgiven, yes. Undone, no," she said, kissing his clipper-shaven pubic area.

Brian's eyes grew heavy as he dozed into a light snore, with his dick in her mouth, believing Michelle would forgive him if she ever found out about his affairs. Why shouldn't she? He was a loving husband. Wonderful father. Could-do-no-wrong son. Drifting into his subconscious, Brian wondered how his mother would feel if she found out, after all of her years of being married to his dad, that his dad had had numerous affairs?

Brian didn't know which felt better: being half-asleep having his dick sucked or his feet massaged. Fluttering his eyes toward the rising sun, he'd peacefully slept the night away with a complete stranger in his arms.

"Wake up. Wake up," he'd heard a voice say.

Widening his eyes, Brian slowly sat on the side of his lounge chair.

The naked woman beside him tapped his leg, asking, "What in the hell happened last night?"

Squinting to diminish the blinding sun from hurting his eyes, he asked, "Damn, it's daylight. Where in the hell am I?" Then he said, "Aw, hell no. Where in the fuck are my clothes?" He covered his dick with his hands. He stared up at a woman who looked down at him. She seemed detached from the fact that he and the woman with him were completely nude publicly.

Brian raced around the pool with his dick flopping in the air in search of his clothes. Maybe they'd fallen over the rail, he thought, leaning to see if he saw anything that resembled clothes or a purse lodged in the sand. *Fuck!* His phone. His wallet. His driver's license. Credit cards. All gone.

"Fuck!" Brian yelled.

The woman with him held her palms against her ears in disbelief. "Where's my purse? My phone? My money? This is all your fault," she cried.

This could not be happening to him. Where were his pants? Who would want them? Fuck! His house and car keys were gone too. He could get spares if he didn't get arrested. Brian walked over to the woman leaning against the rail that overlooked the pool and asked, "Did you see someone down here?"

"Yes," she answered. "About a half hour ago. It was too dark to see his face. He had on long shorts, no shirt."

Fuck! How was Brian going to get home? Even when he got home, how was Brian going to explain to Michelle he was robbed of everything, including his drawers?

CHAPTER 22

Herschel

"Kiss me," Nikki said, rolling over and facing her husband.

Herschel stared in disbelief, looking over his shoulder for someone else to respond. He'd tossed all night wondering if Nikki had confirmed Lexington's inquiry when he'd said Donna was *positive* that she'd caught him getting fucked in the ass by Anthony. Fearing his boy would hear the truth was enough information for Herschel to abandon the conversation between Lexington and Nikki in their bathroom.

Nikki awakened, begging, "Baby, I miss you. Give me a kiss."

Herschel froze. What was Nikki up to? Why did Lexington have to tell Nikki what Donna had said? What did Donna want when she showed up at his back door unannounced?

"You don't care about my being bisexual?" Herschel asked.

"Are you going to make me ask again? Kiss me," Nikki said, straddling her pussy across his dick.

He wasn't feeling up to doing Nikki. She made more money, but she didn't own his dick. "What's gotten into you? Too many of those alcohol-injected honeydew pussy poppers?" he asked jokingly. His dick remained soft and spongy. "You hung out all night with Venus, now you want me to do you? I'm tired too."

"I should start strapping-on and doing you," Nikki said, implying more of a statement than a question.

Nikki eased her middle and ring fingers into his mouth. What if he bit her fingers the way she'd done him? She saturated her fingers with his saliva, then massaged her clit. "Aw, yeah. This feels so fucking great. Herschel, fuck me," she insisted, taking control of his dick. "You do use condoms with Anthony, right?"

Nodding, Herschel forced what little blood she had mustered into his shaft toward his head. Nikki squeezed his dick firm, then sat on him. A low, close ride of her hips against his pubic hairs and his dick engaged his brain. Blood filled his shaft. As disappointed as he was with his wife, she obviously didn't care about his life with Anthony. She bounced her pussy like it was on a pogo stick, making him come quickly.

"Damn, you feel good, baby," Herschel lied.

"I'm giving you my best pussy at sunrise on the day that I'm in heat and ovulating, and all you can say is 'I feel good, baby' when I'm trying to give you a baby?'"

Herschel's forehead buckled. "A what?"

"A baby. I'm ready for us to have one," Nikki said. "And if we're lucky, we're pregnant."

"What do you want from me? You come in here—what, four hours ago?—ease into the bed, wake me up at the crack of dawn, fuck me, because what? Is this your way of patronizing me with the possibility of us having a baby, when I've been asking you to have my child for years? Does everything in our marriage have to be done your damn way, all the fucking time?" Herschel asked, easing from underneath Nikki.

"I don't want anything from you, Herschel. Nothing. Not a damn thing. You can go be with Anthony and I can raise our baby by myself."

"Then do that!" Herschel yelled, making his way to the bathroom. He hated the fact that Nikki knew about Anthony and she was cool with that shit. He wanted her to get mad. Get angry. He needed a reason to stop loving Anthony—not a reason to love him more.

Nikki ranted and all Herschel heard was Donna's voice: *"You two faggots!"*

"Faggot" was such a degrading word. Herschel wanted to stuff a thousand bars of soap in Donna's mouth and make her apologize until they were tired of hearing her voice. Now she had Lexington believing her. No more single husbands threesomes for Herschel. Lexington was not inviting Herschel to hang with him and Brian again.

Attempting not to look obvious, Nikki hurried by him to close the bathroom door before he made it inside with her. He was too slow. Shifting his thoughts, he was thankful for the alone time.

"Fine, you go ahead and use the bathroom. I'll wait out here until you're done," Herschel said, sitting on the edge of the bed with his head in the palms of his hands. Herschel exhaled, thinking, *Another baby. This one would be different. Special. Born with a silver spoon in its mouth. Even the baby wouldn't need me for much.*

His dick hardened. Not for sex. For a much needed piss. Herschel toured areas of his home that they never used. Entering the baby's nursery, he glanced at the pink-blue-yellow-and-green wallpaper border neatly pasted beneath the crown molding. *Wow, a baby with Nikki.* That might be cool if she let him make some of the decisions.

The throb of his dick reminded him he had to piss. "My daughter won't mind if I use her bathroom," Herschel said, growing fonder of the idea of him and Nikki having a baby. Maybe having a baby girl would renew their relationship. As long as he didn't have another gay son, Herschel would do all the things for Nikki that he regrettably hadn't done for Ivory. He'd massage Nikki's stomach every day she was home. Rub her feet. Wash her hair in the shower—the way his boy Brian bragged about doing it for Michelle. Herschel wanted Nikki and him to have the kind of love Brian and Michelle shared. The kind of love that money couldn't buy or barter.

Lifting the toilet seat, Herschel decided today he'd break up with Ivory and Anthony and give his wife a real chance to get to know him. She already knew about Ivory and Kwan.

He squeezed his dick from the base to the head and watched the last few drops of urine plop into the toilet. Staring at his reflection in the mirror, he admired his body. Chocolate cheekbones squaring off into his neatly trimmed goatee. He rubbed the hairs on his dark chest and roller-coaster abs.

His big dick couldn't help but to hang low. Herschel nodded with approval, hoping for a girl.

Turning on the warm water, Herschel washed his hands, ripping a pale green paper towel from the roll. Nikki had told him green was the best neutral color for babies. He tossed the wet paper into the trash, and it fell to the side. Herschel stooped, picked it up, then froze in disbelief, dropping the content in the trash can.

"Damn, that bitch has fucked me again."

Herschel left the nursery, returning to the bedroom where his wife was snuggled underneath the covers, asleep. Snatching the sheet from her body, Herschel stared at her.

Quickly rising from the pillow, Nikki said, "Herschel, what's wrong with you? I thought you had left."

"Lay down," Herschel insisted.

Placing his palms in the arch of her thighs, Herschel spread her labia. He scanned to see what he could find. He licked to see what he could taste. Inserting his middle finger, he desperately probed to see what he could feel. Something had to feel different inside his wife. He had proof in the other bathroom that another man had made love to his wife, but her pussy was covering for her.

"What the hell are you doing, digging in my pussy like you're crazy? What the hell has gotten into you?" Nikki asked, scooting toward the headboard.

Herschel gripped her hips, pulling her toward him. "Shut up," he insisted.

Extending his tongue, he licked her clit. Sliding back the hood with his upper teeth, he sucked his wife's juices, instantly making her cum in his mouth. He knew exactly how to please Nikki. Easing his middle finger into her vagina, he pressed upward against the spongy tissue area, making her come harder and longer. He could continue teasing her G-spot and make her squirt her savory juices all over his face, neck, and chest—but not today.

Easing on top of Nikki missionary-style, Herschel kissed his wife before penetrating her, wondering if the other man pleased her more. Fuck that. Nikki was *his* wife, and if anybody was going to satisfy her best, it was going to be him.

Swaying his hips until his dick found her hole, he splattered wet kisses all over her shifting face, saying, "Baby, I love you. Don't you love me?"

Nikki's hands braced his chest, then pushed. She turned her head to the side and opened her mouth. Before she'd spoken a word, Herschel thrust his dick deeper. "Do you love him more? Is that why you're pushing me away?" he asked, leaning his face to the side to look into her eyes. Eyes that once saw him as a man.

Tears? Tears streaming down her face? He should be the one crying.

"Baby, I'm sorry," Herschel apologized. "Talk to me." He wanted an explanation and confession for what he'd discovered in the nursery bathroom. "Why are you crying?"

"Herschel," Nikki whimpered, "you're a good man. And I do love you, but—"

"Sshhh, no 'buts.' Not today," he said, kissing her lips.

Deliberately he rotated his ass, grinding deep and slow into Nikki's pussy. She looped her hands under his armpits, gripping his shoulder blades, pulling him into her body. The warmth of her breath, the silkiness of her body beneath his, the tightness of his pussy, reminded him of the first time they'd made love. Continuing his slow grind until his wife released her fluids to him satisfied Herschel for the moment.

"Oh, baby. Don't stop. Hold my dick right there. Right there," she whispered, making him throb inside her.

He couldn't impregnate his wife. According to the pregnancy test that was in the nursery, Nikki was already pregnant with some other man's baby. Herschel was determined to find out who he was.

Kissing Nikki on the lips, he eased off her, covered her body with the sheet, showered, stepped into his shorts and T-shirt, then headed to Ivory's. Herschel used his key to unlock the front door.

Ivory was a late-morning riser. He tiptoed into their bedroom. She was sleeping. His lips descended toward her, kissing her gently.

"Huh, what? Oh, hey. I didn't hear you come in," she said.

Herschel removed his shorts, then his shirt, lifted the cover and lay next to Ivory.

Her lips and hips covered his as she straddled on top of him. "Good morning. I'm so happy to see you," she said, rubbing her shaft against his shaft.

Anthony was right. Herschel needed to choose a side and stop teetering. Today he'd make his decision.

"Do you love me?" he asked Ivory.

"Yes, of course I do," she said, easing his dick inside her. "You know I love you."

"How much?" he asked.

"This much," she said, squashing her pussy against his balls, grinding in slow, circular motions.

Ivory felt better than Nikki, but he loved Nikki more than he loved Ivory. Maybe he loved Nikki more because she rejected him more, making him feel like a little boy on the inside, instead of feeling like a man when he was with Ivory.

"Kiss me," Herschel said, pulling Ivory's breast atop his chest.

He held her hips pushing her onto his dick. Each time she rose up, he pushed her down, making her clit feel the abrasion of his pubic hairs. Her mouth opened wider. Her tongue dug deeper into his mouth.

"Um, um," she muffled as he suctioned her tongue.

Her body began trembling. He gyrated faster, kissing her back. Ivory grabbed his ears and started wiggling her pussy. He firmly held her hips against his dick, determined to make her come for him. Her wiggles became tiny shifts, side to side, until her body collapsed on top of his.

"Well, good morning to you too," she said, smiling.

"Ivory," Herschel said, staring into her beautiful brown eyes.

Her forehead wrinkled. He gently brushed his thumb between her eyebrows as she asked, "Yes?"

"Ivory, will you marry me?"

All thirty-two of her teeth appeared as she responded with a resounding "Yes! Yes! I will marry you, Herschel Henderson."

Herschel needed a firm yes from Ivory before asking Nikki

for a divorce. But there was one person he had to tell his decision to, face-to-face. Putting on his shorts and T-shirt, Herschel kissed Ivory, then said, "I'll be back tonight. Ask Kwan—I mean, ask my son—where he wants to go for dinner tonight. I want to be the one to tell him his daddy is coming home for good."

If Herschel was going to raise a child, it was going to be his own. Nikki was not going to have him babysitting some other man's kid while she traveled the world.

Ivory followed him to the living room and stood in the doorway until he could no longer see her in the rearview mirror. Driving to the condo he shared with Anthony, Herschel hoped he'd find Anthony there.

Sliding his key into the hole, Herschel closed the front door behind him. Going directly to Anthony's bedroom, he knocked on the door. No answer. He knocked again. No answer.

"You looking for me?" Anthony asked, walking up behind Herschel with a smoothie in his hand.

Herschel turned around to face Anthony's naked body. "Yes, as a matter of fact, I am."

"Well, damn, you don't have to sound like the police unless you're planning on frisking me," Anthony said, dipping his fingers into his beverage, then sprinkling Herschel's face.

Herschel took the smoothie from Anthony, dipped his dick into the glass, handed it back to Anthony, then said, "Lick me."

"No, you didn't. You gon' make me another smoothie," Anthony insisted, "'cause I ain't drinking that." Smiling, he knelt before Herschel. "But I do love me some strawberry-covered chocolate dick."

Herschel closed his eyes. His throat tightened. A tear escaped the corner of his right eye. This was his last blow job from the only man he'd ever loved. Glancing down at Anthony, Herschel watched Anthony suck his dick like he was slurping the smoothie. Anthony's strong hands traveled up and down his shaft. His jaws tightened, tighter than Herschel's fuck buddy from the gym. What or who was she doing this morning?

Anthony stood, gargled, spat in Herschel's face, then said, "You taste like pussy! That's why you dipped your dick in my drink first? You thought I wouldn't notice? You could've washed that nasty shit off!"

Fuck. There was no arguing the point. "I hadn't planned on us doing anything. I came here to tell you I've made my decision. I came here to tell you it's over. I'm leaving Nikki, and"—Herschel paused—"I asked Ivory to marry me."

Anthony started laughing. "This is too much for me so damn early in the morning. If I weren't laughing"—Anthony laughed louder—"I'd beat your fuckin' ass," he yelled. "How dare you come in here, stick your nasty, stank-ass dick in my mouth, then tell me you're marrying Ivory, when I was the one who stood by you when you were depressed. I was the one who held your ass in my arms when you couldn't sleep 'cause your wife was gone. You, my lover, my friend, are confused and need to get the fuck outta my face," Anthony said, slamming his bedroom door.

Herschel didn't bother following Anthony—and, no, Herschel was not confused. Not anymore. He headed home to pack a few things and tell Nikki of his decision.

Parking in the driveway, Herschel entered their bedroom from the patio.

"Oh, yes! Fuck me harder," he heard his wife scream. "Harder!"

The locks bounced against the man's back as he slammed his dick into Nikki. Her hands were locked onto the headboard. She thrust her ass against Lexington's dick. Watching his best friend fuck his wife should've pissed him off, not turned him on.

Herschel massaged his erection through his pants. It wasn't Nikki that turned him on. Nikki's baby was probably Lexington's. *Let him take care of it,* he thought. *Yeah, right.* If his wife's baby was Lexington's, then Nikki was destined to become a single mom, because all Lexington was going to do was write Nikki a check she didn't need.

Damn. Lexington's fine, sexy ass was beating that pussy up!

"Don't just stand there. Do something."

What the hell? Herschel turned around to face . . . Donna?

"Yeah, that's right. It's me. I knew you two were fucking! I knew it!" Donna yelled, fucking up the mood for everybody, including Herschel.

"Oh, my God!" Nikki screamed, hiding behind Lexington.

God? She knows his name? Herschel thought. He hadn't heard her call on Him outside of having sex.

"Herschel, what are you doing here?" Nikki asked.

Donna entered their house, then disappeared. Which way did she go?

"Um, I live here," he said, squinting his lips. "Well, I used to. I'm moving out today. I just came back to get a few things. Don't stop on my account."

Donna held her right hand behind her back. She ran toward Lexington. He tried to move in front of Nikki, but he couldn't reposition himself fast enough.

"Donna, are you crazy?" Herschel yelled, diving in front of Nikki.

Nikki may not have loved Herschel the way she loved Lexington, but Herschel was no punk. He was man enough to die for Nikki. The object in Donna's hands stabbed Herschel in the heart.

"Ahhh!" Nikki screamed.

"Bitch, are you crazy?" Lexington yelled.

Raising his hands to his chest, Herschel looked at the object, then threw the piece of plastic in Donna's face. "Crazy bitch!" It would've been better if she'd stabbed him with a knife than putting that nasty-ass urine-stained pregnancy test on him.

Donna picked up the test, then tossed it on the bed. Tears streamed down her face. "Yes, I am crazy, and I'm pregnant. The one time I decide to let you make love to me, I end up pregnant again."

Oh, shit. The test wasn't Nikki's? Something isn't right. How did Donna end up leaving a pregnancy test in their bathroom? Fuck! Herschel had proposed to Ivory because he thought Nikki was pregnant with some other man's baby. Fuck!

"Y'all get the fuck outta here," Herschel demanded. "And take that nasty-ass piss stick with you, Donna. You got a lot of nerve coming up in our house taking your damn test."

"And you got a lot of nerve letting a man fuck you in your ass," Donna said, stomping out the door.

Lexington stared at him, waiting for a denial that never came. "Nikki, you need to divorce him," Lexington said, turning his back to Herschel.

Okay, there was an equitable solution to all of this mayhem, Herschel thought, looking at his naked wife. Before he spoke, Nikki said, "Baby, I'm sorry," climbing out of bed.

Was she apologizing to Lexington or him? At this point, it didn't matter. Ignoring Nikki, Herschel packed a suitcase with enough work and casual clothes for a week.

"Herschel, don't," Nikki said.

"Yes, Herschel, leave," Lexington insisted.

Kissing Nikki on the lips, Herschel said, "Since you may be pregnant with my baby or Lexington's, we should all swing tonight until we get fucking up one another's lives out of our systems."

Nikki's jaw dropped.

Rolling his suitcase toward the door, he looked at his wife, then said, "Nikki, you deserve better. I don't want any money from you. I don't want anything from you. I'll call you later."

Herschel missed Anthony already. He sat in the driveway outside their condo and texted, *I love you,* then drove away with a lump, not in his pants but in his throat. This time, Herschel didn't hold back his tears. He cried. Not for Nikki.

Not for Ivory. But for the love he'd lost with Anthony. Anthony deserved better, and he was right. Herschel was confused.

Instead of going to Ivory's, Herschel cruised down Interstate 10, all the way to New Orleans to chill with his mom for a while. Herschel was convinced his lack of parental love and guidance had fucked him up emotionally. If he didn't ask his mother the hard questions that had bothered him since he was a child, Herschel would live his entire life not knowing the meaning of true love.

Did his mother have the answers?

One thing was for sure. Herschel certainly didn't.

CHAPTER 23

Lexington

Lexington did not want another baby by Donna. She'd trapped him once more. That shit wouldn't happen to him again. He knew she wanted him to go to New Orleans with her.

Picking up his cell phone, Lexington dialed the man with the hands that could make his dream a reality. "Yes, may I speak with Dr. Davidson?" Lexington asked.

"May I ask the reason for your call today?" the woman responded.

"Absolutely. In a word . . . vasectomy," Lexington said. "Give me the first available appointment."

Nikki having his baby was cool, but how did he know if it was his? Damn, with her showing up at the sex club, getting her groove on, letting a dude bend her over the chair. Dude's seed could've spilled out of the condom. Lexington wasn't sure if the dude *had* worn a condom that night. She hadn't worn one when she was with him. What if her baby was from Herschel's gay ass?

Lexington helped Donna pack her things. It was time for her to get out of his house.

"Ten years of marriage and this is how we end it," Donna said, sitting down on the job. She sat on the edge of their bed. "If anyone would've fast-forwarded our lives to now, I would've thrown myself down at the altar and said, 'Lord, I can't do this!'"

"Donna, what are you talking about?" Lexington asked, staring at their wedding picture on the wall across the room.

Donna softly said, "Nothing, I suppose. Nothing that matters anyway. I've decided not to have your baby. I'm having an abortion today."

"You're not killing my child, Donna," Lexington protested.

"I'll be done packing in a moment. I don't need your help," she said peacefully.

"Donna, I'm serious. You are not killing my child. I'll take you to court. I have parental rights," Lexington insisted.

Donna laughed, then seriously said, "And you call yourself a man?"

Forget Donna. There was no way he'd let her destroy his seed.

Donna stood before the mirror, glazing on that raspberry lipstick. She combed her hair, then dressed in a pair of white low-rise slacks, a white tank top, and slip-on heels. Suddenly Lexington saw the woman he'd made passionate love to reappear.

"Donna, you think I'm kidding," Lexington said, holding his phone in his hand. "All I have to do is press one button."

His wife walked over to him and kissed his cheek. Her eyes narrowed so close to his eyes, they damn near touched noses. Donna's lips grazed his as she whispered in his mouth, "You want to make that decision. Go right ahead. I'll let you do that. But before you decide, I want you to know. I'm either going to abort your baby, or I'm going to kill you," she said, walking away.

"You're crazy, Donna!" Lexington yelled, following her out the front door to her limo.

Donna didn't look back. She didn't respond. Damn, was that the way he'd treated her, leaving her at home almost every night? Forget Donna. Lexington went into the bedroom, slipped into a pair of shorts, no T-shirt, then walked over to the nightstand to get his Bluetooth. Donna had left the title to the restaurant he'd bought her in South Beach on the bed.

"Whatever," Lexington said, shaking his head.

Lexington needed someone to talk to, so he walked over to Nikki's. Herschel was gone, so he didn't need to call first. Nikki was in bed. Lexington lay beside her. "Hey, you," he whispered.

"Huh? What are you doing here? Oh, hell no. Take your ass home. I do not want your crazy wife over here ever again. Leave, Lexington. Take your married ass home," Nikki said, sliding to the edge of the bed away from him.

Damn, was he that bad of a husband? A friend?

Lexington said, "I sent Donna on her way. She's gone to New Orleans for good. Now we can be together without her interfering." Lexington kissed Nikki's lips. "I want to be here for you and my baby. I want us to have what Brian and Michelle have."

"Brian," Nikki said, laughing. "Are you serious? As much as he fucks around on Michelle, are you serious?"

Frowning, Lexington asked, "How do you know that?"

Nikki laughed harder, holding her stomach, then said, "Everybody knows he fucks around, including Michelle."

Lexington placed his hand on Nikki's stomach. "Seriously, baby. I'm going to be here for you. I'm going to be here for our child."

Nikki asked, "Where're the girls? With Donna?"

Oh, shit! He was so concerned about Donna, Lexington hadn't noticed that Donna left the girls with him. How was he supposed to take care of them by himself? A child's place was with the mother.

"Just what I thought. Go home, Lexington," Nikki said, rolling over. "You're confused, just like Herschel and Brian."

Lexington reached over her arm to touch Nikki's breasts. "Baby, please. I had no idea Donna would be so careless and leave the children."

"Lexington," Nikki whispered, "don't ever touch me again. I want you out of my house right now. I'm not marrying you. I don't want to be with you, and I'm not having your baby."

"Baby, wait. You know me better than this. You mean to tell me you're going to get rid of my baby? You're going to ruin a perfect relationship over something that's not my fault."

"No, Lexington, I didn't ruin our relationship. You did."

"Nikki," he pleaded, then said, "I'll do anything to make

this right. Don't leave me. You're my best friend. Baby, please . . . teach me how to love."

"Is that like teaching an old dog new tricks? You don't even know how to leave when I tell you," Nikki said, rolling over again.

"The girls are fine. I'll leave in a moment. I need you, Nikki."

Lexington kissed her from her lips to her clit. Tossing the sheet out of his way, Lexington spread Nikki's thighs. He did know how to please her. Once her pussy was nice and wet, he eased on top of her, penetrating Nikki real slow so she felt all of his dick, *her* dick, sliding inside her.

His ass rolled, making a figure eight. Imagining her pussy was a baseball diamond, Lexington slid into first, pressing his dick into her left corner pocket. Then he hit third, stimulating her right corner pocket. Fucking Nikki fast, he pounded his dick into second base, nestling his head into the cul-de-sac of Nikki's sweet pussy. Trying not to come, he faked a run for home plate, throbbing his head against her G-spot.

"Damn, when did you learn this shit," Nikki moaned.

"I always have new game for pussy," Lexington said, throwing a fast one into second.

"Yes," Nikki moaned, begging, "let me get on top."

"Hell no," Lexington said, bracing his hands underneath her ass.

He hit first again, making her moan. Third made Nikki scream. Second made her lock her ankles around his waist, over his ass, pulling him in deeper. Lexington brought his dick into home plate. Holding his shaft, he jabbed his head into Nikki's G-spot while his other hand worked her clit.

"Oh, shit. Oh, shit," Nikki screamed, ejaculating all over his dick and balls.

Lexington ejaculated too. Right on her G-spot, then whispered, "We are going to be together. You're not going anywhere."

"You're right, baby," Nikki said. "I'm not going anywhere. You are. And I'm not having your baby. I'm having *my* baby. Lexington, thanks for making me good. That was a good one. But right now, I need for you to get out of my life—and stay out."

CHAPTER 24

Brian

I should call the police on you!" the general manager shouted. "How dare you come to my establishment, with this, with this . . . ," he ranted, gesturing toward the naked woman standing next to Brian in the men's restroom.

"Sir, listen, I apologize. Your bartender served me way too many drinks. I should hold your company liable. You do not want to call the cops," Brian stated authoritatively, trying to establish a position of power.

"You have one phone call and one hour to be off my premises, or, yes, I shall call the cops. I don't care what you claim." The general manager handed Brian his cell phone. "Hurry."

"It's your job and your job reputation you should be concerned about, not whether or not I have a case, because I know the law and so does my attorney," Brian bluffed, taking the phone from the general manager.

One phone call was all Brian needed. Scratching his head, he thought, who was the best person to call? Definitely not Michelle. She'd probably tried to reach him several times by now. God only knew who had his phone and what they'd done with it. Staring down at the woman who'd sucked his dick, he wondered if he had been set up.

I'ma do like Tank said in his song Please Don't Go. *I'ma blame it on the alcohol,* Brian thought.

"Hey," the general manager said, snatching the phone out of Brian's hand, giving it to the woman. "You're taking too long. You, make your call right now," he said, opening the restroom door.

A security guard stood by the door, with his arms folded over his chest.

Brian's eyes narrowed, thinking, *Fake-ass wannabe cop need to get a real job.*

"Good," the general manager said. "Stay right there. I may need you to call the police."

The woman cried into the phone, "I need you to pick me up. I fell asleep on the beach and someone robbed me. I'm so sorry. Please bring me some clothes right away." She was sobbing. "They stole my clothes, my purse, my phone . . . everything." She cried louder, reciting the address of the hotel.

Damn, is it that fucking easy for females to get over? Brian thought. Michelle would've drilled him with ninety-nine questions.

"Last chance," the general manager said, handing Brian the phone.

This time, Brian dialed a number. When she answered, he said, "Can you bring me some clothes and pick me up? I fell asleep on the beach and someone robbed me."

"Brian, what? Are you okay?"

"Other than the fact that I'm alive and standing in the men's restroom naked . . . no, I'm not okay," he said, telling her the address. He was a grown-ass man and he was not going to cry like the woman had done.

Twenty minutes later, the security guard tapped on the door. The general manager opened the door. A tall, slender woman entered the restroom, smiling.

"Girl, here," she said, laughing, handing the woman her clothes.

Brian stared at her, thinking, *What is so damn funny?* He'd thought the woman had called her husband. Women were scandalous!

"Thanks," the woman said, quickly dressing. "I hope everything works out well for you, Mr. Flaw," she said, leaving the restroom.

Oh, hell no! Brian opened the door, alarmed. His mother was outside holding a designer bag.

"Baby, what in the world!" she shouted.

"Damn. Sorry, Mom," Brian said, taking the bag, closing the door.

Stepping into his sweatpants, then pulling his T-shirt over his head, Brian dressed in ten seconds, ran out of the restroom to the lobby in search of the woman he'd fucked last night—pissed that *he* was the one who'd been fucked.

She was gone.

Biting his bottom lip, almost drawing blood, Brian tried to figure out, *Why me?* What had he done to deserve the things that had happened to him?

"Son, what is going on?" his mother asked.

"I'm not sure yet, Mom," he said, trying to answer her question for himself. "Just drop me off at home."

"Well, let's keep this between us. Whatever it is, it had better not be illegal, 'cause your father, grandfather, and all the Flaw men will disown you. Flaw men don't post bail and—"

"I know, Ma, because Flaw men don't go to jail. No, I didn't do anything illegal," Brian reassured his mother, thankful she wouldn't tell his father. The ride from South Beach to his Biscayne Bay home was ten minutes. "Thanks, Ma. I'll pick up the kids tomorrow if that's okay with you."

"But of course it is. You have a lot to take care of today. I love you, sweetheart. Remember, material things can be repaired or—"

Brian finished his mother's statement: "Replaced. People cannot. I know, Ma. I love you too. Please keep this between us, like you said, and don't tell Dad."

Walking up his driveway, Brian noticed several unfamiliar cars. This was not a good time for Michelle to have guests. Had she invited Donna and Nikki over? His stomach churned. Now would be a good time for Brian to run after his mother and get back in the car. But he didn't. He rang his doorbell. Look what he'd been reduced to—ringing the bell! This was his house.

Michelle opened the door. "Brian, where've you been? You haven't answered your phone since last night, and I've called you five times this morning."

Entering his home, Brian said, "Not now, baby. I just want to rest for a . . ." Speechless, he stared at the women sitting on his sofa. Zahra, Carmelita, and the woman from the hotel sat there with their legs crossed, like they were guests on a reality show and he was in the hot seat.

"Oh, those are my mother's guests. She's having some sort of meeting," Michelle said.

"Hello, Brian. How are you?" Zahra asked.

"Fine," he answered, then said, "Michelle, I need to talk to you in private."

"No shit," Michelle said. "How do you know her?"

Brian escorted Michelle to the bedroom. Her mother was comfortably seated on the chaise lounge. "What's she doing here?"

"Mother, who are those women in my living room?" Michelle said, sitting on the bench at the foot of their bed.

"Here," Michelle's mother said, handing Brian a piece of paper. "You see those vows. The ones you promised my daughter. You lied to her. I hired those women to prove to Michelle that you are not the man she thinks you are. What do you have to say for yourself?"

Other than the fact that you're a bitter bitch, nothing, Brian thought. Damn, did she hate him enough to break up his marriage? Brian remained silent. The only thing he could do was admit his guilt, and he'd never do that. Not even now.

Tears poured from his mother-in-law's eyes. "We can talk after they leave, but right now, I want to know if you raped Carmelita!"

Raped? "You're one mentally sick woman. Is that what she said? Is that what you're telling my wife? That I'm a rapist?" Brian asked. "That I honestly raped that woman!"

Michelle's mother smiled. "So you did fuck her."

Bitch! Tightening his jaws, Brian stared at Michelle's mother. What was her fucking problem? She seemed to enjoy her cynical behavior. He was not married to her. "Get out of my house," Brian demanded.

"No problem. I've proved my point. Michelle, you know what you need to do—"

"Ma, get out and take those women with you," Michelle said, standing in front of her mother. "I'll talk to you later."

"But, honey, is this the type of man you want to—"

"Stay married to, Mother?" Michelle asked, then answered, "Yes. Whatever you allege my husband is doing, be aware Brian has never brought anything but love inside our home. Love for me. Love for our children. My husband treats me like a queen. He's a good father. A good man. And I married him for better or for worse, Mother. I love my husband, Mother, and if I had any idea this was what you were up to, I would've stopped you. How dare you bring this foolishness inside my home."

"Baby, you can't be serious?" her mother replied. "You're married to a cheater, a liar, and a man that can't be trusted. You don't know what diseases he might bring home to you. You're lucky if you don't have something now."

No, she is not standing in my house disrespecting me, Brian thought, wanting to kick her out.

"I'm very serious, Mother," Michelle confirmed. "I know Brian isn't perfect. I'm not perfect either. But he's my husband, not yours. Where's Daddy, Mother? Huh? He left you and married another woman. You threw away your husband and he married another woman, and no matter what you say, I'm not throwing away a good man over some other woman's pussy."

Brian wondered what Michelle meant when she'd said, "I'm not perfect either," but at this point, he didn't care. He was in the clear. "Baby, you don't have to explain anything to her."

Michelle snapped, "You need to be quiet. That's my mother and I love her too." As she looked at her mother, tears filled Michelle's eyes. "Mama, there are so many failed marriages out there due to insecurities. I'm not insecure. I can't babysit my husband. There are too many unhappily married people in the world. I refuse to be one of them. There are way too many divorced couples. I'm not letting my kids grow up without a father. I'm not going to be a single mother. I love my husband, and my husband loves me. Mother, sometimes Brian's love is the only thing that gets me through my toughest days. I don't want to sleep in my bed alone every night, cuddling up with morals that can't touch me, principles that can't talk to me, or pride that can't make love to me. I know your intentions were good, but please get those women out of my house so I can make love to my husband. If you think you were going to divide us, I'm getting ready to show my husband how much I love and need him. Mother, the only person that can make me bitter, angry, depressed, or lonely . . . is *me*. Not you. Not those women. Not even society, which feels I should be pissed with my husband, because most of those people are just like you, Mother, they're miserable."

Brian wanted to tell Michelle he had to be on the next plane to Houston to sign his contract to represent Marcus Monty, but the timing wasn't good. This wasn't exactly the ending Brian had anticipated, but the one thing he knew how to do well was keep his mouth shut. Whatever his wife had done—even if she'd fucked another man—Brian would never leave Michelle.

Digging deep into her purse, Michelle's mother tossed his cell phone, keys, and wallet on the bed, then said, "If you lose track of your husband, you can locate him by the GPS device you uploaded on his phone."

Low-down and outright filthy! He never once figured the system was to keep track of him. That's how she'd entrapped him. That phone was being replaced immediately, and Michelle's mother could go to hell with her devilish ways.

Closing, then locking the bedroom door behind her

mother, Michelle said, "Whatever happened, I don't want to know. I'm not saying I don't care. That would be a lie. But my knowing the intimate details about your being with other women isn't going to make things between us better. Brian Malik Flaw, I love you."

EPILOGUE

Lexington

All cried out.

Lexington quickly learned that no matter what he did or said, Donna was done with him. Fortunately, she wasn't serious about leaving Alexandria and Alexandrea in his care. Joint custody one weekend out of the month gave him three Saturdays out of each month to maintain his presence at the sex club. Keeping the girls three days in a row, every four weeks, Lexington had more respect than he was willing to admit for all Donna had done—and how effortless she had made things seem. Inevitably he'd given Donna the main thing she deserved . . . a divorce.

Herschel

It was okay to be gay.

Herschel's visit to his mother was enlightening. He'd confessed to his mother his relationship with Anthony. She replied, "Honey, I've known you were gay all your life. I'm glad you finally figured yourself out. Baby, I love you—no matter what." With his mother's blessings, and the comfort of loving Anthony, Herschel didn't ask Nikki for a divorce. The time had come for Herschel to be man enough to do the right thing.

He canceled his engagement with Ivory, then asked Anthony, "Will you marry me?" That was the happiest day of Herschel's life when Anthony said, "Yes, I will marry you."

Together they filed their divorce papers from their wives, relocated to San Francisco, and legally wedded. Dining. Dancing. Movies. Theater. Concerts. Openly accepting his sexuality freed Herschel to enjoy life, but not with his husband. Anthony was to Herschel what Nikki had never become. Anthony was Herschel's *partner* for life.

Brian

Sixty-nine never felt so good.

Burying his face in Michelle's creamy pussy, Brian circled his tongue over his wife's pussy. Melt-in-his-mouth cotton-candy sweetness seeped, layering her lips with the thickness of a vanilla shake. Sucking her shaft into his mouth, Brian eased his middle finger into her hot, wet pussy, then gently fingered her G-spot. His eyelids closed when Michelle's mouth sucked his dickhead like it had been dipped in watermelon. Damn, that shit felt incredible. Brian exhaled. His wife's energy and love consumed him as he firmly suctioned her protruding clit. Michelle gripped his dick at the base, bobbing his shaft in and out of her mouth. Removing his finger from her pussy, he penetrated her asshole. Bracing her clit between his teeth, he flicked his tongue, making her come as he came in her mouth. Brian had Michelle's mother to thank. What she believed would rip their marriage apart had made them come . . . closer together.

Book Club Questions

1. Do you love yourself? I ask this question first because most people either don't know how to love themselves or they think they love themselves, yet they allow others to abuse them.
2. Married, divorced, or single, have you had sex with (or dated) a married person? Before you answer, think, have you dated or sexed a person without inquiring about his or her marital status (i.e., a one-night stand, a short-term relationship, etc.)? Was the relationship fulfilling? Why?
3. After reading *Single Husbands*, do you feel the characters in this novel violated their marriage license? Why or why not?
4. Has reading *Single Husbands* changed your outlook on marriage? Why or why not?
5. Would you have or have you had sexual intercourse with your friend's spouse or mate? If so, would you ever tell your friend?
6. Do you know any women or men who are married but live like they are single? Do you envy their relationships or lifestyle?

7. If you knew for a fact that your friend's spouse or mate was cheating, would you tell your friend? Why or why not? Have you ever lusted after your friend's mate?

8. Could you have an open marriage, knowing that both you and your spouse were permitted to have sex outside the marriage? If so, would you want to know your spouse's sexual partner(s)? Why or why not?

9. Is it possible for one person to satisfy all of your sexual needs and fantasies? Before you answer, what are your sexual needs and fantasies?

10. Should the person who earns more money in the relationship or marriage be permitted to control the relationship? What emotional impact, if any, do finances bear on a relationship?

11. After reading *Single Husbands,* how would you write or rewrite your marriage vows? Do you believe marriage vows are important? If the vows are broken, what can a person do to make them enforceable? What are the laws of marriage?

12. Would you divorce your spouse for sexual and/or emotional infidelity if everything else in your marriage was perfect? Why or why not?

13. Would you go to a sex club with your spouse or mate? Would you participate in sexual activities with other club members? Could you be comfortable watching someone else have sex with your spouse or mate?

14. What's the freakiest thing you've done sexually? Would you do it again? Are you try-sexual?

HoneyB Tips

If you've never been to a sex club or swingers club and are considering going after reading *Single Husbands,* here are my suggestions:

1. Know what pleasures you want to derive from going to a sex club before you get there. Don't set your expectations high on your first visit. In fact, I recommend being a voyeur on your first visit or joining in with a small group in a private room. Most folk can sense the amateurs right away, so chill for a moment. Act like you're a veteran.

2. Be safe. There are so many places to choose from. Do your online research ahead of time. Ladies, invite a friend to go with you. I find that most people—men and women—want to experience a sex and/or swingers club at least once. So trust me, don't hesitate to ask that friend to go with you.

3. If you're planning your first visit, don't ask the person you're dating, or the person you're attracted to, to go

with you. Ten times out of ten, it'll ruin your relationship beyond repair.

4. Be prepared. Read the acceptable attire and club rules online before going to the club. Almost all clubs require you to bring your own alcohol. For the BYOBs, you can also premix your drinks to your liking, but you will probably be required to let the bartenders on duty serve your alcohol to you.

5. If it's a club you've never visited, I highly recommend that you call ahead (there should always be a phone number listed online) with your questions. Drive by the club during the day. Ask to tour the club, preferably during the day, but definitely before you pay. I've found some clubs unsanitary. Just like a restaurant, always check the restrooms for cleanliness and hygiene supplies. Also, check the showers. Most people don't use the showers at the club, but you want to make certain they're clean. This signals the standards for the club.

6. Bring your own condoms—ladies especially. Your body is your responsibility. Trust me, some guys will try to hit it raw, especially in the private rooms. Don't let them. Most clubs provide condoms but they may not supply quality brands. Also, if you're doing a ménage à trois, and the guy is double-dippin', make sure he changes the condom between penetrating others. Trust me, he won't care, but if you don't know the other person (and even if you do), you don't know what, if any, STDs they may have.

7. Ladies, do not go to sex clubs with your man just to appease him. Neither of you will be happy. I observed a threesome at a sex club where the man anxiously wanted to fuck both his woman and their invited partner, another female. His woman clearly did not allow him to perform oral copulation or vaginal penetration with the other woman the entire time. However, in the dressing room, I observed this same man begging to taste the woman's pussy before his woman came in. And, yes, the woman did allow the guy to do so. A man is going to get his; so, ladies, you should too.

8. Get your sexy on! Your body type or size only matters if it matters to you. There is somebody for everybody at the sex club, and a lot of men are curious about plus-sized women. They specifically want to have sexual experiences with all types of women.

9. Beauty starts on the inside. Don't go to a sex club if your self-esteem is low that day. Go when you're ready for the overall experience. Don't worry about how others will judge you if you tell them you went to a sex club. It's your life. Tell them what HoneyB would say, "Don't waste your life trying to live mine."

10. Be great to yourself and live in the moment.

Honey Bits

Ladies, do you wanna look better . . . just a little bit? Do you want to get sexy . . . just a little bit? Test a small area of your body to avoid allergic reactions. Well, here are a few of my Honey Bits:

1. Put your best face forward. Smile often, it's free. If your face is bland like mine, I do recommend permanent makeup. Nothing drastic. Start off slow. I jumped in and had my eyebrows, eyeliner, and lips done the same day. That was way too much. Focus on one area at a time. And do get referrals and recommendations from previous clients before having any services done. Ask your girlfriends. Some of them may have permanent makeup and you don't know it.

2. Exfoliate your face and body twice a week. If you can't afford facials and body scrubs, there are do-it-yourself products you can buy. The grocery store has the best natural products. Fresh lemon juice and sugar mixed is the best hand scrub. Rubbing the inside of fresh peaches in circu-

lar motions on your face and body works wonders. One cup of plain yogurt mixed with a tablespoon of turmeric, located in the spice section of your grocery store, tightens your skin. Leave it on for ten minutes, shower off, and you'll notice a tighter and smoother feel immediately.

3. Take care of your hair. Licensed stylists don't always know what's best for your hair. Don't be reluctant to ask what products are best for you. Shampoos that are alcohol-based will dry out your hair. Use a silk shampoo. And make certain your conditioner has protein in it. If you have locks like I do, and you're experiencing hair loss or damage, I highly recommend you e-mail Davette Mobry of Beverly Hills in San Antonio, Texas, at IBraid@satx.rr.com.

HoneyB Safe: Don't Get Stung

I can't say that every woman wants to fuck a professional athlete, so I'll speak for myself. This particular person is definitely high-profile, so I won't disclose his identity. Based upon this novel, *Single Husbands,* trust me: the obvious is not so obvious. Don't waste your time trying to decode names, places, or characters in this or any of my novels, trying to figure out my sexual partners. Actually, his name is insignificant; the situation I found myself in was jaw-dropping.

I wanted to sex one of the players on this team for years, so when I had the opportunity, I did, but I didn't necessarily fuck the one I fantasized about the most. The man I had sex with, on about a half-dozen occasions or so, was wonderful, from oral copulation to deep penetration. He had a great personality, sense of humor, and commitment to his family. I never wanted to be his woman or his wife. I was in control and very clear about our friendship with benefits.

Now, I'm not the kind of woman to bring drama to any man's front door. Never have. Never will. It's not productive or necessary, because there is a plethora of dicks hanging around longing for a pussy to get into. But when this man—whom I considered a friend—called himself, putting me, HoneyB—a single and uncommitted woman—in check, he'd basically fucked up, and fucked with the wrong woman. I'm about as nice as women come (and cum), but nonsense and bullshit from men (irrespective of their status) with double standards, I can't digest or comprehend.

I'm going to paddle doggie-style into this situation. This piece is not written with malicious intent; which is why I will not mention his name, but he's smart. He's never confronted me again. Did he not remember that I am from New Orleans, Louisiana? Southern women are the most loyal group of women, until you cross us. Once a man screws up, I will pull out the pushpins, the voodoo dolls, his baby picture, call the two-headed lady, and whip out the grigri bag on his ass if I have to. Just ask my ex-husband if you see him. I treat men the way they treat me. No better. No worse. I'm a Virgo and I don't believe women should be submissive to men. Partners, yes. Submissive, hell no! What for? Don't get me started.

Anywhoo, my flight landed and I headed to my favorite rental car agency, National. I love being an Emerald Club member at National Car Rental because I get to select the car of my choice. It's with the same discerning discretion that I choose my lovers. After signing my car contract, I saw a familiar face walk in. This woman, I don't label her as a friend, but we'd seen one another on several occasions. Retrieving our cars, we headed to our hotel on the waterfront, checked in, and later met at the bar for drinks.

I'm not shy, and for anyone who knows or has hung out with me, they realize that I play hard and work harder. Anyway, we were joined in the bar area by a gentleman whom we both knew and everyone was having a funtastic time. I gave them a glance at a photo of my Brazilian wax. Anyway, judging by the expression on the gentleman's face, I said, "Oh, you've seen this picture before? Your boy showed you, huh?"

Without getting a verbal response from him, the woman said, "Oh, my gosh. That's why he was so persistent in having me send him a picture. You started this." She was referring to my at-that-time lover.

We laughed and continued drinking. But knowing that the guy sitting at the table with us was a personal, way-back friend of my lover, the woman looked at me kinda intrigued. The short of it was obvious. We'd fucked the same guy. The difference between us was she was white and had been married for almost three decades.

Over the next three days, we hung out together and she probed for information about my interactions with him. She told me about how he fucked this fat woman (by the way, a different personal friend of mine told me plus-sized sistahs got it going on, so I'm just reiterating what I was told) but couldn't get to her pussy, so he fucked her in the crevice of her thigh, and I told her about how he'd fucked this eighty-year-old woman who practiced Tantra. The old lady had sucked his dick and had made him come instantly. So while he couldn't disclose this story to a lot of folks, he told me he went back to the older woman to see if she could do it again . . . and she made him come again.

The white woman had mentioned that she overheard him call her a "pink toe," aka white girl, to one of his friends shortly after he'd finished fucking her, and I briefly mentioned my ménage à trois with him. Our stories went back and forth and she begged me not to tell him, because she wouldn't want anything to get back to her husband.

"Not a problem," I said, and meant it.

Well, after being back home in the Bay Area for a few days, I received a phone call from him that kinda went something like this.

"I'm calling to say I'm disappointed in you. What right did you have to discuss our business with anyone else? You don't know who she knows or if she knows my wife. That's why I was skeptical about getting with you in the first place. You're not the media, but you do have the ability to put things out in public with your books."

I listened until he was finished talking, then told him, "You need to be disappointed in your damn self. I am sick and tired of married men fucking around, then trying to control the situation and everyone involved in it. Once you fuck somebody, the situation is out of your control." He should've learned that from the mistake of another professional athlete on his team.

And, yes, I did say he's married. Don't act like it's just me, when both Oprah and Barbara Walters publicly announced they had been involved with married men too. Some of y'all too, so shut your "I'm a born-again Christian, I don't do those things no more so I'm better than everybody else" mouths. Anywhoo . . .

Ignorance is amazing. This man still said he was disappointed in me, and who he fucked was his business. He was grown and he could be with whomever he wanted.

No doubt that was on the real, but I told him, "If you're

concerned about what others are going to say, you need to stop fucking around on your wife."

It stuns me how men, in their minds, justify their infidelity. Now, granted, I don't need a man to meet my financial obligations. I can have sex and keep it in perspective. I honestly enjoyed having sex with this man and would have continued. I never called him the next day, next week, or even the next month after each time we had sex; that's how I roll. Have fun, take the dick and run.

If I was in his hometown or near where he was, I'd give him a shout-out to see what was up, or vice versa. In fact, on our last rendezvous, he phoned his secretary to say he was gonna be late to a meeting (he had to drop off the kids) just so he could fuck me early one Tuesday morning before I left town. We sat and talked about what was happening in our lives; then we had sex. It was great and just what I needed before heading to the airport, and exactly what he wanted before starting his workday.

I know where he lives and he knows where I live, but he's never been to my home and I've never been to his. My rule of thumb for married men is "If I can't kick my heels up at your house, you can't kick it at my place." Married men have to meet me at a hotel—and not just any hotel, a nice hotel—and they have to pay for everything. Now, don't go judging me when I done told y'all both Oprah and Barbara Walters admitted to being involved with married men. It happens, and married women need to stop pretending that it doesn't happen. I've never thrown a man down, whipped out his dick, and raped him until I came, but I would like to. My point is, married men—just like the characters in this book—are heavily pursuing single and married women for sex.

This note is for married men who do fuck around. It pays to keep the woman outside of your home happy so she doesn't wreak havoc in your life, because—oh, yes, indeed—like it or not, women have more power than they exert. So don't mistake a woman's kindness for weakness. A smart man will take time to find out what a woman wants, even if she doesn't want or need a thing from him. Too many athletes think that because they have big dicks (some of them are buff but have little dicks, ladies; but the man I'm talking about has one of the biggest, prettiest dicks I've ever seen) women should be grateful to be with him. Bullshit!

My other note to married men is to stop talking so damn much about your wife and kids. This man constantly talked about his wife, kids, in-laws, special occasions, birthdays, holidays, barbeques, his dogs, horses, his multiple houses, and how he had to hook up with me later after he'd called his wife from the home phone. He disclosed where her favorite hangout spot was (which is one of my favorite places too) so we couldn't meet there and where his favorite spot was. I knew exactly where he lived. I knew one of his favorite restaurants, where he'd ordered takeout for our ménage à trois. I mean, if I had ill intent, he'd voluntarily given me all the information I needed to know to screw up his personal life, including an eyewitness.

But I never brought drama to his front door. Never. Ever. My motto is "Never fuck around with anyone who has nothing to lose." The best thing he could've done was not fuck that particular white woman and he shouldn't have tried to check me, HoneyB.

Men need to realize that whether they like it or not, whether it's his woman or his wife, women are in control. Ladies, don't let any man check you over some bullshit. And, fellas, you need to think with the right head. Never piss off the woman that can bring drama to your front door. I'm reiterating this, because men don't hear shit we say the first time. You might want to believe that your wife would never accept another woman's word over yours, but that's not always true.

I was extremely considerate of this guy by not mentioning him by name. But I could tell you what his dick looks like, what his ass feels like, and what he tastes like . . . but I won't.

Acknowledgments

I thank the Creator for blessing me with you, the person who has chosen to read *Single Husbands*. I pray your life is filled with self-love, peace, and prosperity. FYI, HoneyB is my scintillating pseudonym; Mary B. Morrison is the name my parents gave me at birth. I write under both names.

Always and forever, I thank my son, Jesse Bernard Byrd Jr., for all the priceless moments we share together, simply being mother and son. Remember, no one can deny what you deserve, for what they hold is theirs to keep. Nor can anyone control your destiny. Stay focused. Keep making great accomplishments. I am always proud of you.

My world of writing wouldn't be the same without my scintillating editors, Karen R. Thomas and Selena James. My wonderful agents, Andrew Stuart and Claudia Menza, I appreciate all you do.

Both of my parents have made their transitions into eternity—my mother when I was nine years old, and my father when I was twenty-four years old. They blessed me with the greatest siblings—Wayne Morrison, Andrea Morrison,

Derrick Morrison, Regina Morrison, Margie Rickerson, and Debra Noel.

Much love to Richard C. Montgomery, George Pearson, Roy Campanella, Felicia Polk, Marissa Monteilh, Kimberly Kaye Terry, Emma Rodgers, Vera Warren-Williams, Michele Lewis, Kim Mason, Eve Lynne Robinson, Mother Bolton, and Sarah Brown, aka Indie Jackson.

Feel free to hit me up with a piece of your world at www. MaryMorrison.com. Peace and prosperity.

Unconditionally Single

by *Mary B. Morrison*

Prologue

I've been single all my life.

The day I entered this world, the second the doctor severed my umbilical cord, I had to make it on my own. Crying. Screaming. Like most kids, I did what I had to do to get attention.

Obviously, my mother fed me, changed my diapers— basically, she did what she had to do for me, but not much more. I guess she'd grown tired of catering to me and my sister or doing for us instead of taking care of herself. I didn't ask to be here. She could've prevented our pain and suffering. But no. She decided to have not one but two babies for men who didn't want her. Yet, she wanted her life to be hers, I supposed.

My mother's new man became her new priority. Kicking

me out of the house when I was sixteen, she was done sacrificing for me. Sitting in the funeral home, grieving over my sister's casket, I never understood why my sister got to stay home until she'd died.

Survival was a skill I'd learned early in my lifetime. Like I said, I had to make it on my own. My only other option was to join my sister. I wasn't ready to die, then or now. A few major mistakes here and there. Marrying two abusive men for the wrong reasons. I did what I had to do to live another day.

I said, "Fuck you!" to any "holier than thou" motherfucker who degraded prostitutes. Did they think they were better? Fuck them. They were different. Definitely not better. Maybe they had a better life. Parents who gave a fuck about them and shit. Bet they weren't homeless like me.

After two divorces, I chose to become a prostitute. Not the kind that walked a beat in 100-degree heat on the back streets, sucking dicks and turning tricks for twenty bucks. No, that wasn't where you'd find Lace St. Thomas.

I was in an air-conditioned ranch house, with my own room, servicing my johns for eleven years. I had no shame in what I had to do. Survive. Recession. Depression. Didn't matter. Pussy was always in demand. I made lots of money prostituting. I earned more money after I quit to become a madam. Experience served and paid me fifty grand . . . a night.

Overseeing thirteen high-priced, drop-dead gorgeous escorts who earned us $10,000 an hour made me wealthy, and my boss, Valentino James, wealthier. I enjoyed my job. Most of the time. Until my top escort dropped dead after being shot in the head by my boss.

Men. They thought they ruled the fucking world, when, in fact, all they did was fuck up their world and everybody in it. Truth be told, women are wiser than men. I supposed . . . until I fell in love with Grant.

Illegally, I inherited $50 million from my ex-boss, and I unexpectedly experienced multiple heartaches caused by the man I loved. Perhaps I was better off by myself, but there was a part of me that wanted to get married. I wanted to love someone who loved me for me. Settle down. Have a few babies. Live a peaceful life. No matter how hard I tried, shit continued to happen.

My boss wanted his millions back. Fuck that. I thought I wanted my man back. Forget that. Neither one of them owned me. Unconditionally, this was my life. The fact that I had a pussy between my legs didn't mean I was less than a man. A man wasn't shit without a woman. I learned that prostituting. I learned a lot more about men when I was a madam. They wanted free pussy, but they were willing to pay for good pussy. Sexy pussy. Tight pussy. Experienced pussy. Hell, bad pussy could make a dime if it was attached to the right mind.

It was my prerogative to pamper my pussy any way I damn well pleased. Sometimes a woman had to be sweet. Sometimes she needed to be bittersweet. Then there were times a woman had to be a straight-up bitch. I'd mastered all three.

If I had to suck a dick or shoot a man in his damn head, I wouldn't hesitate. A woman unsure of herself would miss out on opportunity after opportunity, lying in her grave, wondering, *What if?*

Curled in the fetal position, kidnapped, locked in the back of some motherfucker's SUV, I had what my assailants didn't know I possessed, but they would soon find out. I had my gun. They'd kidnapped the wrong bitch. The minute they opened the trunk, I opened fire.

What the fuck? Not these two fools! I should've known.

First, I fired at my ex-boss, Valentino, the one without the gun. He jumped in the wrong direction for him, right for me. One of the two bullets I fired at him hit his ass in the side. Then I shot Benito Bannister, my ex-man, the idiot with the gun. Valentino was stupid for letting Benito have the gun. Benito had never shot or killed anyone. They deserved to die. Both of them.

"Fuck!" I underestimated that idiot Benito.

We exchanged fire. *Pow!* I got his ass too. Right in his shoulder, although I aimed for his head, right between his eyes. *Pow!* My gun fell to the ground. I didn't realize I'd been shot until blood soaked my red jacket. I couldn't feel a thing.

"Let's go, nigga!" Valentino yelled, getting in the driver's seat. "Lock that bitch in the fucking trunk! I'ma personally kill her ass execution-style!"

Not if I kill you first, I thought.

Benito reached for my legs. I kicked this stupid ass in his face. What smart attacker would lean face-first into his subject? My stiletto punctured his chin.

"Nigga, let's roll. The fucking cops are coming!" Valentino yelled.

"Damn, Lace. You gon' pay for that shit," Benito said, gripping the trunk.

I'd stopped answering to Lace when my sister died. I'd buried myself and assumed her name, Honey. Exhaling, I heard the sirens. For the first time, I was happy to hear police sirens. Jumping out of the trunk, I picked up my gun, then yelled, "Punk!" firing at the SUV, shattering the back window. I looked down at my shoes surrounded by a puddle of blood. My blood. I wanted to throw up but couldn't. Frisking my body, I couldn't feel where I'd been shot.

"Drop the gun!" were the last words I'd heard before my body collapsed to the ground. I figured, if the police thought I was dead, they wouldn't shoot me.

My Pussy—My Prerogative

by Mary B. Morrison

My pussy
My prerogative

The last time I'd checked
My pussy was attached to me
Not some wannabe lover
Claiming my pussy
Was his pussy
And reciting the same line
To the other
Pussy in his face
After I cum
He's gone without a trace

You see this pussy
That's between my legs
Is attached to a head
With brains
That can drive a man insane

MY PUSSY—MY PEROGATIVE

My pussy
My prerogative
To give
Or to keep
To remain celibate
To sell a bit
Or to creep
Or to freak

To snap
Or to wrap
Around a man's head
In and out of bed

Unconditionally
My pussy is
My prerogative

Wanna taste
Wanna slide into first base
Second? Seconds?
Third? Thirds?
My pussy has the first and final words
On whether your dick's worthy
Not
If your dick is dirty
Your pockets are dry
You're a selfish lover
Your back hurts

You cum before my pussy gets wet
You leave right after your cum is dry
Don't ask me why
I refuse to let you fuck me
Just take your dick
And let my pussy be
Free to choose
The right stroke
The right man
The right lover
The right dick

Unconditionally
For as long as I live
It's my clit
My pearl
My pussy
My world
My prerogative

Cum correct
Or don't cum at all